PAYBACK

JOSEPH BADAL

SUSPENSE PUBLISHING

PAYBACK
by
Joseph Badal

PAPERBACK EDITION
* * * * *
PUBLISHED BY:
Suspense Publishing

Joseph Badal
COPYRIGHT
2020 Joseph Badal

PUBLISHING HISTORY:
Suspense Publishing, Paperback and Digital Copy, May, 2020

Cover Design: Shannon Raab
Cover Photographer: iStockphoto.com/ Albert Pego

ISBN: 978-0-578-64043-3

JOSEPH BADAL'S BOOKS & SHORT STORIES

THE DANFORTH SAGA
EVIL DEEDS (#1)
TERROR CELL (#2)
THE NOSTRADAMUS SECRET (#3)
THE LONE WOLF AGENDA (#4)
DEATH SHIP (#5)
SINS OF THE FATHERS (#6)

THE CURTIS CHRONICLES
#1: THE MOTIVE
#2: OBSESSED
#3: JUSTICE

LASSITER/MARTINEZ CASE FILES
#1: BORDERLINE
#2: DARK ANGEL
#3: NATURAL CAUSES

STAND-ALONE THRILLERS
THE PYTHAGOREAN SOLUTION
SHELL GAME
ULTIMATE BETRAYAL
PAYBACK

SHORT STORIES
FIRE & ICE (UNCOMMON ASSASSINS ANTHOLOGY)
ULTIMATE BETRAYAL (SOMEONE WICKED ANTHOLOGY)
THE ROCK (INSIDIOUS ASSASSINS ANTHOLOGY)

DEDICATION

Payback is dedicated to John W. Badal, Robert G. Badal, Karla J. Peska, and Janice C. Badal, my siblings who have given me their unwavering support and who never fail to make suggestions that have positive impact on my work.

ACKNOWLEDGEMENTS

To my readers, thank you for your loyal support. You virtually keep alive my passion for writing. Your kind feedback and suggestions are invaluable, and your reviews make a difference.

I have been fortunate to have had reviews and blurbs for my novels written by many successful and prolific authors, including Mark Adduci, Tom Avitabile, Parris Afton Bonds, Steve Brewer, Catherine Coulter, Philip Donlay, Robert Dugoni, Steve Havill, Anne Hillerman, Tony Hillerman, Paul Kemprecos, Robert Kresge, Jon Land, Tosca Lee, Mark Leggatt, Michael McGarrity, David Morrell, Michael Palmer, Dennis Palumbo, Andrew Peterson, Douglas Preston, Mark Rubinstein, Meryl Sawyer, and Sheldon Siegel. I know how busy these men and women are and it always humbles me when they graciously take time to read and praise my work.

Many thanks to Karla Ponder and Carole True for their comments and suggestions. You each contributed in a meaningful way to making *Payback* a better read.

Kudos to Donna Pedace who bought the naming rights at a charity auction to the main character in *Payback* for her husband Bruno.

I want to recognize John Byram for doing a superb job of editing *Payback*. Every author needs a top-notch editor, and John certainly is as top-notch as they come.

Finally, many thanks to John & Shannon Raab at Suspense Publishing for your confidence in and support of my writing.

PRAISE FOR JOSEPH BADAL

"*Payback* is a twisty tale packed with turnabouts, betrayals and double-crosses galore. Joseph Badal's steamy, scintillating crime tale crackles with color, authenticity and a plot that combines the best of Joe Finder and Harlan Coben. A thriller of rare depth and pathos, *Payback* pays back on every page, making it one of the true must-reads of 2020."

—Jon Land, *USA Today* Bestselling Author of the *Murder, She Wrote* Series

"Pick up a Joseph Badal book and you can be assured of a couple of things even before you turn the first page. The bad guys are going to be really bad, and it may take a while, but they are going to get what's coming to them. In *Payback*, Bruno Pedace is being set up to take a fall for the securities fraud committed by his partners at Sy Rosen's Wall Street firm. Bruno escapes, but his career has been destroyed and he is being hunted by a contract killer. When Bruno comes roaring back with a little help from a colorful cast of characters that includes a tough-skinned social worker, some hard-working cops and a few Mafia pals, he concocts an ingenious way to get even. He'll have to deal with a few more hitmen and an assassin who is as deadly as she is lovely, but readers will enjoy joining Bruno and friends as they rise to the occasion in the action-packed climax of this taut tale of revenge and retribution."

—Paul Kemprecos, *#1 New York Times* Bestselling Author

"*Payback* has everything: an intriguing, single-minded protagonist; cunningly evil bad guys; well-drawn settings; a possible romance; and, best of all, a complex plot based on dark revenge. Author Badal never runs short of clever ways to challenge readers' assumptions as the absorbing, action-filled plot brilliantly unfolds."

—Anne Hillerman, *New York Times* Bestselling Author

"Joseph Badal reigns supreme in the thriller genre, and he's done it again with his intense thriller, *Payback*. Badal is a skilled stylist. His

attention to detail allows the reader to easily go with the flow of his skilled storytelling. His settings are believable whether they exist in southern California or on an island off the coast of Vietnam, the streets of New York or a bank in the Caribbean. Extended tension keeps the story moving, and just when the reader is ready to take a breath, Badal adds another twist, a colorful character, or a blood-pounding action scene. Multiple, intriguing threads come together as Badal orchestrates the story, urging the reader to pull for Bruno as he fights to do the right thing and redeem himself. *Payback* could very well be Badal's best work yet."
—John Carenen, Award-Winning Author of the *Thomas O'Shea Mystery* Series

"A terrific read! Joseph Badal takes a break from his series characters and pens a white-hot standalone thriller filled with suspense, intrigue, and revenge. Social worker Janet Jenkins and financier Bruno Pedace are finely drawn characters who are worth rooting for—not super-human heroes found in more pedestrian thrillers. Badal's expertise in the world of high finance shines in this gripping story. With a finely tuned, fast-paced plot, the narrative in *Payback* hurtles forward to a satisfying conclusion. Highly recommended."
—Sheldon Siegel, *New York Times* and Amazon Bestselling author of "The Dreamer"

"When Bruno Pedace is framed by his business partners, he takes the needed exonerating evidence and runs. For nearly a decade all is well, but when his past comes calling in the form of a skilled hit man, Bruno must employ all of his skills to escape death and bring down his former partners. A fast-moving story with great characters."
—D.P. Lyle, Award-Winning Author of the *Jake Longly* and *Cain/Harper* Thriller Series

"Joseph Badal handles a complex, international world with aplomb. It's a one-sitting read!"
—Steven F. Havill, Award-Winning Author of "Less Than a Moment," a *Posadas County Mystery*

PAYBACK

JOSEPH BADAL

PART I

PROLOGUE
NINE YEARS AGO

"Oh, Annie," Bruno Pedace said, grief heavy in his voice.

Annie Donohue stopped trying to halt the flow of her tears, which dropped torrentially onto her silk blouse. She looked down at her lap while she kneaded a handkerchief in her hands, shuddering sobs racking her body.

"Why didn't you come to me? I could have put a stop to it. I'm a partner of this damned firm; not some flunky."

She made a snuffling noise and cleared her throat. It took several seconds for her to speak. She looked up at Bruno, held his gaze for a moment, then dropped her eyes to her lap again.

"I couldn't do that," she said. "He would have fired me. I need this job. You know that. What would I do with four kids at home and no husband?"

"I never would have let Sy Rosen fire you," he said.

She scoffed. "You're a partner, but Sy Rosen is the managing partner. What could you do against someone like him?" After a beat, she added, "Look what they're planning to do to you. They're turning everything over to the SEC in two days, after the markets close on Friday."

Her sobs began again. Bruno sat behind his desk and waited for her to compose herself. When she did, she looked up again, this time meeting his gaze.

"Rosen told you all of this?"

She blurted a laugh, but there was no humor in it. She said, "A bottle of wine and a little massaging of his ego is all it takes for Sy Rosen to divulge his deepest, darkest secrets." She shook her head, a sour cast to her mouth. "I'm sick about this, Bruno."

"Tell me again everything he told you."

"He said the SEC is investigating all the Wall Street firms for fraudulent mortgage securities transactions. He knows that the company won't be able to stand up to the scrutiny of such an investigation. The sub-prime mortgage securities the firm created were full of false data. None of the loans in those deals should have ever been made. Rosen is livid about your opposition to Rosen, Rice & Stone underwriting those fraudulent securities. That's one of the reasons they're setting you up to take the fall."

"One of the reasons?" he asked.

"Yes." She swallowed hard, looked into his doe-like brown eyes for a moment, then stared into the middle distance. "He said you were born to be a victim. I remember exactly what he said about this." She huffed a mighty sigh. "He told me, 'Bruno Pedace is the perfect patsy. His own wife was sleeping with one of the partners.'"

When Annie stopped talking, Bruno said, "What else?"

"The senior partners have forged documents to make it appear that you put the mortgage deals together, that you knew the loans were bad, and that you believed you could get away with it. Rosen said they'd make the case that you hoodwinked the managing partners by doctoring the data about the mortgages." She groaned, then added, "They've created emails and internal memos in which you supposedly set up the scheme to defraud the partners and our investors. Your name and signature are all over those documents."

Bruno stood, came around his desk to where Annie sat, and took hold of her arm. He helped her to stand and told her, "I want you to go out to your desk, go about your business, pretend that nothing's happened."

"They'll know I told you."

He shrugged. "That's probably right, Annie. But if they fire you, I want you to call Jim Kennedy. He'll file a sexual harassment suit against Rosen and the firm that will fix you for life. The moment

Rosen hears from Kennedy, he'll want to settle with you out of court. You understand?"

She nodded. "What are you going to do, Bruno? You could go to prison."

He patted her shoulder. "Don't worry about me. I'll figure something out."

"I'm sorry, Bruno. I'm so sorry."

"It's okay, Annie. Go on now. I've got some thinking to do."

She moved to the office door, but as she gripped the door handle, she turned and said, "Rosen's dangerous, Bruno. He'll do anything to protect himself and the firm."

After Annie Donohue left his office, Bruno considered his options as he paced. He could go to the SEC and tell them what he knew, but, based on what Annie had told him, the senior partners had constructed a trail of false documents that would be difficult if not impossible to disprove. And if he stayed and fought the ultimate charges, his assets would be wiped out, and there was no guarantee he'd win in the end. As far as his assets went, the vast percentage of his personal wealth was in his stock in Rosen, Rice & Stone. There would be no way he could liquidate that interest.

He concluded that he had only one option: run. A terrible pain hit his stomach, as acid had filled it. *Running is what I've been good at my entire life*, he thought. *Annie's correct. Rosen is a very dangerous man. He's not above having me killed.*

He stopped pacing, took his cell phone from his suit jacket pocket, and called his T.D. Ameritrade broker.

"Herman, it's Bruno."

"Hey, Bruno. How're things?"

"All's good. How quickly can you liquidate my account?"

"All of it?"

"Yes. I have an opportunity to buy a larger percentage of the firm's stock. It's an opportunity I can't pass up."

"Everything's in marketable securities. I can probably sell everything today, depending on what price you want on your holdings."

"Sell everything at market."

"You could get hammered doing that."

"Just do it, Herman. Then transfer the proceeds to my bank account. Get it done today."

Bruno terminated the call, then snatched a set of keys from his desktop and walked quickly to his office door. *Calm down*, he told himself. He opened the door and moved slowly through the waiting area. He smiled reassuringly at Annie, then looked straight ahead as he exited into the hall, went to the emergency staircase, and descended three floors to the vault.

CHAPTER 1

"Mama, are you trying to kill yourself?"

Maybelle Jenkins frowned. "Sugar, you gotta stop harassing me about eating. I'll eat when I feel like it."

Janet Jenkins stared down at her mother and felt an ache in her heart. She remembered how tall and beautiful the old woman had been. How people used to say Janet was the spitting image of her blue-eyed, auburn-haired, long-legged mama. That Maybelle was the most beautiful woman in all of Mississippi. Even down to the freckles on her perfect nose, her neck, and shoulders. Now, she towered over her mother, who seemed to shrink a bit every year, looking more like a sack of bones. Only when she smiled—a rare occurrence—did Maybelle resemble the woman she'd once been.

Despite her frustration and worry, Janet Jenkins smiled. The strains of Mississippi flowed through her fifty-seven-year-old mother's speech in a sing-song cadence that reminded her of growing up in the south. Then she shuddered as though a cold breeze had hit the back of her neck. The mellifluous sounds of her youth were about the only things she didn't regret about those early years.

"You're wasting away," Janet said. "That dress just hangs on you, Mama."

Maybelle showed a wan smile as she cocked a hip and touched the side of her face. Putting on an exaggerated southern drawl, she said, "Ah am fashionably thin, *mah* dear. Today, that's all the thang, ya know?"

Janet felt a headache coming on. "There's nothing fashionable about starving yourself."

Maybelle waved a dismissive hand. "You're gonna be late for work."

"I'm not leaving until you promise me you'll eat your breakfast."

"All right, I promise."

Janet squinted at her mother and then shook her head. "If you drop one more pound, I'm taking you to the hospital. And you know what they'll do to you."

A fearful expression crossed Maybelle's face, immediately replaced by anger. "Don't you even think about it. The last time they stuck so many things in my hands and arms I was bruised for a month."

Janet wagged a finger at her mother. "Then stop starving yourself."

"All right. All right. Get yourself gone."

The drive from her rented bungalow in El Segundo to her job in Redondo Beach was sometimes a bumper-to-bumper, thirty-minute slog in traffic that flowed like molasses. Other days, the trip was a fifteen-minute, nerve-wracking rodeo of careening SUVs, sports cars, and luxury sedans jockeying to gain an advantage. Today, traffic moved erratically, but quickly. Janet planted her rusted twenty-year-old Chevy in the middle lane, as she always did, and kept a wary eye on the manic NASCAR-like race flowing around her. She knew from experience that if she didn't maintain perpetual vigilance, some idiot on a cell phone in a one hundred thousand dollar automobile might cut in front of her and then suddenly hit his brakes. Her front bumper was already held in place by baling wire. If she lost her wheels, she'd be in real trouble.

The spring sunlight slashed through the driver's side window and played games with her vision. She tried to slant her sunglasses to block out the sun's rays, but that did little good.

Errant thoughts of her mother invaded her brain. She understood the old woman's problem. It wasn't physical; it was psychological.

Maybelle Jenkins was, plain and simple, depressed. She'd been that way for as long as Janet could remember. Ever since Marvin Jenkins ran off with some chippie he'd met in a Tupelo dive. Maybelle was twenty-nine at the time, but was already worn out from cleaning rich women's houses, taking in laundry, and suffering abuse at the hands of her heavy-fisted, lazy, philandering husband. Not yet thirty, she already showed signs of defeat and disillusionment.

Janet was eleven when Marvin Jenkins abandoned them. She remembered the look in her mother's eyes that day. The lead up was bad enough. He'd been more abusive than usual. The names he called her mother. The way he ridiculed her appearance. The way he'd thrown her across the room and then kicked her while she was sprawled on the floor of their three-room, broken-down shack. Yeah, that had all been bad enough. But the worst was when he bent down, laughed, and said, "I never loved you. You were nothing but a piece of ass to me." He laughed again and added, "And you ain't even that no more."

The scene replayed in Janet's mind. She'd watched and heard the whole thing from the cracked-open closet door. Her brain was saturated with the memory. No matter how she tried to obliterate the nightmare, it came back, unbidden, without warning. But the worst of the memory had been her mother's reaction. While Janet tried to help her up off the floor, she'd met her mother's tearful gaze and saw a depth and breadth of anguish and hopelessness as she'd never observed before. It was at that moment that she vowed to never let a man abuse her in any way.

The first and only time Rory Brownell hit Janet, on her nineteenth birthday, six months after their wedding, Janet walked out, gathered up her mother, and left Mississippi in their new Impala—a gift from Rory's parents on their wedding day. She would have preferred to put more miles between her and Rory, but the Pacific Ocean stopped her. She reverted to her maiden name as soon as she arrived in California. That was twenty years ago.

As she shook her head to try to clear it of the memory, an ear-splitting screech sent her heart racing. She slammed on her brakes and skidded to a stop inches from the back bumper of a black Tesla.

The driver of the luxury car shot her arm into the air, middle finger extended.

Janet's heart beat as though it wanted to escape her chest. She took a long, deep, calming breath and watched the Tesla speed away, leaving a six-car space between them. In a matter of a few seconds, other vehicles filled that space. *Nature abhors a vacuum*, she thought, and laughed, but without any humor. Everything suddenly seemed eerily quiet except for the beating of her pulse in her ears. Then a rap concert of sounds penetrated her senses—horns blaring, stereos banging and thumping, engines roaring. She shook her head to clear it and removed her foot from the brake pedal.

CHAPTER 2

"Where the hell are you, Casale?" Sy Rosen demanded.

Giovanni "Johnny" Casale didn't like Rosen's tone of voice, but he figured he could put up with it considering the amount of money the investment banker had already paid him…and was going to pay him. "Las Vegas," he answered. "I had a lead that the guy might be here."

"You're a couple hundred miles east of where you should be."

"What d'ya mean?"

"One of the ATC bonds just surfaced in Los Angeles."

"I'll be damned. I wondered when he'd run out of dough and cash in one of the bonds. My God, it's been eight years."

"Almost nine. I'll send you an email with the contact info for the broker who cashed the bond."

"I'll get right on it," Casale said, unsuccessfully trying to keep the excitement he felt from his voice. "What was the value of the bond?"

"They're each denominated at one hundred thousand dollars."

"So, he still has a bunch more of them?"

"That's right. Nineteen of them. One point nine million dollars."

"Like I said, I'll get right on it." After a beat, Casale said, "I gotta ask, Mr. Rosen. Why the hell hasn't the guy skipped the country? I mean, with that kinda money, he could be livin' large some place like Mexico."

Rosen sighed. "His passport's still in our vault."

"Hell, he could buy fake ID, get a fake passport."

Rosen scoffed. "Not everyone runs in the circles you do, Mr. Casale."

Casale didn't really buy Rosen's explanation, but he decided there was no reason to argue the point.

"And don't forget our arrangement," Rosen blurted. "If you… permanently solve my problem, your fee will double."

After the phone call from Sy Rosen, Casale went back to his room at Caesar's Palace. While he packed his suitcase, he thought about what he needed to do before he got on the road: *buy a pistol and ammunition; rent a car.* He'd calculated that driving from Las Vegas to Los Angeles wouldn't require much more time than taking a cab to the Las Vegas airport, waiting around for an hour, flying to LAX, and renting a car there. Besides, there was no way he'd be able to board a plane with the pistol he planned to buy.

On the way from his room, euphoric about the news Rosen had passed on, he sat down at a blackjack table. *This is my lucky day*, he thought. But he quickly dropped three grand. He blamed his losing streak on his inability to concentrate. The thought of the fee Rosen had promised him diverted his attention from the cards. *Two hundred thousand dollars. Twice that if I permanently solve Rosen's problem.* The cocktail waitresses who cruised past the blackjack table also diverted his attention. Their skimpy outfits left little to the imagination. But they pissed him off. None of the women showed any interest in him. Despite his stature—six feet, two inches tall—his athletic build, and his Latin good looks, women reacted to him as though he had leprosy. His sister had once told him that he scared the crap out of women because he looked at them as though they were prey. He'd laughed at that. Because that was exactly how he perceived women: prey.

Once I find Bruno Pedace and get paid by Rosen, I'll have all the women I want, he thought.

Sy Rosen spent a couple hours on the telephone, then checked his tie and collar in the mirror in his private bathroom. He wiped away imaginary dandruff from the shoulders of his Armani suit jacket, and flicked off a lint particle on a lapel. He showed his "master of the universe" smile, then wheeled around and moved to the conference room adjacent to his office for the meeting he'd called.

"What's up, Sy?" Richard Stone asked. "I have a golf game with Jack Leonard in two hours."

"To hell with Jack Leonard," Rosen groused.

"Leonard's one of our best clients," Partner Karl Rice said.

Rosen glared at the two men, in turn, and forced himself to maintain a neutral expression. Short, overweight, and lazy, Rice and Stone disgusted him. He said, "You remember those bonds that Bruno Pedace included in the financial disclosures we had to file with the SEC?"

"Sure," Karl Rice said. "What's the big deal? He only had a couple million dollars' worth of those ATC bonds."

"One of those bonds just surfaced."

"After all this time?" Stone said. "Unbelievable."

"So what?" Rice asked.

"The private investigator I hired is on his way to California, where the bond was cashed in."

Rosen noticed that Rice suddenly looked nauseated.

"What the hell's your problem?" Rosen barked.

Rice swallowed hard and blew out a loud breath. "None of this would have happened if we hadn't set up Bruno. Your strategy was to deflect the SEC's attention from us onto one of the second-level partners. It didn't accomplish a damned thing except to chase away one of the best people in the firm. The SEC never did a damned thing to us or, for that matter, to any of the Wall Street firms."

Rosen scowled at Rice. *Fuckin' wimp*, he thought. He didn't need anyone to remind him that the Securities & Exchange Commission was on the warpath almost a decade ago, looking to place blame on investment bankers who sold mortgage bonds backed by subprime loans. How could he have known that nothing would come of it? His plan had been to make one of their executives the fall guy so that none of the senior partners became an asshole cellmate of Bernie Madoff.

"What eats at my gut," Rice continued, "is that Bruno was the only guy here vehemently opposed to us selling subprime paper."

Rosen shot Rice a venomous look. "The fact that Pedace's wife got killed in a car wreck on the way home after meeting you in a hotel room is probably eating at your gut, too."

Rice slumped in his chair and muttered, "Asshole."

"Hah," Rosen shouted. "I won't argue with you about that. My being an asshole is what's made us one of the top Wall Street companies."

"What's the P.I. going to do?" Stone asked.

"Recover the documents," Rosen answered.

"And, if Pedace doesn't cooperate?" Rice said.

"Don't worry about that. I assure you, he'll cooperate."

"What the hell does that mean?" Rice said.

"What do you think it means?" Rosen said.

Rice stood and said, "Pedace was with us for eighteen years. Eighteen years! We ruined his life and now you're telling us some guy you sent to California is going to kill him."

Rosen glared at Rice and then looked at Stone. He spread his arms in a helpless gesture. "Did I say anything about killing anyone?"

Stone shrugged.

Rosen said, "How many times do we have to go over this?" He chuckled. "Bruno Pedace was the perfect fall guy. He was a cipher."

"Bullshit," Rice shouted. "He was the best junior partner we've ever had. The guy was a market genius."

Rosen felt his face go hot. He suspected that he looked as though he was about to explode. "So what? We can always find market analysts. They're a dime a dozen."

"Nonsense," Rice said. "Good market analysts are worth their weight in gold and Pedace was the best I've ever known."

Rosen shook his head. "All he did was work. He had no personal relationships. Hell, Rice, you were *shtupping* his wife. The guy couldn't even keep his own wife happy; he gave no emotion to anyone. He had no friends or allies inside the firm. He was the perfect victim."

Rice dropped back into his chair, looking sick at heart. Rosen shot him a contemptuous look. "You two need to remember that

Pedace betrayed *us* when he took those confidential documents."

Rice glared at Rosen. "If you hadn't been sleeping with Pedace's assistant and sharing your darkest secrets with her, he would never have been warned of what was about to come down and wouldn't have taken the docs."

The room went quiet for a few seconds. Then Stone added, "Remember that when Pedace took off, his stake in the company was worth at least twenty-five million. Today, it would be worth more than twice as much. Maybe we could negotiate something with him."

"How the fuck are we going to negotiate with Pedace if we can't find him?" Then Rosen stood and, in a low, menacing tone, said, "I'm going to say this one last time. If the documents that Pedace took ever fall into the hands of the SEC, we're toast. It's one thing for the commission to ignore billions of losses caused by the sale of subprime mortgage loans, if the investment bankers claim that it was all due to bad judgment. It's an altogether different matter if there's proof that fraud was perpetrated." Rosen sneered at Stone, then at Rice. "You won't like prison."

Rice hung his head.

Stone said, "If those documents are potentially so harmful, why the hell hasn't Pedace turned them over to the SEC?"

Rosen spread his arms and said, "How the hell would I know what's going through his mind?"

What Rosen didn't say was that he had suspected all along why Pedace had gone underground and hadn't released the stolen documents. *Bruno Pedace may have been a personality-less cipher, but he wasn't stupid. He knew if he ever surfaced with the documents, his life wouldn't be worth a damn. I would have eliminated him.*

CHAPTER 3

"A glorious start to another day in paradise," Frank Mitchell announced to the staff gathered in the conference room at St. Anne's Shelter for Women & Children.

"What happened, Frank?" Janet asked.

"It's a bad one," Mitchell answered. "Mother's in the hospital with broken bones. Father crashed through a police roadblock with three kids in his pickup truck. He was the only one wearing a seatbelt."

Janet felt momentarily nauseous, but she swallowed and focused on what she knew would come next. As St. Anne's outreach social worker, among her other responsibilities, it was her job to make the first contact with their clients. Five years on the job hadn't quite made her impervious to human suffering, but she'd developed a psychological thick skin that helped get her through the day. *One day at a time*, she told herself repeatedly.

Mitchell turned toward Janet. "You'll need to interview the mother in the hospital." He paused for a second. "It's Jasmine Essam."

"Oh, no; not again," Janet said. "Does she know about the crash...her kids?"

Mitchell shook his head. "Looks like you'll have the job of informing her."

"Shit," Janet muttered.

"My sentiments exactly," Mitchell said.

"What set off the husband this time? His eggs overcooked?"

"A neighbor told the police he was pissed off because his wife didn't cover her head when she went outside to collect the mail. The neighbor saw Essam run outside, smack her in the head, and then drag her inside. Heard the man shouting, the woman pleading, and the kids screaming. The neighbor called 9-1-1."

Redondo Beach Detective John Andrews asked, "Who's the broad in the blue suit? She's built like a brick—"

Five feet, eight-inch Detective Hugo Rosales poked a finger in Andrews's chest and glared at the six feet, two-inch, blue-eyed, blond-haired surfer boy, who'd grown up in Southern California. Andrews had transferred to the Redondo Beach PD from the LAPD with a reputation as a womanizer and a partier. Rosales had an almost Puritanical attitude about how women should be treated. His *abuela* had instilled that in him from an early age.

"How is it you always know exactly the wrong thing to say at any given moment?"

"Jeez, Hugo, what'd I say?"

Rosales, a fireplug-of-a-man, with jet-black hair, mahogany-colored eyes, and swarthy skin, poked Andrews again. "You and I've been partners for a total of two weeks. I hoped the word on you was wrong, that you couldn't be as bad as I heard. I guess I was mistaken."

"What the hell's your problem? I was just—"

Rosales grabbed a fistful of Andrews's right arm and pushed him through the open door of a linen closet on the third floor at Presbyterian Hospital. He shifted his hand to Andrews's chest and pressed the man against a bare wall.

"Focus on why we're here. There's a woman in a room down the hall who was beaten to within an inch of her life by her monster-of-a-husband, and who doesn't know yet that the guy was responsible for the deaths of her three kids. Maybe you could think for a minute how we'll be able to get a statement from the woman considering the circumstances."

"Get outta my face, Rosales, before I knock you on your ass."

Rosales gave Andrews a toothy smile, dropped his hand, stepped back a foot, and then rammed his hand back into the taller man's chest. "Anytime you want to go one-on-one with me, you let me know." He stepped back again and walked out into the corridor. He spotted Janet Jenkins—'the broad in the blue suit'—outside the victim's room and moved toward her.

"Hey, Janet," he called out.

She turned in his direction and smiled.

"Well, well," she said, "the RBPD must have finally gotten smart. It sends me the best and the brightest for a change."

At that instant, Detective Andrews walked up, stuck out his hand, and introduced himself to Janet.

She half-smiled and shook his hand.

Rosales said, "Good to see you. It's been a while."

"Too long," Janet said. "I just got here. What's happening?"

"Mrs. Essam's surgery was successful. She'll be in a leg and an arm cast for at least six weeks. They reset her nose, but she'll need plastic surgery at some point."

"What about the husband?" Janet asked.

Rosales breathed out noisily. "I can't believe the paramedics brought him here. He's down in the ER right now. But, apparently, all he has are cuts and bruises. He'll be transported to city jail pending arraignment."

"The charge nurse told me I can speak with Mrs. Essam now," Janet said. "The doctor okayed it."

"You'll have to wait for us to interview her," Rosales said.

Janet nodded. "You going to tell her about her kids?"

Rosales grimaced. "No, we'll leave that to you."

"You're a hell of a guy, Hugo."

"That's what they tell me, Janet."

CHAPTER 4

Janet took an elevator down to the first level and bought a cup of coffee in the hospital cafeteria. Someone had left a copy of the morning paper on the chair next to hers. She scanned the pages of the front section, but couldn't concentrate on the stories about Middle Eastern wars, lone wolf terrorists, another bombing in Paris, and political in-fighting in Washington. She had more than enough violence to deal with right here at home.

She checked and answered emails on her phone and, when a half-hour had gone by, dumped her empty cup in a trash can and returned to the elevators to take her turn with Jasmine Essam.

In the hallway as she approached Mrs. Essam's room, a man in a white lab coat hurried from the doorway.

"I'm Janet Jenkins from St. Anne's Shelter. Are you treating Jasmine Essam,"—she noted his name tag—"Dr. Zelden?"

It took him a few seconds to look up from the cell phone in his hand. "Yes."

"Have you told Mrs. Essam about her children, Doctor?" Janet asked.

"Uh…no. I didn't think it was my place."

Janet detected cowardice in the physician's eyes and weak mouth. She'd long ago become an expert at evaluating men's character. *He didn't think it was his place. What a load of crap.*

She was fully prepared to do the dirty work the doctor was

afraid to do, but that didn't mean she had to like it. She was about to tell the man off, but stopped herself. She didn't do "confrontation" well.

The man suddenly looked over Janet's shoulder and said, "I think I'm needed in another room."

Janet said, "Well, can you at least tell me if she's well enough for bad news?"

"Her heart's strong and she's pretty much come out of the anesthesia. Yes, I think she can handle the news about her children."

"Mrs. Essam," Janet said, her voice as soft as a lullaby. "My name is Janet Jenkins. I work with St. Anne's Shelter for Women & Children. I'm here to assist you in any way I can."

The woman stared at Janet for several seconds. "I remember you," she finally said, her words slightly slurred, her voice strained.

"Yes, we talked after the last...incident with your husband."

"Where are my children?" she asked weakly.

Janet cast a shadow over the woman's face as she leaned forward. "All I want you to focus on right now, Mrs. Essam, is getting well. And you'll need assistance after you're released from here. We have a room ready for you at St. Anne's Shelter until you're ready to return to work."

The woman gave Janet an odd sort of look. She squinted and her nostrils flared.

"What do you mean *you have a room for me*?"

Janet's shoulders slumped. She realized she'd made a mistake. Mrs. Essam was more alert than she'd anticipated.

"I just meant that you'll be able—"

"What is your name again?" Essam asked.

"Janet Jenkins."

"Ms. Jenkins, where are my children? Are they okay? Those two policemen who were in here a few minutes ago dodged my questions. Now, I've got the feeling that's what you're doing, too."

Janet sighed and took the woman's hand. "After your husband beat you, a neighbor called 9-1-1. When the paramedics arrived, your husband and children were gone."

A pained expression spread over the woman's face. She squeezed

Janet's hand so hard that Janet had to force herself not to show pain.

"What did he do?" Essam asked. "Please, what did he do?"

"The police put out an Amber Alert and found him driving erratically on I-5. They tried to pull him over, but weren't successful. They stopped traffic on the interstate and set up a roadblock two exits ahead. Your husband tried to run the roadblock."

"Oh my God. What did that drunk do?"

Janet closed her eyes for a couple seconds, and steeled herself to meet Essam's frightened gaze. When she opened her eyes, her breath caught in her chest. Mrs. Essam's face told Janet she'd already finished the story in her mind.

A banshee-like low moan came from the woman. She released Janet's hand and covered her eyes with that hand. Tears leaked from beneath her fingers and her lips trembled.

"Mrs. Essam, I—"

A shriek halted Janet. She stepped into the hall, hailed a nurse, and said, "You'd better get the doctor in here." When she came back into the room, she looked down at Mrs. Essam just as she removed her hand from her face. Janet's heart seemed to stop when their eyes met. It was as though she'd been transported back twenty-eight years to that shack-of-a-home in Mississippi. To the moment she'd tried to help her mother off the floor after her father beat her and then walked out. Mrs. Essam's eyes—full of grief and hopelessness—looked just like her mother's eyes had looked that day. Every time she'd remembered that look, she'd tried unsuccessfully to describe it. Now, staring into this woman's eyes, the description finally came to her: death stare. It was as though Mrs. Essam had given up on life and now accepted death as the only logical resolution to her grief. *It might be only a matter of time before she takes her own life,* Janet thought. Maybelle had attempted suicide three times, and Janet had found her each time and called for help. It hit Janet at that moment—starvation was just another form of suicide.

CHAPTER 5

"You okay?" Frank Mitchell asked.

Janet shook her head. "This one got to me."

"It's hard, Janet. I wish I could say something to make it easier."

Janet wanted to tell Frank what she'd seen in Jasmine Essam's eyes. But it was too personal and, besides, she wasn't certain anyone would understand the effect that death stare had on her. Not just today, but for the last twenty-eight years.

Janet cleared her throat. "Frank, I'm going to take a walk. I'll be right back. Okay?"

"Of course. Do you want me to go along?"

She waved a hand. "Thanks, but no. I just need to clear my head."

Janet didn't pay any attention to where she walked. She just headed north, toward Hermosa Beach, on the PCH. When she came to the Hermosa Beach boundary line, she realized she'd been gone for over thirty minutes. She reversed direction, then crossed the PCH at Herondo Street and walked under the big Redondo Beach welcome arch at the top of North Catalina Street. The smell of the ocean came to her on a stray breeze and the sun felt good on her back. She rolled her shoulders and continued down North Catalina.

She'd wanted to wipe her mind clean of the look she'd seen on Mrs. Essam's face, but the more she attempted to erase it, the more intense the look became in her memory. She'd gone about a block toward Beryl Street when she heard a high-pitched shout, "Stop it. Leave me be." Two paces down, a narrow alley led from the sidewalk to the side door of a small commercial building. Ten feet into the alley, two burly teenagers stood over what appeared to be an elderly man who gripped the handle of a brown leather briefcase. The man was fighting to maintain his hold on the briefcase as though his life depended on it.

Janet had never been one to look for trouble, and she sure as hell never thought of herself as a fighter. But something about that day, from the conversation with and worry about her mother, to the drive to work, to the experience with Mrs. Essam, had built up anger. There were too many victims and too much unchallenged evil.

"Hey, what are you doing?" she shouted.

The two young men released their holds on the briefcase and turned toward her. They looked stunned. As though they couldn't believe anyone, let alone a woman, would interfere.

"Get lost, bitch," one of them growled as he stepped forward.

Janet reached into her jacket pocket and palmed her pepper spray. Frank had ordered that all the social workers at St. Anne's be armed with the stuff in case some angry spouse came after them. After an irate husband had driven Janet off the road one night, she'd concluded that pepper spray wasn't enough. For almost two years, she'd carried a pistol she'd bought, but then put it in the table next to her bed, where it had laid undisturbed for the past four years.

The thug was less than four feet away when she pressed the plunger on the canister and sprayed him between the eyes. He stopped dead in his tracks, threw his hands at his face, and screamed. Janet cuffed him on the side of his head with her left hand and pulled him from the alley. Then she advanced on the second kid.

"Hey, lady, we was just foolin' around."

"Get out of here or I'll call the police."

The kid sidled past her, grabbed his buddy's arm, and disappeared up the sidewalk.

The old guy was now slumped against the building wall, the briefcase wrapped in his arms. Janet moved in front of him and squatted.

"My name's Janet. You okay, sir?"

The guy's eyes danced around as though he was high on drugs. Now that she had the chance to get a better look at him, she guessed he was closer to fifty. His week-old stubble, weathered skin, pure gray hair, and the weary look in his eyes made him look older. Much older.

"You live around here?" Janet asked.

The man shrugged. His eyes continued to pinball.

Janet stood and extended her hand. "Let me help you up."

He took her hand, stood, and then leaned against the wall. He still hugged the briefcase as though it was a baby.

"Listen, I've got to get to my office. Is there someone I can call to pick you up?"

He shook his head.

"You going to be okay?"

He nodded.

She gave him a once-over and then smiled. "I have to go. You can come with me to my office. We have a nurse there who could check you out."

The man shook his head again.

Janet pressed her lips together and walked away. She glanced back over a shoulder and smiled at the man.

The man watched the woman walk away. He moved to the top of the alley and looked left, the way his attackers had gone. He breathed a sigh of relief; they were nowhere in sight. He wondered if they'd been sent to find him. A vein of ice seemed to hit his backbone and he shuddered at the thought that they'd finally tracked him down. But then he pushed away the thought. The attackers were nothing but teenagers, not hardcore muscle.

He looked to the right and saw the woman, now half-a-block away. *She said she had to get to her office. It must be close*, he thought. *After all, she's walking.*

He set off after her, the briefcase cradled in his arms. *It would be good to know where she worked.*

It took Johnny Casale four hours on I-15 to make the trip from Las

Vegas to Los Angeles. He arrived at 10 p.m. and took a room at the Beverly Hilton. After a room service burger, fries, and a glass of merlot, he went to bed, and dreamed about money and women.

DAY 2

CHAPTER 6

Casale knew that the financial markets opened in New York City at 9:30 eastern time, which meant that investment houses on the west coast probably opened at 6:30 a.m. He parked in the lot on the side of the Forsythe Investment building on North Beverly Drive in Beverly Hills and approached the unoccupied reception desk. Behind it were two rows of glass cubicles, six on either side of a central aisle that ran to the back. Two private offices were visible at the rear of each row of cubicles. He spied a twenty-something woman in a glass-enclosed room that was obviously a kitchen/break room at the back, beyond the private offices. She waved at him and raised a finger to signal that she would be with him momentarily.

The woman came forward and greeted him with a big smile. "Sorry," she said, "I was making coffee. Would you like a cup?"

Casale shook his head. "No, thanks." He stared into her eyes and took some satisfaction when she seemed to cringe and looked away. He handed her a card. "I'd like to speak with one of the partners."

The woman glanced down at the card and said, "Private Investigator? New York?"

He smiled and said, "Yeah. Have gun, will travel."

She frowned. "Excuse me?"

Casale guessed the young woman had never heard of the old television show. *Ah well*, he thought.

"Sweetie, how 'bout you tell one of the partners I'd like to talk with him about an urgent matter?"

The woman scrunched up her face and seemed to be about to say something, when Casale squinted, gave her his "street cred" predator look, and barked, "Now!"

Her eyes went wide. She mouthed a couple silent words, turned, and marched down the central aisle. Fifteen seconds later, a distinguished-looking, white-haired man of about the same age as Casale, stepped out of the far right-hand office and peered at him. The receptionist stood behind him and pointed at Casale. The guy said something to the woman, after which she scurried back toward the kitchen. Then the man came forward. He stopped a few feet from Casale, looked down at the business card the woman had given him, and then glared at Casale.

"You got a problem with my receptionist, Mr. Casale?"

Casale was surprised the guy not only pronounced his name correctly—Ca-sal-eh, but he spoke with the traces of a New York accent, and he eyeballed him as though he might take a swing at him. He smiled and answered, "No, I don't have a problem with her. I told her I wanted to talk to you and here you are."

"New York, huh?"

"Yeah. Queens, to be exact."

The guy now wore a humorless grin.

"You, too?" Casale asked.

"Brooklyn."

"I didn't get your name," Casale said.

The guy showed a toothy grin and said, "I didn't give it to you."

Casale waited.

Finally, the man said, "Forsythe. Charles Forsythe."

"You don't look like a Forsythe."

It was Forsythe's turn to not respond.

Casale scoffed. "Probably wanted to fit in out here."

Again, there was no response from Forsythe.

"You got ten minutes for me?" Casale asked.

Forsythe waved a hand. "Let's go back to my office."

The office was large, spacious enough to accommodate a credenza, desk chair, and desk, with two more chairs and a tray table in front of the desk, and a three-seat couch and coffee table at the opposite end of the room from the desk. It was richly appointed, with a Persian carpet and what appeared to be original paintings of California landscapes.

After Casale sat in a chair in front of the desk, Forsythe stared at him for a couple of seconds, then said, "So, what brings you to California?"

Casale made a production of pulling a small note pad from an inside jacket pocket. He flipped open the cover and turned to a page. He then made eye contact with Forsythe. "You ever heard the name, Bruno Pedace?"

He looked for some sort of tell from Forsythe, but caught nothing.

"Why?"

Casale shrugged. "He took something that belonged to my client."

"Musta been something valuable for you to come this far."

The P.I. looked toward the open door and waved in the direction of the hallway. "I see you got a number of people working for you. Maybe one of them heard of Pedace."

"That's possible."

"Maybe you could ask them if they did a transaction for him. Cashed in a one hundred-thousand-dollar bond."

Forsythe's right eyelid twitched.

Casale leaned forward and, in a lowered voice, said, "Let's not jerk each other around, Forsythe. I suspect no one cashes in a one hundred-thousand-dollar bond around here without a partner signing off on it. All I want to know is where the guy who cashed in that bond lives. I know it was Pedace. I walk outta here with that information and I'll be indebted to you. Maybe I do you a favor one day. But if I leave here empty-handed, you'll have a new enemy."

Forsythe's face colored momentarily and his eyes narrowed. But there was no fear in his expression. Casale was convinced the guy was no white-collar softie.

"If this Pedace is a client of this firm, there's no way I'll give you any information about him. But since I've never heard of him, I can't help you."

Casale groaned, then stood. "That's too bad. You're making a big mistake."

Forsythe said, "Mr. Casale, I'm asking you real nicely to leave my office. If you don't do so in the next few seconds, however, I'll throw your ass out."

Casale pointed a finger at Forsythe and opened his mouth to say something, when Forsythe leaped from his chair. "If you think I'll be pushed around by some *chooch* from Queens, you're badly mistaken. *Hai capito*? Now get the hell out of my office."

Casale pointed at his business card in the middle of Forsythe's desk. "You got my cell number. Call me if you change your mind."

The Starbucks sign nearly seduced Janet. She was tempted to pull off the PCH and go through the drive-thru lane. She could almost taste and smell a double mocha cappuccino. But Janet couldn't easily edge into the left turn lane and decided that was good, after all. She couldn't afford to splurge, not with paying for her mother's medications and doctor visits. At fifty-seven, her mother had the health expenses of an eighty-year-old.

She put the cappuccino out of mind and wondered how Jasmine Essam was doing. She would call the hospital as soon as she got settled at her desk.

As Janet entered the St. Anne's lobby, Mary the receptionist raised a finger and said, "Mr. Mitchell wants to see you in the conference room."

Janet thanked her and used her passkey to enter the office area. She swung by her office and dropped off her purse and jacket, picked up a legal pad and pen from her desk, and walked through the office area toward the conference room at the back. Her stomach did a quick flip-flop when she entered the room. Seated around the table were Frank Mitchell and Detectives Rosales and Andrews. A dark cloud seemed to hang over the room.

"Ah, Janet, come in and take a seat," Mitchell said.

Janet sat on the same side of the table as Mitchell, directly across from the two detectives.

"Go ahead, Detective Rosales," Mitchell said.

Sparks seemed to shoot out of Rosales' eyes. Janet knew him well enough to recognize how angry he was.

Rosales said, "As I told you, Mr. Mitchell, I could kill someone right now. I can't believe the stupidity of some people."

Janet's gaze drifted from Rosales to Andrews and back to Rosales.

"What happened, Hugo?"

"They made a mistake at the jail and released Rasif Essam."

Janet's mouth dropped open. "Mrs. Essam could be in danger. What—?"

Rosales raised a hand. "As soon as we discovered what had happened, we put uniforms outside the hospital and on Mrs. Essam's floor. He'd have to be nuts to try to get to her there."

Janet slowly shook her head. "I'd say that a man who nearly beats his wife to death and then, in a drunken rage, is responsible for the deaths of his three children, qualifies as a nut job."

Rosales gave a brief nod. "Listen, it's not Mrs. Essam we're worried about. She's got plenty of protection. It's you people here. Essam raised holy hell in the emergency room last night about St. Anne's interfering with his life." Rosales fixed his eyes on Janet. "He had special words for you. Even while he was booked, he still ranted about you and how you corrupted his wife's mind the last time you helped her."

"You mean the last time I helped her after her sick husband kicked the crap out of her."

Mitchell said, "The RBPD has offered to post a guard on our building. A police officer will escort all employees to their vehicles."

Janet forced a smile. "I'm sure the RBPD will find Mr. Essam and put his butt back where it belongs."

Detective Andrews said, "Ms. Jenkins, I assume you have an unlisted phone number at home."

Janet blurted a laugh. "In this business, I'd be insane to have a listed number. The only phone I've got is my cell."

"Good," Andrews said.

"What are you doing here?" Jimmy Duffy asked Rasif Essam. "I heard on the news that the cops are looking for you."

"I have to get out of town, but I need your help."

Duffy wheeled his chair backward and stretched to reach his

home office door. He closed it and then wheeled back to his desk. "What's going on, Rasif?"

"It was all a misunderstanding. You know Jasmine. She's always breaking the rules. I had to teach her to—"

"Rasif, the news said you nearly killed her and then crashed into a police car at a roadblock." Duffy showed Essam a sympathetic look and said, "I'm sorry about your children."

For a moment, Essam seemed unable to speak. Tears came to his eyes. "That damn Jasmine. It's all her fault."

"Were you drunk again?"

"What does that have to do with anything?" Essam growled as he stepped toward Duffy.

Duffy backed up in his chair, but he could go only a few inches before he hit the desk.

"Are you going to help me or lecture me?"

"I don't want any trouble, Rasif."

Essam took a step away and backed into a chair. "There won't be any trouble. All I need is an address."

"You could look in the phone book or go on the Internet."

"I already tried. The address and phone number aren't listed."

Duffy pressed his lips together and groaned. "All right, what information do you have?"

"I know a name and a workplace. I also have the plate number on a car." He handed over a slip of paper.

"The easiest hack will be of the California DMV."

"How long will that take?"

Duffy laughed. "Minutes. I break into that system a couple times a week." As he tapped away at his computer keyboard, he asked, "Who is this woman?"

"The one who put all sorts of Western ideas in Jasmine's head. The last time Jasmine and I…argued; the police brought this woman to our house. She took Jasmine and my children to her shelter and kept us apart for a week."

Duffy stopped typing and spun around. "What are you thinking?"

Essam made a dismissive gesture with a hand. "Nothing for you to worry about. I just want to frighten her a bit."

"*Then* what are you going to do?"

"Go back to Egypt. There's nothing left for me here."

CHAPTER 7

St. Anne's Shelter was housed in a 1930s-era three-story mansion bequeathed to the organization in 1951 by a wealthy couple. It took up half a block of prime Redondo Beach residential property. The neighbors in the area had raised a ruckus about the house being converted to a battered women's shelter, but the Catholic Church had ultimately won out and got the zoning it needed. The inside of the facility had changed dramatically over the years. The first-floor windows were barred and every wing was security-controlled. The electrical and plumbing systems had been modernized. But, the exterior was essentially the same as it had been for over eighty years: pitched slate roof, white dormer windows, and gray stone walls. The site was elevated several feet above the street and surrounded by two acres of grass studded by gigantic oak and sycamore trees. A concrete city sidewalk defined two sides of the property and a three-foot-high stone wall separated the lawns from the sidewalk. The parking area was on the right side of the building.

A man sat on the stone wall at the front left corner of the St. Anne's property. His feet dangled over the sidewalk. He'd stationed himself there at 1 p.m. and had alternately kept an eye on the facility's front entrance and the parking lot, between reading pages of a dog-eared copy of Michael Lewis's *The Big Short*, a story that detailed the mortgage market crash of 2008. He put a hash mark on the inside front cover of the book as he turned the last page. There were now eighty-five hash marks there. He didn't actually read the words anymore. He'd long ago memorized every one of them. He now turned pages as he recited words.

The angle of the sun told him it was approaching 6 p.m. when the door opened and the woman exited. She turned left on an interior walkway, away from where he sat, and moved toward the parking lot. He quickly slipped the book into his briefcase, closed the case, dropped to the sidewalk, and called out, "Oh, miss, hello."

The woman turned around and looked at him.

"It's me, miss. You remember?"

The woman cut across the lawn toward him, smiled, and said, "Of course, I remember you. How are you?"

"I'm fine, thank you."

"What are you doing here?"

He lowered his gaze, coughed, and said, "I want to apologize for my poor behavior yesterday. I didn't thank you for helping me. And it was terribly rude of me not to introduce myself." He performed a brief half-bow, and said, "My name is…Cecil Rosandich."

The woman smiled again. "Well, it's nice to meet you, Mr. Rosandich. My name is Janet Jenkins. Is there something I can do for you?"

"No, no, quite the opposite. I wanted to thank you for your help and give you a small reward."

"Your thanks are more than enough. No reward is necessary. I'm sorry, but you'll have to excuse me. I'm running late."

The man raised a hand. "Please, I'll only take another minute of your time." He opened his briefcase and removed a packet wrapped in a paper towel, secured with several rubber bands. He extended the packet to the woman. "Please accept this gift as an expression of my deep appreciation." He half-bowed again.

The woman bent and took the packet. "Thank you, Mr. Rosandich. I appreciate the gesture. But I really must go."

He nodded, picked up his briefcase, and walked away.

Janet watched him and felt a pang in her heart. She'd got a really good look at him this time. His suit appeared to be of excellent quality, perhaps custom made. But it was frayed at the collar and cuffs. His shirt was now more gray than white and was also frayed. His polished wing-tipped shoes were wrinkled with age and wear. The tie, although neatly done, was stained. Despite the worn appearance of his clothes, the man appeared to be well-groomed. His fingernails were clipped; his gray hair was cut short and appeared to be clean. But what made the greatest impression were his eyes—startlingly blue and intelligent, and his articulate speech. Despite her first impression in the alley, she now thought, *he's no ordinary homeless person.*

"Jeez," Janet mumbled as she walked past the building to her car. "I wonder what his story is."

She unlocked her car and slipped into the front seat. After she tossed the package the man had given her onto the passenger seat and placed her purse beside it, she started the Impala and drove away.

Jimmy Duffy had been unable to concentrate since Rasif Essam left his home. It wasn't because he'd given the woman's address to Essam. That's what he did for a living—provide information to people for a price. Hell, he'd hacked classified databases for years and given information to all sorts of people and organizations. But Essam was a fugitive from the law. Duffy had told his wife, Sarah, what he'd done for Essam. His usually calm and gentle wife had thrown up her hands in exasperation and screamed at him for a full minute. She'd finished her tirade with, "I've told you to stay away from that man. He's evil. What if he doesn't get out of the country and is captured by the police? What if he tells them you gave him the woman's address?"

After Sarah stormed from his office, Duffy leaped from his chair, paced for a minute, and then growled, "Damn."

He moved back to his desk, pulled open a desk drawer, and selected one of a dozen burner phones there. He plugged it into a charger cord and waited until it powered up enough to call 9-1-1.

The tension in the unmarked was palpable. Detective John Andrews was still pissed at his partner, Detective Hugo Rosales, about the way he'd manhandled him in the hospital. Rosales still harbored a grudge about Andrews's chauvinistic reference to Janet Jenkins. He would have been angry if Andrews had disrespected any woman, but he was especially angry because Andrews had used gutter language to refer to a woman he respected and who'd become a friend of his wife, Carmela.

Rosales was just about to say something to Andrews, in an attempt to clear the air, when the car radio squawked and the dispatcher announced their call sign.

Andrews responded, "This is Bravo 23. Over."

"Bravo 23, we just received a call about fugitive Rasif Essam. A male caller said he believes Essam is on his way to the residence of a Janet Jenkins. 1428 Brockhurst Lane in El Segundo."

"Did you alert El Segundo P.D.?" Andrews asked.

"They're on the way."

Andrews signed off as Rosales pulled a U-turn and drove toward El Segundo. "Damn! Damn! Damn!" he cursed. Then he handed his cell phone to Andrews and said, "Look up Janet Jenkins's name in my contact list. Try to reach her."

Andrews pulled up Jenkins's number and called it, but it rang without being answered. He left a message.

As he goosed the accelerator, Rosales cleared his throat and said, "Listen, I shouldn't have put my hands on you. It was unprofessional."

Andrews grunted. "Is that an apology?"

Rosales cleared his throat again. "Yeah, I apologize."

After a good fifteen seconds passed, Andrews asked, "You gotta tell me why you reacted as you did. Jeez, Hugo, I was just admiring a piece of—"

"You weren't admiring a piece of ass; you were disrespecting a fine woman who I think the world of."

Another few seconds passed before Andrews asked, "You got something going with her?"

Rosales shot a glance at Andrews, expelled a loud breath, and muttered an extended curse in Spanish.

CHAPTER 8

Two drive-bys of the bungalow in El Segundo in his wife's Toyota van left Rasif Essam frustrated and angrier than he was already. There was no vehicle in the gravel driveway on the side of the house; no garage either. He could see no lights on inside. His left foot tattooed the floorboard and his hands beat a riff on the steering wheel.

He thought, *I can't wait around here forever. Some damned cop might drive by and spot this van.* He sorely wanted to punish Janet Jenkins. He'd come to the point in his thinking that what had happened to his family was all because of her. But, if she wasn't home, he could still harass her; make her sorry. He'd trash her shitty little house.

He parked the van in the lot of an Asian market and walked two blocks back to the bungalow. After he eyeballed the houses on either side of Jenkins's place, to make certain there were no nosy neighbors, he fast-walked down the driveway to the rear door, found it locked, and kicked it in. He quickly went through the kitchen into a small dining room that opened onto a living room.

Essam scoffed as he glanced around. "Nothing of value in here," he muttered. He moved toward the bottom of the staircase to the second floor, when a shrill voice called from the top of the stairs, "Is that you, dear?"

Essam took in a big breath and charged upstairs.

Janet was listening to KKGO radio when she heard her cell phone ring. She tried to grab her purse, which had slid up against the passenger door, but couldn't quite reach it. *I'll deal with whoever it is when I get home*, she thought. Then she sang along with Carrie Underwood's *Jesus, Take the Wheel*. She knew her voice was professional quality and wondered what her life would have been like if she'd moved to Nashville, rather than to L.A. She interrupted her singing, blurted a laugh, and said, "Dream along with me." Despite bumper-to-bumper traffic, she was making decent time and hoped her mother had eaten the lunch she'd left for her in the refrigerator. She then picked back up with Underwood.

"Who are you?" Maybelle Jenkins cried, her heart quickening, her breathing erratic. "What are you doing in my house?"

The man grabbed her arm and dragged her to the bedroom at the rear of the second floor.

"Stop it," she yelled.

The man threw her on the bed, pointed a finger, and shouted, "Where's Janet Jenkins?"

"She's not here."

"I can see that, you old bitch. When will she be here?"

Maybelle shrugged and lied, "My daughter is out of town on business."

"You're full of shit, old woman."

She tried to stand, but the man slapped her and knocked her back on the bed. She stared at the man and, for an instant, thought she saw her former husband, Marvin. The guy had the same beady black eyes. Her stomach burned and her heartbeat quickened even more.

"You wait here," the man ordered. "You leave this room and I'll break your scrawny neck." He walked out and closed the door after him.

Maybelle heard the *clomp-clomp-clomp* of his footfalls as he went back downstairs. She took in a series of deep breaths to calm her heart, then went to the window on the side of the back bedroom that overlooked the driveway.

Essam went to the kitchen and removed a butcher knife from a rack. He returned to the living room, sliced the couch and chair cushions, and tipped over the television. In the dining room, he repeatedly marked the table with the knife and then shouted a huge "Yeah!" when he pulled the breakfront off the credenza and watched it crash to the floor.

Back in the kitchen, he went to work on the food, flatware, and dishes in the drawers and cabinets. He was about to topple the refrigerator when he heard a car motor and the crunch of tires.

Maybelle saw Janet's Impala pull into the driveway. She tried to open the window, but it was painted shut. She banged on the glass so hard she thought it would break. But Janet apparently didn't hear her. "What the heck are you doing?" she muttered. *Get out of the car*, she silently pleaded.

Janet kept the motor running while she and Patsy Cline finished the last part of *Crazy*: *And I'm crazy for lovin' you*. She switched off the radio, turned off the ignition, and sighed because she didn't know in what state she'd find her mother. She stretched out and grabbed her purse, opened her door, and planted her feet on the driveway. Then she remembered the package the man had given her. She reached back to get it when she heard her cell phone ring again. She moved her hand to pull the phone from her purse when there came a loud crash and a shower of glass landed on the car roof, on her legs, and at her feet. She yelped and felt her heart leap. She peeked up at the house. At that moment, her mother stuck her head out of the broken second-floor window, screamed, "There's a man in the house," and then tossed something that landed with a *thud* on the car roof and slid down the windshield onto the hood.

"My God," Janet cried when she spotted her .38 revolver resting there. She dropped her purse in the driveway, rushed from the car, and snatched the pistol.

"Essam, *ese hijo de puta*," Rosales growled as Andrews shouted directions at him.

The flashers in the unmarked's grill were on and Andrews had placed the bubblegum light on the car roof. The siren was going full blast. But rush hour traffic was a mess and even the drivers who wanted to make way for the police vehicle had no place to go.

"El Segundo PD will get there before we do anyway, "Andrews said, not sounding particularly confident.

Rosales continued to grumble and curse in Spanish. Then he said, "Try Janet's phone again."

As he redialed the number, Andrews said, "You know the guy who called 9-1-1 about Essam might have been a prank caller."

Rosales shot a quick scowl at Andrews. "Right. How'd he know Janet's address?"

A gap opened in traffic and Rosales slipped into it and hit the gas.

As Janet moved to the back door, she shouted at her mother to crawl under the bed. But then she saw a man in the window frame, his arm around her mother's neck.

Janet gasped when she saw the door hanging open and through the doorway the condition of the kitchen. Her heels crunched on debris as she crossed into the dining room. More of the same there and in the living room beyond. She rushed toward the staircase— the pistol down at her side, and turned to look up to the second floor. She stopped; her breath caught in her chest. Rasif Essam stood at the top of the staircase. He had one arm around her mother's throat and a knife raised in his other hand. Janet moved her gun hand behind her back.

"You couldn't keep your nose out of my business, could you, bitch?"

"Let my mother go, Mr. Essam. Then you and I can sit down and discuss this."

"It's your fault my children are dead."

This guy's delusional, Janet thought. "Come on, Mr. Essam. We can talk about it after you release my mother." As she waited for a response, she made eye contact with Maybelle and noticed anger and determination in her expression. *Please don't do anything stupid, Mom,* she thought.

Essam lifted Maybelle with one arm and moved down two steps.

Janet heard sirens as she backed up toward the front door. Essam must have heard them, too, because he said something in a foreign language that sounded like a curse. His eyes went wide.

"Please let my mother go," Janet pleaded. "You can go out the back. You still have time to get away."

Essam coughed a laugh and roared.

At that moment, Maybelle lowered her head and bit Essam's forearm. He screamed, jerked his arm away, and then shoved Maybelle at Janet. Her mother's frail body flew toward the bottom of the stairs. Janet stepped forward to try to catch her but had barely covered half the distance from the door to the bottom step when Maybelle's head struck the final on the top of the balustrade with a *thunk*. Before she could take another step, Essam ran down the stairs, knife extended, roaring with rage, hatred in the set of his mouth and in his eyes.

Janet brought the pistol from behind her back, aimed, pulled the trigger, and tensed in anticipation of the weapon's noise and kick. But nothing happened as the hammer fell on an empty chamber. The man now blotted out her view of the staircase as he attacked. She pulled the trigger again and this time the weapon boomed, the percussion of the fired bullet ricocheting off the room's hard surfaces. Essam landed against her and drove her back into the front door. Her head struck the door and the wind went out of her lungs. Her gun hand was pinned between their chests as they fell to the floor. Stunned, she tried to push Essam off her as he continued to vent his anger in massive, maniacal shouts and curses. Then he lifted up and raised the knife.

Still stunned, but aware enough to realize her predicament, she pressed the pistol against Essam's chest and pulled the trigger.

A loud *oof* escaped the man as the noise of the weapon again careened around the room. Spittle dribbled from his mouth as he made animal-like sounds. He drove the knife downward. Janet screamed in agony as the blade penetrated her left shoulder. Then Essam fell away onto his back, his breathing labored, blood staining his white shirt.

Janet rolled to her side and gawked at the handle of the knife as though its presence made no sense. She got to her knees and placed the pistol on the floor at the bottom of the staircase. She attempted to stand but failed, and had to crawl to her mother.

"Mama," she rasped. "Talk to me, Mama."

Janet turned her mother onto her side and gasped. The side of Maybelle's head was crushed. Blood covered the wood floor and the edge of the throw rug. "No, no, Mama," she wailed, as tears clouded her vision.

The inside of her skull felt as though it was filled with mush and the sound of crashing waves on a beach roared in her ears. She had a crushing headache. Then the banshee-like screams of sirens seemed suddenly overpowering. They made her head hurt even more. But amid the noise and pain in her head and the sounds of sirens, she heard a gurgling sound and looked over her left shoulder. The movement sent searing pain through her and she screamed like a wild beast. But she shunted the pain aside and leaped from her knees onto Essam's back just as the man grasped the pistol. She beat the back of his head with her fists and then clawed at his face. But he threw an elbow backward and connected with her side, sending a wave of pain through her ribs. She fell back onto the floor and saw through a veil of tears Essam roll onto his side and slowly bring the pistol around toward her. In that moment of clarity, when she knew she was about to die, Janet scrambled to her knees, jerked the knife from her shoulder—blood flowing down her arm, and plunged it into Essam's chest. Her pain-, rage-, and terror-driven screams ricocheted off the walls. Then she pushed him onto his back, and straddled him. As she peered into the fading light in his eyes, she raised the knife and struck…again…and again…and again.

CHAPTER 9

Charles Forsythe pulled out of his office parking lot at 8:00 p.m.

"Long friggin' day," Johnny Casale muttered as he watched from a parking space across the street. He followed Forsythe to a restaurant in Beverly Hills, where Casale looked at the dashboard clock and thought, *better call it a day.*

"Holy shit, what a mess," Detective John Andrews groused as Hugo Rosales drove to Presbyterian Hospital. "Hope Jenkins had a permit for that pistol."

Rosales gave Andrews a squint-eyed look. "In most states, I'd say that shouldn't make a difference. It was obviously self-defense. But this is friggin' California, after all. The first thing our *pinche* D.A. will do is bring firearms charges against her and then wait to see how the media reacts."

"Probably right," Andrews said. "But, now that I think about it, she'll get off for sure, don't you think? I mean, it was self-defense all the way."

Rosales shrugged. "Essam brutally beat his wife, killed his kids, and was subject to a fugitive warrant when he broke into Janet's house. Then he murdered Janet's mother and tried to kill Janet. Even in California, that constitutes reasonable cause. But, as I said, this *is* California."

"Gotta give her credit. That gal fought like a wounded tigress.

Can't believe what she did to that maniac."

"Couldn't happen to a nicer guy," Rosales said.

They were almost at the hospital, when Andrews said, "Listen, Hugo, I want to apologize for what I said before about Janet. I didn't mean anything by it."

After a long beat, Rosales said, "I appreciate it. But it's not just wrong to disrespect women; it's bad for your career. Hell, the RBPD chief is female, as are two members of the Police Oversight Board."

Andrews nodded.

Frank Mitchell sat in the surgical waiting room, his elbows on his thighs, his gaze fixed on the coffee-stained carpet beneath his feet. Other St. Anne's staff members had come in and out of the hospital during the night, but they'd all gone home by 11 p.m. The news about Janet Jenkins was "as good as can be expected under the circumstances." That's the way the surgeon had put it. Mitchell knew there was nothing he could do for her, but he couldn't make himself leave. After all, she had no one else. He was just about to see if he could find a cup of coffee when Detectives Rosales and Andrews walked in.

"Hey, Frank," Rosales said. "You hear anything?"

"Yeah. She's out of surgery and already in a room. Surgeon said something about the knife wound in her upper left chest causing her to drop a lung...whatever the hell that means. Apparently, the knife she used to kill Essam was the same one he stuck in her. If you can believe it, she took it out of her chest and used it on him. Could have severed a vein or an artery when she pulled it out."

"So, what are you doing here? You look like death warmed over."

Mitchell hunched his shoulders and spread his arms. "I was just asking myself that a few minutes ago." He swallowed hard. "You know she doesn't have any family. No friends that I know of. All she did was work and take care of her mother. I just—" Tears came to his eyes and his throat burned.

Rosales came over and put a hand on Mitchell's shoulder.

Mitchell used a hand to wipe away his tears. "You know, we've had a lot of close calls at St. Anne's; but this is the first time one of our people was badly injured." He swallowed hard again and said,

"Oh, God. And her mother."

Andrews said, "I'm going to find a nurse. See if there's news."

Rosales took the chair across from Mitchell. "Did you know she had a pistol?"

Mitchell sat up straight and said, "Yeah. Janet told me she'd bought one several years ago after an incident. I encourage all our social workers to carry pepper spray, but never suggested they carry guns. But, after today, I might do just that. Pay for them all to get concealed carry permits. Our work involves dealing with some bad people." He choked up again and couldn't continue for a few seconds. "As far as I know, Janet hadn't carried the thing with her in a while."

"Having that pistol probably saved her life."

Mitchell met Rosales's gaze and nodded.

Rosales stood. "Let's all go home. Maybe things will look better in the light of day."

DAY 3

CHAPTER 10

Janet wasn't certain if she was alive or dead. Everything was pitch-black and she felt as though she floated on mist. She heard the noise of a long groan and wondered where it came from. Then a voice.

"Ms. Jenkins, my name is Alice Higgins, your nurse."

The groan again. This time, she realized it had come from her.

"You're in Presbyterian Hospital. You've had surgery. Everything went well."

Janet made a sound in her throat that came across like a growl. She tried to speak, but nothing came out except another growl. Then she felt a straw placed between her lips and she sucked in cool water. She finally said, "My mother?"

The nurse touched her arm. "The doctor will be in shortly. He'll explain everything to you."

Janet attempted a response, but her head went fuzzy and she drifted off.

Johnny Casale had been awake all night thinking about his meeting with Charles Forsythe. His instincts told him that threatening the investment guy with physical violence was a non-starter. The man had grown up on the streets of Brooklyn. He needed to come up with another way of intimidating him. One thing he'd learned over the years was that no one was a saint. He'd discover what Forsythe's weaknesses were and then exploit them.

The sun sent a slanted ray of light through a slight gap in the hotel room curtains. Casale looked at the clock on the bedside table and grumbled about the time: 6:35. He rolled to get out of bed when his cell phone rang. He snatched the phone off the table, looked at the screen, and recognized Sy Rosen's private number.

"Fuck," he barked. He answered the call and forced himself to keep aggravation out of his voice.

"You find him?" Rosen shouted.

"I'm close. I met with a partner of the firm that traded the bond for Pedace."

"And?"

"He's not cooperating. But I assure you that won't last."

"How can you be so sure?" Rosen demanded.

"I know people, what motivates them, Mr. Rosen. That's why you pay me big bucks."

"Casale, my patience is about exhausted. You resolve this matter or I'll fire your ass and hire someone who can get the job done."

Before Casale could respond, Rosen terminated the call.

7 DAYS LATER
DAY 10

CHAPTER 11

The receptionist at St. Anne's had noticed the man sitting on the wall in front of the shelter the day after Janet was put in the hospital. And every day since then. She remembered that Janet had mentioned the man a couple days before she was attacked. Every day, the man followed the same routine: arrive at 8:00 a.m., sit on the wall, circle the property once every hour, eat a sandwich he'd take from his briefcase, leave at 5:00 p.m.

On the third day, she'd gone outside and asked him if there was something he needed.

"I'm waiting for Janet," he'd told her.

"You know she's in the hospital?"

"I do."

"It may be a while before she returns to work."

"I'll wait."

Casale had shadowed Forsythe's movements for forty-eight hours after his meeting with the man. He'd discovered nothing he could use against him. He came to work early and left late. Other than the first night when he'd followed him to a restaurant, Forsythe had gone straight from his office to a palatial residence in Beverly Hills.

On the third day of trailing Forsythe, the man had driven to LAX, parked in a long term lot, and taken a shuttle van to the American Airlines terminal. There was nothing Casale could do but drive away from the airport and hope that Forsythe would soon return to Los Angeles.

Janet was released from the hospital on the sixth day after being admitted. The morning after her release, she stood outside her surgeon's office and used a tissue to blot her tears. Every thought about her mother brought on another crying jag. She'd wailed at the walls of her hospital room and shouted at God for days. The wailing had now stopped, but her anger with God had only increased with each day.

Her surgeon had advised her to take two more weeks off from work, but there was no way she would comply with his instructions. She wanted the doctor to remove the drainage tube in her shoulder and to pronounce her well enough to return to work. She left her work clothes—dark blue suit, white blouse, and black pumps—in her car, and wore jeans, a baggy T-shirt, and cross trainers into the medical office.

"How are you doing, young lady?" the white-haired surgeon asked as he sallied into the exam room.

"What do you say all the time? As well as can be expected under the circumstances."

The doctor chuckled. "I do say that, don't I? I'll have to come up with another line. Well, let's have a look at you."

Janet pushed the shirt off her left shoulder and stared at the ceiling. The surgeon slowly removed the bandage and thick gauze pad and clucked for a few seconds.

"Looks good, Janet. Another week or so and you should be almost as good as new."

"I want you to take this damned thing out," she said, pointing at the drainage tube.

The surgeon pushed back on his wheeled stool and stared wide-eyed at her. "You've still got discharge from your wound. I hope you're not thinking about going back to work."

"If I don't go back to work, I'll go crazy."

The man looked at her and slowly shook his head. "You need rest; time to recuperate. It'll be at least two weeks before you feel like yourself again."

Janet clenched her jaws. "Either you take it out or I'll do it myself. Bandage me up so I can get to work."

The doctor squinted at her. "You ever call Dr. Shapiro?"

Janet felt her face warm. "Not yet."

"You should call her, Janet. She's handled a lot of patients who've been through traumatic experiences, including men and women who've been in combat. That's what you went through—combat."

She nodded. "Maybe I'll call her today."

The surgeon looked at her through hooded eyes. She could tell he didn't believe her. He sighed loudly and then removed the tube and bandaged her arm. As she stood to leave, he said, "For God's sake, make sure you finish the antibiotic series I gave you."

A minute later, in her Impala, she attempted to calm her breathing and her pulse. It was all she could do to keep from screaming obscenities and hammering her hands against the steering wheel.

'*Feel like yourself again*,' the doctor had said. Those words made her want to scream.

She gripped the steering wheel as though she wanted to break it, as the vision of her mother's crushed and bloody skull and lifeless eyes came to her. Then the picture of her mother's face the day Marvin Jenkins abandoned them resurfaced. The grief and hopelessness in her mother's eyes so many years ago were as vivid as though it had been yesterday when her father's final betrayal had occurred.

Through narrowed eyes, Janet looked through the windshield at the medical building. "No, Doc. I'll never feel like myself again. The old Janet Jenkins will never be back."

On the way to St. Anne's, Janet turned on her radio. But the strains of C&W music didn't seem to fit her mood. She switched it off as she stopped for a red light. The driver to her left, a guy in a Mercedes sports car, glanced at her, raised his eyebrows, and then winked. Janet flipped him the bird and grimaced. She felt momentarily embarrassed about her reaction, but then she thought, *screw him*.

She pulled into the St. Anne's parking lot and rocked her head left then right. She was relieved there was little pain and not much stiffness in her shoulder. She opened her door and reached for her purse, mentally thanking the cop who'd found it in her driveway and left it for her at the hospital. Then she noticed something on the passenger side floor. *What the hell?* She bent over, looked closer, and saw the package Cecil Rosandich had given her a week ago. The sight of it made her chuckle. It had been there in her unlocked Impala for the past week. *Thank God it's nothing valuable*, she thought, *or it might have been stolen by one of the neighborhood derelicts.*

She reached down and picked up the package, placed it in her lap, and removed the rubber bands and paper towel wrapping. What she saw caused her to do a double take. At first, she thought she was looking at funny money. But when she examined the bills, she discovered there was nothing "funny" about them. There were two bundles of cash. Each one had a strap around it that read: $10,000. She slammed the car door closed and locked herself in.

"Holy shit," she exclaimed. "Twenty thousand dollars in my unlocked car for seven days." Then a thought hit her: *Where would a guy like Cecil get this kind of money?*

Janet looked around as though she expected someone to look in at her. She stuffed the money in her pocketbook, reopened the door, and stepped out. Then she opened the back door, took out her work clothes, closed both doors, and locked the car. She slung her purse and her clothes over her good shoulder. As she exited the parking lot and walked past the corner of the building, she looked at the stone wall down by the front sidewalk, hoping that Cecil might be there. She was surprised at how disappointed she felt when she didn't see him.

Inside the lobby, the receptionist greeted her with a hearty, "Welcome back."

"Mary," Janet said, "have you seen that guy hanging around lately? Wears a suit and tie. Carries a briefcase."

Mary said, "Oh yeah. I saw him out there seated on the wall the day after you were injured. He was there every day after that. One day, I asked him what he was doing. He said he was waiting for you." Mary's face seemed to sag. "He seemed really upset about you being injured. Isn't he out there now?"

"No. When did you last see him?"

"Yesterday. Same as usual." She moved to the front window. "This is the first day he didn't show."

"Okay, thanks. Let me know when you see him next."

Janet was suddenly worried. *If anyone discovers the man carries around large sums of cash, his life won't be worth a damn.*

Rosandich sat on a bench at a bus stop on the PCH and read for the hundredth time the article in the newspaper about the break-in and assault at Janet Jenkins's house. The article had been the only thing he'd read since learning about her being hurt. He hadn't touched his copy of *The Big Short*. Every day since he'd read about the assault, he'd camped out at the shelter, hoping her car would be in the lot. He'd barely slept for the past week. He huffed a sigh as he stored the newspaper in his briefcase, closed it, and pushed off the bench. He felt terribly guilty about being late today. He'd overslept.

CHAPTER 12

"You're certain you're ready to come back to work?" Frank Mitchell asked. "You look pale."

Janet smiled. "I was going bonkers at home. And I'm pale because I've been cooped up indoors. I couldn't be readier to be back at work. I hope you have a case for me."

Mitchell returned her smile. "I'm thrilled to have you back. We were short-handed as it was. With you gone, we couldn't keep up. You bet I have a case for you. In fact, I have three cases."

Janet groaned. "Maybe I'll take a couple more weeks." Then she laughed when Mitchell's face sagged. "Just kidding, Frank."

Mitchell picked up three case files from his desk and handed them over. "Start with the top one. It's a doozy."

"Aren't they all?"

Janet went to her office and dropped the files in the middle of her desk. She removed her purse from a desk drawer, placed it on her lap, opened it, and looked inside. The thought crossed her mind that she'd imagined the money. But there it was. *I could use it to pay off my credit cards or make a down payment on a new car*, she thought. As soon as that thought was gone, she knew what she had to do. She'd find Cecil and return the cash. She wondered again where it came from but then shook her head and compressed her lips. "It doesn't make any difference," she muttered.

She slipped her purse back into the desk drawer, pulled the top file on her blotter toward her, and looked at the name on the tab: Claudia Barkley. She flipped open the cover. Photographs apparently taken at a hospital were clipped to the file's inside front cover. Janet had seen worse, but these photos, for some reason, shocked her more than usual. The situation report told the story: fifth reported abuse incident to the RBPD; fourth hospitalization; no charges pressed against the husband by the victim after the previous incidents; husband intoxicated and taken into custody pending formal complaint filed by spouse.

Janet went back to the photos and felt her temperature rise as her heart rate accelerated. "What the hell," she whispered as she took long, slow, calming breaths. She'd never had this sort of reaction before. She closed her eyes and continued to slow-breathe. But the face of Rasif Essam sprang into her head. She rubbed her hands over her face and tried to will away the memory of the man she'd killed. But, instead, the memory segued to her being on top of Essam, repeatedly stabbing him. Detective Rosales had told her she'd stabbed the man twenty-seven times and that the El Segundo Police Officer first on the scene had a difficult time taking the knife away from her.

Eyes now open, Janet closed the file and thought getting some fresh air might be a good thing. She left her office and moved to the front lobby.

"Mary, I'll be back in a few minutes," she told the receptionist, who was on the telephone, but nodded and waved.

Her eyes drifted to the front wall. She was pleasantly surprised to see Cecil Rosandich seated there. As soon as she stepped down to the interior walkway, he slid off the wall and moved toward the steps that led to the raised yard. He stopped at the bottom of the steps and, briefcase hugged to his chest, said, "I heard you were hurt."

"I'm fine now, Mr. Rosandich."

"I'm glad to hear it. The papers said your mother was murdered and that you killed the man who attacked the two of you."

Janet nodded.

"That was a very brave thing to do, Ms. Jenkins."

Janet tipped her head to the side and spread her arms. "Maybe you could call me Janet."

He lowered his head and looked down at his feet, like an embarrassed schoolboy. Still looking down, he said, "Only if you call me Cecil."

"I'd like that, Cecil." She stepped down to the sidewalk and asked the man to sit on the wall. After he did so, she sat a couple feet away from him, his briefcase between them. While the two of them stared out at the street, Janet said, "I can't keep the money you gave me. It wouldn't be right."

He turned and tapped her arm. Janet looked at him. He smiled and she again noticed his sky-blue, intelligent eyes. She also noted his straight patrician nose and wonderful smile.

"What else would I do with my money?"

"I don't mean to insult you, Cecil, but you could use some new clothes."

He looked down and fingered the lapels of his jacket, then looked back at her. "I guess I could do that." He hesitated a moment and then added, "But I want you to keep the money I gave you."

"I can't do—"

He dropped to the sidewalk and wagged a finger at her. "Why do you want to insult me?"

"I'm not insulting—"

"That's exactly what you'd be doing. I won't hear of it."

Janet made eye contact with him and finally nodded. "Okay, Cecil."

He raised a finger. "But, do me a favor. Don't deposit the money in a bank account all at once. Make several deposits of less than ten thousand dollars each."

"Why?"

"Deposits of ten thousand or more are reported to the Treasury Department." He grinned and added, "You wouldn't want the Feds to think you're a drug dealer."

Rosandich's explanation made Janet wonder if there was another reason he didn't want her to deposit all the money at once, but she let it go.

The man gave her a glowing, toothy smile. "Maybe you could go with me to buy some new clothes. My wife used— I'd like to have your input."

Janet smiled back. "That's a deal. Meet me by my car at five."

Janet watched him walk away, then shook her head and went back to her office. She booted up her computer and googled Cecil Rosandich. There was nothing.

CHAPTER 13

"This car is about as worn out as my clothes are," Cecil said, as Janet drove north on the PCH.

She laughed. "It's old, all right, but I'd have to argue with you that it's in worse shape than your suit."

"Huh. I'll have you know this is a Hickey-Freeman. Even in its present condition, it's still a Hickey-Freeman. This car was and always will be nothing but a Chevrolet."

Janet shot a glance at him. "That's a pretty snobby thing to say."

"Oh, sorry, I...."

Janet had a revelation that the man didn't process humor very well. "I was just kidding, Cecil."

"Oh, I see."

"How long have you been in Redondo Beach?"

"About nine years."

"Where did you come from?"

Rosandich shrugged. "Here and there."

"What have you been doing since you came here?"

Out of the corner of her eye, she saw his head shake. "Nothing really."

"Come on, Cecil, don't tell me you've been wandering the streets all that time."

He shrugged again.

"Do you have family here?"

When he didn't answer, she gave him a long look. He appeared agitated. His hands repeatedly wiped the top of his briefcase on his lap and his head shook from side-to-side as though he had palsy. Then he suddenly grabbed the door handle and shouted, "Let me out here. I want to get out now."

Janet pulled off the PCH into a supermarket parking lot. "Please, Cecil, forgive me for getting personal. I meant nothing by it. I'm just concerned about you."

The head-shaking transitioned to repeated nodding. But he said nothing as he opened the passenger door and moved to the pavement. He walked toward a hardware store and disappeared around a corner.

"Dammit," Janet said under her breath. She watched the corner which Cecil had gone around, hoping he might return. But, after five minutes, she gave up hope and drove away. She thought about going home and ordering a pizza, but decided instead to go to the hospital and check in on Claudia Barkley.

Detectives Rosales and Andrews waited outside Claudia Barkley's hospital room for word from her physician that they could talk with her. Rosales paced while Andrews leaned against the wall opposite Barkley's room.

"You're wearing through a lot of shoe leather," Andrews said as Rosales passed him for about the hundredth time.

Rosales stopped in front of Andrews. "I can't help it. These cases get to me."

"Jeez, Hugo, it's all part of the job. You gotta go with the flow."

Rosales glared at his partner; shook his head. "I'm going outside. Can't stand the smell of this place." Andrews watched his partner walk away.

"What the hell is his problem?" Andrews muttered. He moved toward a chair in the hall when the social worker, Janet Jenkins, stepped off the elevator and moved toward him. He stopped, cleared his throat, stood up as straight as he could, and adjusted his tie.

"Hey, Janet," he said. "Back on the job already?"

She nodded. "Yeah. First day back."

Andrews looked at his watch. "It's six. Working late?"

"I thought I had a thing tonight but it fell through at the last minute."

Andrews gave her a sympathetic look. "Only an idiot would stand you up."

Janet tilted her head, smiled, and, while making eye contact, said, "It wasn't that sort of thing. But thanks, anyway."

Andrews felt a flutter in his stomach as he looked into her eyes. He'd noticed before that they were hazel, but he hadn't realized just how green they were. He cleared his throat again and took in a deep breath. But the flutter remained.

"What's going on with Mrs. Barkley?" Janet asked.

"We're waiting for the doc to give us the okay to talk with her. She's in really bad shape."

"You working solo tonight?" she asked.

"No. Hugo stepped out for a minute." He looked down the hall in the direction Rosales had gone and then stared down at the floor. "He seems unusually upset."

"What do you mean?"

Andrews waved his arms around and pressed his lips together. When he looked back at her, he said, "I don't know. He said these domestic abuse cases are getting to him."

"That's understandable," Janet said.

"Yeah. It seems like half the cases we handle are battered women."

"It's more than that," Janet said.

Andrews peered at her and waited.

"You don't know, I take it."

"What?"

"Hugo's father beat his mother to death when Hugo was just a kid."

Andrews knew his mouth had dropped open, but he was too surprised to close it. Movement to his left drew his attention away and he turned to see Rosales coming toward them. At that same instant, Claudia Barkley's doctor exited her hospital room.

"Hello, Janet," Dr. Stanley Stark said as he stepped forward, shook her hand, and gave her a questioning look. "Glad to see you back, but isn't it a bit too soon, considering?"

"I'm fine, Stan. Just tired."

Stark turned to Rosales and Andrews. "You won't be able to talk with her tonight. Maybe tomorrow."

Janet tipped her head toward the hospital room. "What's her condition?"

The doctor's features changed. He looked suddenly morose. "Bad, Janet. Ruptured spleen, broken ribs, busted nose and jaw. The worst part is that she was four months pregnant with her first child. She lost the baby."

Andrews expected to see sadness on Janet's face but, instead, her eyes had gone to pinpoint lasers and her clenched jaw twitched. He noticed her hands bunched into fists.

"This is the fifth reported incident," she said.

Rosales interjected, "She's refused to file formal charges each time."

Stark nodded. "I see it all the time. These women are lacking two things that make them perpetual victims. Lack of self-esteem and lack of financial resources. They're typically brainwashed by their husbands to believe they deserve the treatment they get and that they can't make it on their own."

Rosales said, "That woman better figure out a way to sever her relationship with Thomas Barkley. The beatings he's given her have gotten worse each time. The next time he very well might kill her."

Rosandich hugged his briefcase and pounded it with a fist. He repeatedly intoned in cadence with his footsteps, like the lines of a chant, "Why? Why? Why? Stupid! Stupid! Stupid! Why? Why? Why?" He turned off the PCH and hiked up 3rd Street, huffing as the incline of the asphalt became steeper. At Gentry, he turned left and then crossed Prospect to the park.

Even after sitting on the ground, up against the fence that separated the grass from the basketball courts, he continued his chant, berating himself for reacting badly to Janet Jenkins's questions. He knew she was just being friendly, not nosey. But he'd been on his own for a long time, during which he'd never shared personal information with anyone. *Sharing can be dangerous*, he thought. *Even deadly.*

CHAPTER 14

Janet's body trembled from anger, as though she'd overdosed on caffeine. The images on the photographs in Claudia Barkley's case file scrolled through her brain like a never-ending horror slide show. Dr. Stark's description of the woman's injuries was the audio that accompanied the pictures. When she pulled into her driveway, she couldn't remember anything about the traffic or the time it took her to drive from the hospital. She looked to her left at her rented home. Her empty home. Sure, her mother had been a financial and emotional burden. But they'd been a team. And when she'd been bone-weary or psychically-drained after a long day of dealing with beaten-down women, abusive husbands, and cops who had seen it all, her mother seemed to sense her mood and would revive her. Maybelle Jenkins always knew what to say when Janet was down. Janet smiled as tears ran down her cheeks. She mimicked one of the last things her mother had said to her: "Ah am fashionably thin, *mah* dear. That's all the thang, ya know?" She grimaced at herself in the rearview mirror and said, "Oh, Mama."

She carried her purse to the front door, unlocked and opened it, and then stepped inside. She lifted the throw rug she'd used to cover the blood stains in the entry, expecting to find them gone. But they were still there.

"You bastard, Brennan," she cursed. She'd talked with her landlord yesterday and he'd again promised to get everything back to normal today. She moved to the back door and shouted, "Dammit," when she saw the landlord hadn't replaced the door, either. The door that Rasif Essam had broken was still nailed to the frame.

Janet placed her things on the dining room table, took her cell phone from her purse, and dialed Brennan.

"Hello."

"Mr. Brennan, this is Janet Jenkins. I see you didn't do the work you promised to do today."

"I'm a busy man, Ms. Jenkins. I'll get around to the repairs as soon as I can."

Janet had always avoided conflict at all cost. She'd had half-a-dozen issues with Brennan and had always let him push her around. He never did work when he said he would. "When do you think that will be?" she asked.

"As I said, as soon as I can."

"Okay, Brennan," Janet said, her voice suddenly strident and threatening. "Here's the deal. I'm not paying you rent until the repairs are complete. And, first thing tomorrow morning, I'm filing complaints against you with the California Consumer Affairs Department, the Housing and Community Investment Department, and the Health Department. Then I'll call my attorney and I'll also call the local television stations and remind them I was almost murdered in the house you own, that my mother *was* murdered, that you haven't done a thing about making the repairs you promised to make. Just imagine how the blood stains on the floor and the nailed-shut back door will look on television."

"Now wait a minute. I told you I'd fix everything good as new. You can't get away—"

"Watch me, Brennan. I can and I will. You'd better hire a good attorney, because by the time I'm finished with you, I'll own this house."

Janet terminated the call and counted aloud. "One-two-three-four-fi—" Her cell phone rang. She recognized Brennan's cell number.

"What?" she answered.

"I'll take care of everything first thing tomorrow. What time do you leave for work?"

"8 a.m. But I think it would really be good if you had your crew here at 7:30." She ended the call, shucked her suit jacket, and removed the packet of money from her purse. She felt its weight and decided it was time to rent a safety deposit box.

Janet replaced the cash in her purse and carried it upstairs to her mother's bedroom. She'd slept there for the last three weeks, waiting for Brennan to fix the window in her own room. She changed into pajamas, then returned to the kitchen and reached for the bottle of chardonnay that had been in the refrigerator for months. But she remembered that alcohol and antibiotics didn't go well together. Instead, she removed a can of ginger ale, opened it, poured a glassful, and moved to the living room. After she sat on the couch, she remembered again what her doctor had said that morning about feeling like herself again. She thought about her conversation with her landlord, sipped the soda, and scoffed. The old Janet Jenkins would never have stood up to Brennan; or to anyone, for that matter. At least, that was the way things had always been when it came to standing up for herself. She muttered, "Feel like myself again, my butt."

DAY 11

CHAPTER 15

Janet's first stop on the way to her office was Claudia Barkley's hospital room. "How many times has this happened, Mrs. Barkley?" Janet asked.

The woman moaned as she shifted slightly to her left side, as though she didn't want to look at Janet. But her eyes were swollen-shut, so she couldn't see anyone anyway.

"We can play this game all day, ma'am, but sooner or later you'll have to make a decision."

"Wha…are…you…talkin'…'bout?"

Mrs. Barkley's jaw was wired shut, so her words were so slurred that Janet could just make out what she'd said.

"Police records show you've called 9-1-1 five times and been hospitalized four times." Janet lowered her voice. "I'll bet there have been other times he beat you when you didn't call for help. Is that right?"

Barkley didn't react, other than to close her swollen eyes.

"Your dead child can't testify. You need to go to court and testify against your husband."

The woman suddenly sobbed, which quickly evolved into a long moan.

Janet felt anger rise inside her, pushing aside any sympathy she had for the woman. "Listen to me," she growled, "he almost killed you this time. The next time, he might do just that. Holy God, woman, at least stand up for your unborn child."

Janet walked around the bed and watched tears leak from Barkley's eyes. Her shoulders rose and fell in cadence with low, groaning sobs that racked her body.

"My…baby," she moaned. "My…poor…baby."

Janet waited.

After a minute, Barkley said something that was indecipherable.

"What was that?" Janet asked.

"Wha'…would you…do?"

"What would I do?" Janet repeated. "I'd decide to live."

Outside the hospital room, Janet conferred with Detectives Rosales and Andrews.

"The doctor said we can talk with her now," Rosales said.

"You won't get much out of her. Between the emotional trauma of losing her baby, nearly being beaten to death, and her fear of living alone, she's barely cooperative. Plus, her broken jaw makes speaking difficult."

"We'll try," Rosales said.

"Did you talk to the husband?" Janet asked.

"Oh yeah," Andrews said. "When he was brought into the interrogation room, the first thing he wanted us to do was pray with him for the soul of his dead child. He wants us to bring him here so he can apologize to his wife."

Janet huffed and whispered, "Dear Jesus."

Rosales nodded. "It's the same old story. The wife has no skills. Maybe she could get a job slinging burgers in a fast food joint, but she can't make enough to live independently. Her husband works union construction and has health and life insurance through his employer. Without her husband, she wouldn't make it."

"*With* her husband, she's not going to make it either," Janet said, barely suppressing her red-hot rage.

After opening a safe deposit box in a bank a couple of miles from St. Anne's, Janet tried to pull an idea from the recesses of her brain that might permanently help the women she worked with. The drive to her office was as hectic as usual, so she needed to pay close attention to traffic, but she found that difficult to do while trying to spark her creative synapses.

In the lot at the shelter, she parked, but remained behind the wheel, letting the sun warm the left side of her face. The gerbil in her brain ran frenetically but nothing came to mind that would make a revolutionary difference. She smacked the steering wheel and cursed at the futility of her work. She felt there wasn't a thing she could do to change the pattern of abuse: psychopathic abusers and their pathetic, dependent victims. The men wouldn't change and neither would the women. At least not if the women lacked self-confidence and resources.

She was deep into her thoughts when a shadow fell across her face. She jumped and reached for the .38 revolver she now carried in her purse. As her fingers wrapped around the pistol grip, she looked left and saw Cecil. He stood three feet from her door, wearing a forlorn expression. She released her hold on the .38 and threw open her door, forcing Cecil to step back.

"Damn, Cecil, you scared me."

He dropped his gaze. "I'm sorry, Janet. I...I...just wanted to apologize for...you know...yesterday."

Janet slammed her door, stepped forward, and placed a hand on his shoulder. "You have nothing to apologize for. I shouldn't have gotten so personal. I—"

He waved her off. "I've had almost no one to trust for so long, I've forgotten how to trust. Maybe...maybe you could give me another chance."

Janet lowered her hand and extended it. "Let's shake on our trusting one another."

He tentatively accepted her hand and lightly squeezed it.

Janet felt as though her heart was breaking when she saw tears in his eyes. She gripped his hand with both of hers. "How about we get together for dinner tonight right after work? I know a nice little Italian place."

He beamed. "That would be nice." Then he backed up again and spread his arms. "You notice anything?"

Janet couldn't believe she hadn't noticed; he was no longer wearing his old, worn-out blue suit. He'd replaced it with a blue blazer, white shirt, gray tie, and dark-gray slacks. His new shoes gleamed.

"You look very spiffy, Cecil."

"Got 'em off the rack at Macy's. Didn't even need altering." He smiled and added, "Got a haircut, too."

"I don't know, Cecil. My little Italian place might be too informal for the likes of you."

The edges of his mouth dropped and his eyes again looked sad. "Oh, no, if it's where you want to go, I'm certain it'll be fine."

Janet touched his arm. "I was pulling your leg."

"Oh. I guess that's another thing I've forgotten. Humor."

The pain in her heart returned. She forced a smile. "I'll see you right here at seven. I need to work late tonight. A lot of cases."

CHAPTER 16

The threat of being fired by Sy Rosen hung over Johnny Casale like a black smoke cloud. Yesterday, he'd had to tell Rosen that the Beverly Hills investment broker, Charles Forsythe, had flown out of LAX several days earlier and had not yet returned.

"Forty-eight hours, Casale," Rosen had screamed. "That's all you got or you're fired."

Casale had staked out Forsythe's offices every day since the guy had gone to the airport. His morale was in the toilet and he'd almost reconciled that he'd lost the big finder's fee, when Forsythe showed up at 8:00 a.m. Casale watched the office through most of the day, until Forsythe pulled away at 3:30 p.m. in a black Audi R8. Casale let three vehicles fill the space between them, then pulled into traffic and followed.

Smart guy, Casale thought. *Getting out of Brooklyn and coming out here. Nice car. Looks like he's got it made.*

He followed Forsythe two blocks up North Beverly Drive, then the guy turned right onto Burton Way. At La Cienega, he went left and drove past Cedars-Sinai Medical Center. After about a mile, he turned right onto Willoughby Avenue and pulled to the curb in front of a one-story bungalow halfway up the block on the right. It was a nice enough neighborhood, but way too downscale for a guy driving a one hundred seventy-five-thousand-dollar car. Casale pulled into a parking place half-a-block past the Audi and watched his rearview mirror. Forsythe remained in his car. Then, after a few minutes, a white Mustang convertible pulled into the bungalow's driveway. Casale raised the binoculars from the front passenger seat, twisted to the right, and planted the glasses on a young woman—maybe thirty years old—who exited the Ford. She wore a white nurse's uniform that, even from six houses away, showed off her voluptuous figure. *Yeah, looks like he's got it made, all right.*

Janet took a sip of water and placed the glass on the table. "This place isn't fancy, but the food and service are good. The menu's a bit funky...both Italian and Greek, but I really like coming here. My mother and I—" She stopped, shook her head, and didn't finish.

Rosandich nodded. "It reminds me of a place near where I grew up."

Janet almost asked him where that was but didn't want to instigate another episode like the one they had yesterday.

But he smiled and said, "Go ahead. You can ask me where I grew up. In fact, ask me whatever you want." He smiled again. "On one condition. I get to ask about you."

She drank more water and said, "Okay. Where are you from?"

"Brooklyn." He hesitated for a long moment, as though he'd gone back in time, remembering his childhood. "I was an only child. My mother worked as a seamstress in the garment district. My father died in a construction accident when I was five years old."

"Is your mother—?"

"She passed away right after I graduated from college."

"Where'd you go to school?"

"Ah, I...I went to Boston College."

Janet sensed he had just lied to her. She said, "I went to USC at night while I worked days."

"What did you study?" he asked.

"I received my degree in counseling and social work. I worked days and weekends as a companion to a handicapped elderly woman."

The man's face drooped, making him look a bit bloodhound-ish. "That must have been difficult...working and going to school."

She shook her head. "It wasn't as bad as it might have been. The lady I cared for slept most of the time. I was able to study while on the job."

"I saw in the newspaper that your mother lived with you." He swallowed and took on the droopy look once again. "I'm sorry about what happened."

"Thank you. I miss her a lot."

He took a long drink of water as an uncomfortable silence fell over them. A waiter came by and took their orders. After the waiter walked away, Cecil said, "Tell me about your job."

Janet compressed her lips and squinted. "Not a happy subject."

"It's okay if you don't want to talk about it."

She wagged her head. "I don't mind talking about what I do. You just might not want to hear it."

He smiled. "How bad can it be?"

"Pretty bad," she said. "Our mission at St. Anne's is to provide a safe place for abused women and children. Sometimes that abuse is gruesome."

He looked off at a corner of the room and didn't immediately respond. When he did, his eyes had gone hard. "Men who abuse women should be hung in public," he said in a staccato monotone.

Janet blurted a small laugh. "We don't do that sort of thing here." She laughed again. "But that would surely make my life a lot easier. So many of our cases involve repeat offenders."

"Why do women stay with men like that?"

"Keep in mind that abuse doesn't just involve men abusing women. There's child abuse and elderly abuse, too. St. Anne's just handles abused women and their children. And the reasons most women stay with their abusers include children, love, guilt, fear, pride, embarrassment, financial independence—or a combination of those. It's very possible the victim is unaware that he or she may be locked into a cycle of violence. But the common factor in most cases is dependence. Emotional and financial."

"There's nothing you can do about that?"

"Smarter people than me have racked their brains trying to come up with a solution to the problem." She blurted the laugh again, lowered her voice, and added, "Short of hanging abusers in public, no one's solved the problem yet."

He looked off in the near distance again. After a full ten seconds, he said, "You mentioned that these women are both emotionally and financially dependent on their abusers. If you could solve the financial problem, what would you do about the emotional side?"

"That's a good question, but awfully theoretical. I mean, how could we ever resolve the financial side of the problem?"

"Humor me," he said.

"Okay. When I said that the women are often emotionally dependent, I meant that they have been so badly verbally abused that they no longer have any self-confidence. So, I guess what I would do is—if the money was there—place them in a supportive environment and enroll them in a training program that would develop skills that would allow them to make it on their own."

He nodded like a bobble-head doll. "That would be good. We should figure out a way to make it happen."

Warming to the topic, Janet said, "I'm working a case now where I'm afraid the husband will ultimately beat his wife to death. She's in the hospital now…for the fourth time." She shook her head. "She was pregnant and lost her baby because of the most recent abuse."

"Oh, my God. How awful. But won't her husband be put in prison?"

She shrugged. "If the wife testifies against him, he could draw a long sentence. But, if she won't testify, he's likely to get a short-term sentence or probation. Or, nothing at all."

"How much money would it take for her to support herself while she acquired the skills to have a career?"

Janet spread her hands. "I haven't thought about it, but I'd guess, maybe, thirty, forty thousand dollars a year, tax-free. Rent, tuition, food, transportation, and so forth. It would be even more if she enrolled in a four-year degree program. Of course, we encourage our clients to work while going to school. Even a menial job gives them the satisfaction of earning their own money. And there are scholarship programs available from some educational institutions."

"That's all?"

She chuckled. "That's a lot of money, Cecil."

The waiter brought their salads and placed them on the table. While they ate, Janet tried to draw out Cecil on other subjects, but he'd retreated into himself and didn't seem to want to discuss anything.

After he paid the check with cash and they'd gone back to her car, she attempted one more personal question: "Cecil, where do you live?"

He looked across the seat at her and replied, "Oh, here and there."

Johnny Casale wondered if Charles Forsythe planned to spend the night with the young nurse. It was now 7:45 p.m. Forsythe and the woman had been inside for over four hours. But, just as he was about to give up and drive off, the two of them walked out of the house. The woman hugged, then kissed Forsythe. He patted her on the ass, then moved to his car.

Casale watched Forsythe speed down Willoughby Avenue and then go right at the first intersection. He stepped on the gas and followed the broker for a couple of miles, back to Beverly Hills, where he pulled into his gated residence on Carmelita Drive. Casale whistled as he drove away.

CHAPTER 17

Nikos Pappadopoulos untied his stained apron, pulled it over his head, and rolled it into a ball. After he tossed it into a basket, along with other dirty linen, he washed up in the bathroom and then changed into clean clothes.

"*Eteemee eesay*, Voula?"

His wife raised a finger in the air, telling him to wait a minute. His heart swelled as he watched the best-looking girl ever produced by the Island of Patmos tally the day's receipts. For about the millionth time, he asked himself how he'd gotten so lucky.

A minute went by before Voula raised her head and said, "I'm ready, Niko."

He smiled at her and knew what would come next. The same game they played every night after they closed Pappa's Café.

"You want to guess the total?"

"Of course, *koukla mou*. But I'm always off."

She pulled a slip of adding machine tape from an apron pocket and waved it in the air. "Come on, Niko, you've got to win one of these nights."

"Okay, okay." He rubbed his chin and waggled his head. "I have a feeling tonight's the night. We had good traffic today. All three meals, we turned the tables at least once. So, I guess…two thousand, eight hundred…no, no, I'll change my guess to three thousand, four hundred, and eighty-five dollars."

"Ha," she exclaimed, "not even close." She slapped the tape on the counter and read off the number there: "Four thousand, one hundred eleven dollars."

Nikos shook his head and groaned, "I never get close to the actual number, *koukla mou.*"

Twenty minutes earlier, Pappadopoulos had estimated the day's receipts to within twenty-two dollars of the actual number. He'd calculated years ago the average amount a customer spent in the café—fourteen dollars and sixty-three cents—and could tell from the pre-printed numbers on the hand-written order tickets the waitresses used how many tickets had been used on any day. But their daily ritual gave Voula so much pleasure. The joy on her face reminded him of the young girl he'd married forty-one years before. All the work and aggravation that came with running a restaurant were more than compensated for by the smile she showed when they played their nightly guessing game.

"*Eemay kourasmeni, agape mou. As pame.*"

"I'm tired, too, Voula. But I was hoping Cecil would get here before we locked up. He might not have eaten yet."

Voula came over and hugged him. She looked up into his soulful brown eyes and kissed his cleft chin. "You know why I love you so much, Niko?"

"My good looks and Olympian physique?"

"Of course," she answered as she pushed away and eyed his bulldog jowls and massive gut. "But, most of all, I love your heart. It's the biggest heart I know."

Pappadopoulos felt his face warm.

"The way you take care of Cecil, the way you worry about him, will earn you a place in heaven someday."

He placed his hands on her shoulders. "With you in my life, I'm already in heaven."

She playfully slapped his chest and said, "Stop it."

He was about to lead her to the back when the door there opened and Cecil Rosandich entered.

"Hey, Voula. Hey, Nick. I thought I might have missed you."

Nikos smiled at Rosandich. "I'm sorry, but the kitchen is closed."

"That's all right, Nick. I ate with a friend tonight."

Voula said, "You're wearing new clothes and got a haircut." She shot a mischievous look at Nikos and said, "Perhaps Cecil has a girlfriend?"

Nikos wrapped an arm around Voula. "Don't tease our friend." Then he looked at Cecil and said, "Maybe we'll see you in the morning."

Rosandich nodded and followed them to the back door. He watched them get in their five-year-old Buick and drive away. Then he locked up after them, changed his clothes in the tiny two-room apartment at the back, and went to work on the restaurant. He would make certain the place was spic and span for when Nick and Voula arrived at 5:30 the next morning. It was the way he paid them back for letting him use the apartment for the past nine years.

DAY 12

CHAPTER 18

It was after 1:30 a.m. when Cecil finished cleaning up the café. While he'd worked, he'd massaged the idea that had germinated during dinner with Janet Jenkins. As a seedling, the idea frightened him. But, as it grew and grew, the idea made ever more sense. The documents he had were worth a lot of money. Hidden in the ceiling of his apartment, the documents were doing no one any good. He knew that his old partners at Rosen, Rice & Stone had to be aware by now that he'd cashed in one of the bonds. That meant they were probably investigating the bond's trail. They'd obviously know where it had been traded. Someone would surely contact Charles Forsythe.

I need to leave California, he thought. *But, before I do, I'll call Rosen.*

He felt a flash of anger. *Those bastards ruined my life.* But the anger quickly metamorphosed to fear. His body trembled as though electrified. He'd thought many times about turning the documents over to the government. But he knew, without his testimony, the documents would be nothing but worthless paper and flash drives. And he feared that neither the SEC nor the FBI would be able to guarantee his safety. His old partners would find a way to eliminate him.

He used a ladder from the café's storage room to raise a ceiling tile in the apartment's bedroom, dragged out the plastic-wrapped bundle of documents, and dropped it on the bed. After he put away the ladder, he firmed up his plan.

At 5:30 a.m., Casale watched Forsythe pull into the parking lot next to the Forsythe offices, leave the vehicle, and enter the building. Two hours earlier, Casale had spray-painted the lenses of the security cameras that spied on the parking lot. Under cover of darkness, he now pulled into the lot, ten yards behind Forsythe's parked Audi, opened his rental car's door, and lit the cloth fuse in the bottle of gasoline. He waited a few seconds, then tossed the bottle under the Audi and quickly drove away. He saw flashes from flames as he turned out of the lot, onto the street.

Fifteen minutes later, Casale pulled up to a Mickey D's drive-up window and bought a coffee and an Egg McMuffin. Then he drove into a parking slot and waited. He devoured the Egg McMuffin, slurped the last of the coffee, and was considering a run to the men's room, when his cell phone chirped. He answered the call with a low "Yeah?" and waited.

"I got your message."

Casale recognized the Brooklynese undertones in Forsythe's speech. *I'd better handle him carefully*, he thought. *He could be recording this call.* "Who's this? Do you know what time it is?"

"Oh, you wanna play games," Forsythe said. "The only one you hurt this morning was my insurance company." Forsythe muttered something unintelligible and then added, "You know that information you wanted from me? Well, go fuck yourself and the horse you rode in on." He hung up without waiting for a response.

Casale looked at his cell phone as though it was a strange appendage. "What the hell," he rasped. The reaction he'd just gotten from Forsythe was so different from what he'd expected, he felt butterflies erupt in his gut. *Why would Forsythe deny knowing Bruno Pedace? Especially after his fancy car was destroyed?* He tapped the phone against his chest while he thought about what had just happened. He needed more information. He placed a call.

"Sal? Johnny."

"Hey, *pendejo*, I heard you was hangin' out in Lost Wages."

"I'm in L.A. now. You wanna do me a favor?"

"*Como no*! For my usual fee."

"I know that. Despite being married to my sister, you don't do nothin' for free."

"Gotta pay the bills, *amigo*."

"I need a full background write-up on an investment broker in Beverly Hills named Charles Forsythe. He's originally from Brooklyn. Changed his name to Forsythe when he moved to California."

"Changed it from what?"

"How the hell do I know? Earn your fee and find that out."

"That's it?"

"No. See if there's a connection between Forsythe and a guy named Bruno Pedace."

"How much time do I got?"

"I want something by noon today, California time."

"That'll cost you double."

"Jeez, Sal. You keep jackin' up your rates, I'll dump you and find an Italian who can do the job."

Sal laughed. "No, you won't, Johnny. You know you can't trust the *goombahs* and, besides, your sister would cut off your balls."

Casale scoffed, then asked, "And how *is* my sister?"

At 11:00 a.m., Rosandich used the office phone in Pappa's Café to call Charles Forsythe.

"Jeez, where the hell are you?" Forsythe asked.

"Why? What's wrong?"

"There was a guy from the old country in here asking about you. I think that bond you cashed in got your old partners' attention."

Old country was code for New York City. "No surprise there."

"I wanted to contact you as soon as this *mook* walked out of here, but without a phone, how the hell am I supposed to reach you?"

"I-I'm sorry. I can't risk it."

"That's fine and dandy, but that *mook* blew up my car this morning."

"Oh, my God, are you okay?"

"Yeah, yeah; no one was hurt. But this thing just escalated to a new level."

Rosandich took a moment to catch his breath. Rosen was now closer to him than he'd been at any time over the last nine years. Nine years of being frightened every time a stranger looked at or talked to him. He knew Rosen, Rice & Stone wanted the documents he'd taken. He also suspected they wanted him out of the picture. Permanently.

"I-I need your help, Charlie. I want to redeem the rest of my bonds."

"All of them?"

"Yeah. All one point nine million."

"That's a lot of cash."

"I'm leaving California and I don't want anything with me that will leave a trail. When you get the cash from the bonds, convert it to cashier's checks." He cleared his throat and then said, "I also have some documents. I want you to call Sy Rosen and tell him you'll send him the documents in return for the firm sending you forty-five million dollars."

"Forty-five million? How'd you come up with that number?"

"That's the number I need."

"You sure about this? You actually believe they'll pay that kind of money?"

"Absolutely. I'll messenger the documents to you. I want you to open a safety deposit box and put the docs in it. Then messenger the box key to my attention at St. Anne's Shelter in Redondo Beach."

"Sure," Forsythe said. Then he asked, "Where are you going?"

Rosandich's hands vibrated as fear flooded his nervous system. "Better I don't say."

"Bruno, don't you think—?"

His throat tightened as he yelled a warning: "Don't use that name. Someone could be listening."

"Sorry…Cecil."

"You tell Rosen I'll sign a non-disclosure agreement that states I'll never say a word about what I know. Tell him there are no copies of the docs."

"You know the non-disclosure agreement won't be enforceable."

"They know me, Charlie. They know that I would never go back on a promise."

"It's about damned time you went on the offensive. But why don't you just come out of the dark and go to the SEC?"

Rosandich's throat tightened again. "You think the SEC can protect me from my former partners? They'll whack me before I could ever testify. Besides, you think the SEC will pay me forty-five million?"

Forsythe said, "How do you want to do this?"

"I'll call you with the details. In the meantime, call Rosen."

"Okay. Be careful, my friend."

CHAPTER 19

Janet wanted to scream. After a wasted thirty minutes with a non-communicative Jasmine Essam, and a fruitless hour with Claudia Barkley, she marched out through the front door of Presbyterian Hospital and ran into Hugo Rosales.

"You look as pissed off as I feel," Rosales told her.

Janet pointed up at the building. "Mrs. Barkley won't testify against her husband and Jasmine Essam just wants to die."

"Well, I've got more bad news. A judge let Barkley out on a ten-thousand-dollar bond. He only had to put up a thousand in cash, which his brother provided."

"Holy shit," Janet cursed. "He might come straight here."

"I'm putting a uniform on her room as long as she's in the hospital." He shrugged. "But after that, all bets are off."

"Oh, God. We could provide a room for her at St. Anne's, but I wouldn't be surprised if she refused it."

Rosales's expression turned sour. "I understand there's a quarter-million life policy on the bastard through his work. Maybe he'll fall down a flight of stairs and crack his head open."

"From your lips to God's ears," Janet said.

Rosales's eyebrows caterpillared along his forehead. "You know I was just joking about him falling down stairs, right?"

She felt her face go hot. "Of course," she said. "Of course." She showed a smile, but didn't think it came across as genuine.

On her drive back to St. Anne's, Janet considered Claudia Barkley's situation. The frustration she felt just seemed to expand to the point where it might blow off the top of her skull. To make matters worse, the Barkley woman was just one of many in a similar predicament.

Sal Trujillo jack-hammered his feet on the wood floor of his second-floor home office. He knew the thumping always drove his wife crazy, but he was pumped about the information he'd found for his brother-in-law, Johnny Casale. The phone continued to ring, which caused him to become more agitated and to thump his feet faster and heavier.

"That you, Sal?"

"Finally, Johnny. What the hell are you doing out there? Going to the beach?"

"Beach, my ass. What d'ya got?"

"I'll send you an email, but here's what I came up with. Charles Forsythe was born Carlo Massarino and grew up in Brooklyn. Has a brother and a sister who still live there. He attended Regis High School, which, as you probably know, ain't easy to get into. He was all-state in wrestling. From there he went to Harvard on a full ride. He worked on Wall Street for a dozen years and then moved to California. He changed his name to Forsythe shortly after he made the move. Married a girl from an old-line California family. Got three kids and four grandkids."

Casale scoffed. "Changed his name so he'd fit in better out here. Hard to believe that sort of thing would be necessary."

"I suspect changing his name had nothing to do with fitting in," Trujillo said. "You remember when the Justice Department went hot and heavy against the Families back here?"

"Of course. It was a bad time for a lot of my friends. That RICO statute took down the Mafia."

"Well, Carlo Massarino's father was a made guy with the Luccheses. Carlo did everything he could to avoid being tainted by his father's mob connections. When things got bad here, he put three thousand miles between him and his family and changed his name."

"I see," Casale said. "Makes sense."

"Yeah. But Johnny, I gotta warn you. Carlo Massarino, or Charles Forsythe, whatever you call him, is a tough sonofabitch. His father wanted him to take over the family business, if you know what I mean. It broke the old man's heart when his eldest son moved away and changed his name. Carlo had the toughness to be a Mafioso and the brains to be the heir to the Lucchese organization."

Casale reflected on the toughness Forsythe had already shown. He didn't doubt a word of what Sal had just said. "What about Pedace?"

Trujillo chuckled. "I thought I recognized the name when we talked this morning. He disappeared about a decade ago. The SEC put out a warrant on him. They wanted to talk to him about his possible role in a mortgage securities scam."

"Anything else?"

"What are you doing out there?"

"Cut the bullshit, Sal. What else did you find out about Pedace?"

Casale listened to the dead air over the line. He visualized the wheels turning in his brother-in-law's brain. The bastard was about to raise his fee again. Before Sal could respond, Casale said, "I warn you, Sal. You try to jack up your fee on me, I'll never do business with you again. Sister or no sister."

"Okay, okay, Johnny. You're gonna love it. Pedace and Massarino grew up on the same block in Brooklyn. They attended Regis and Harvard together." Trujillo blurted a laugh. "But here's the capper. Massarino and Pedace went to work at Rosen, Rice & Stone after they graduated from Harvard. I called a retired priest who taught at Regis when Massarino and Pedace were there. If you can believe it, he still remembers the two of them. You know what he told me?"

Casale vented a loud breath and said, "What, Sal?"

"He said Massarino was the second brightest student they ever had at Regis. But Pedace was the brightest kid he's ever known. Made Massarino look average. He said Pedace had skipped two grades and was a shy, socially-inept boy who kids picked on. At least, until Massarino took Pedace under his wing. He protected Pedace like a kid brother."

"Looks like he's still doing that," Casale muttered.

"What was that, Johnny?"

"Nothing, Sal. Thanks. You did good. Send me your bill."

Casale hung up and paced the length of his hotel room. He'd already decided that Charles Forsythe was no pushover. Physical violence would probably just stiffen his back more. "I got one play," he said under his breath.

CHAPTER 20

It was mid-afternoon when Janet's intercom chimed. "Yes, Mary?" she answered.

"Ms. Jenkins, you have a visitor."

"Did you get a name?"

Mary's voice dropped as she said, "I asked him but he said he'd rather not give me his name. It's the same man who asked about you when you were in the hospital. The guy from the front wall."

"Okay, Mary. Tell him I'll be right there."

She shook her head as she stood, wondering what Cecil was up to now. She fast-walked to the lobby and found him pacing, briefcase in hand. He immediately turned toward her and rushed over.

"We need to talk."

"Okay, Cecil. Can we get together after work?"

"Oh, no, that won't do. We need to talk right now."

The wild-eyed, flushed look on Rosandich's face worried Janet. Usually quiet, almost passive, he now appeared to be wired, as though on drugs.

"Are you okay, Cecil?"

"Yes, I'm fine. But we must talk right now. It's important."

Janet glanced at Mary and wondered if she should have her call Frank Mitchell, but decided against it and invited Cecil to follow her.

They had barely sat down in her office, Rosandich having placed his briefcase on the floor beside his chair, when he popped back up and shut the office door. Before she could object, he scooted back to his chair, leaned forward and, in a low voice, said, "I have a solution to your problem."

Janet ran through a mental checklist of all her problems and finally asked, "Which one?"

"The abused women," he said. "Allowing them to gain their independence." He jumped to his feet again and paced in front of her, waving his arms around like a marionette.

Janet stood, moved around her desk, and took Cecil's arm. "I want you to sit down and calmly tell me what's going on."

When they were both seated again, she poured him a glass of water from a carafe on the credenza behind her desk and pushed the glass toward him. As he drank, she watched his eyes to see if she could detect any sign that he might be high. But his pupils looked fine.

He placed the glass back on the front of her desk. "From what you told me, it appears the solution to the problem of your clients gaining their independence is two-fold. They need to be separated from their abusive husbands and they need the financial resources to make it on their own."

When he paused, Janet nodded.

"Okay," he said, as he took his briefcase from the floor beside his chair and placed it on his lap, opened it, and withdrew a quarter-inch stack of paper. He replaced the briefcase next to him and handed over the papers.

"What's this?"

"Research I did at the public library."

She riffled through the papers. "You did this all today?"

He looked at her as though he didn't understand the question. "The library is a wonderful place to do research. Did you know they now have computers which you can use for free?" He didn't wait for an answer. "I found that your organization serves an average of seventy-five women and one hundred eighteen children per year. You house and feed the women and their children for no longer than ninety days, at which point they must find their own accommodations. In most cases, they wind up returning to their husbands and the abuse cycle begins all over again."

Janet raised her eyebrows and nodded.

"Your website says you have dozens of volunteers who provide daycare services, counseling, job training, etc., which means, if you had the physical facilities and the financial wherewithal, you wouldn't have to turn your clients loose until after they had the training, education, and psychological stability to get a job and be on their own."

"Those are big *ifs*."

He held up a hand. "I'm not finished," he said impatiently.

"Sorry. Go ahead."

"There's a financial pro forma in that package. You can study it later, but the summary conclusion is that you need three times as many residential units as you have on site here. And you need an annual revenue increase of three million, seven hundred and fifty thousand dollars."

Janet was beginning to lose patience. All the figures he was throwing around were pie-in-the-sky numbers that weren't attainable. "That's all good, Cecil, but—"

He held up his hand again and whispered, "Another minute, please."

She sighed exasperatedly and leaned back.

"Did you know there's a foundation in Omaha, Nebraska, that will match one-for-one any gift over five million dollars donated to organizations that help abused women?'

She shook her head.

"So, if your organization was the beneficiary of a forty-three-million-dollar donation, the Omaha foundation would match thirty-eight million of it. That would give you eighty-one million dollars. If you put that money into a real estate investment fund that generates five percent, for instance, your annual income off that investment would be over four million dollars. Or, more than the increase in your budget that I mentioned." He spread his arms and added, "Of course, if the real estate fund paid six percent, rather than five percent, that would give you an extra one point one million dollars in income."

Janet hated to discourage Cecil. He was obviously excited and had done a lot of work in putting together his study, but he was also delusional, obviously off somewhere in la-la land. This time, she raised a hand. "Cecil, this is all well and good, but"—she leaned forward, put her folded hands on the center of her desk, and raised her voice enough to show her frustration—"where the hell are we going to find forty-three million dollars? And you forgot something. How in God's name can we triple the capacity of our residential facilities?"

"Oh, yes, I meant to mention that. The Archdiocese of Los Angeles just put out a request for proposals on a fifty-unit apartment house donated to the Church by the Robert N. Franklin family. I called Mr. Franklin's business manager this morning and told her what I had in mind. She told me she would intercede with the Church on St. Anne's behalf."

"How'd you get through to her?"

"I told her I was Bishop Flanagan."

Janet just stared at him wide-eyed. She felt her pulse leap. On paper, everything he'd told her sounded wonderful. She smiled, trying not to look patronizing. "But what about the forty-three million?"

"Oh that," he said.

"Cecil, I'm…"—she looked down at her hands and sighed—"we have a doctor on staff who I would like you to see."

He chuckled. "There's something I want you to do before you set up an appointment with a psychiatrist. Open your computer and search the name Bruno Pedace. P-E-D-A-C-E."

Janet was beyond being frustrated. "Cecil, this has to stop."

He turned serious, his face going angry-red. "Just do that one thing for me. Please."

Janet was exasperated, but she booted up her desktop and Googled the name Bruno Pedace. At the top of the postings, a photo popped up. She stared at it for several seconds, then looked across at Cecil, then back again at the computer screen.

"What the hell?"

Rosandich smiled, again lifting his briefcase to his lap. This time he took out a small red paper pouch, which he placed on her desk.

"That's a key to a safety deposit box a friend of mine just opened. What's now in the box is worth forty-three million dollars."

Janet looked back at the computer screen and, in a louder voice than she'd intended, said, "It says here that you're wanted for questioning by the Securities & Exchange Commission. Did you steal this money?"

He compressed his lips and wagged his head. "I said it was *worth* forty-three million dollars. I didn't say it was money."

Janet was inclined to think the man had lost his mind. "St. Anne's can't get involved in anything illegal."

"Janet, why don't you let St. Anne's attorney decide if there's anything illegal here. I assure you, there will be no problem." He smiled and said, "Do you want the money, or not?"

Janet collapsed into her chair and expelled a long, breathy, "Jesus, Mary, and Joseph."

Charles Forsythe had for hours considered how he would deal with Sy Rosen. He'd handled tough negotiations with hard-nosed clients many times. But everything he knew about Rosen told him the guy was beyond hard-nosed. He was a sociopath who was motivated by winning as long as the reward for winning was dollar denominated, regardless of pain and suffering he might cause. His trepidation about the call to Rosen was that he didn't believe the man would agree to pony up forty-five million dollars. *Well, here goes*, he thought.

It took dropping Bruno Pedace's name to get through to Rosen.

"This is Sy Rosen."

"Mr. Rosen, my name is Charles Forsythe. I'm a broker in Beverly Hills. My client, Bruno Pedace, has documents he claims are important to you. He's willing to sell them."

Rosen scoffed. "What documents are we talking about, Mr. Forsythe?"

"I don't know. I haven't looked at them. But Mr. Pedace told me they are papers and storage devices he took with him when he left New York. He feels that you would be happy to get your hands on them."

"Let's say that's true. What would the price be to acquire these items?"

"Forty-five million dollars."

Rosen coughed, then said, "Are you serious?" he asked in a slightly higher voice. He then laughed. "Get real, Forsythe. Tell your client I'm not interested."

Forsythe felt as though a thousand butterflies had erupted in his stomach. Rosen's reaction was what he'd feared it would be. He sucked in a slow, quiet breath and then did what Bruno had told him to do. "Mr. Rosen, I've been instructed to inform you that you have exactly one hour to commit to wire forty-five million dollars to the account number I will send you via email as soon as we terminate this call. If you commit to send the wire, it must be deposited to my brokerage escrow account by no later than 9:00 a.m., Pacific time, tomorrow morning."

"And what happens if I decline your *generous offer*?"

"My client will contact a certain federal commission and will make himself available to provide sworn testimony in a court of law." After a beat, Forsythe added, "If you prefer to not avail yourself of the hour grace period, please advise me of that now so the documents can be immediately transmitted."

After five seconds of silence, Forsythe said, "Are you still there, Mr. Rosen?"

Rosen responded with a grunt.

"Should I interpret your silence as a declination of my client's offer?"

Another few seconds went by before Rosen shouted, "I have your number on my console. I'll call you back within the hour."

Forsythe replaced the phone in its cradle, leaned back in his chair, and expelled a relieved breath. He shook his head and whispered, "I'll be damned."

He instructed his secretary to hold all calls except for one from a Sy Rosen. Then he tried to focus on financial reports but was too excited to concentrate. He watched his desk clock tick away the seconds and minutes between wandering around the floor of the brokerage office, pretending to observe what his employees were doing. Fifty-five minutes went by before his phone rang.

"Mr. Rosen is on the line for you, Mr. Forsythe," his secretary

106

told him.

"Keep him on hold for one minute, Celine, then put him through."

Forsythe drummed the floor with his heels while he waited for the minute to pass. When his console rang, he took a deep breath, exhaled, then lifted the receiver.

"Forsythe."

"Sy Rosen here. I need some assurances."

"Go on."

"Are there any copies of the documents?"

"No."

"How would the documents be transmitted?"

"They're in a locked bank bag inside a safety deposit box. The key to that box will be sent to you or to whomever you delegate as your representative as soon as funds are received. I'll email you the combination to the bank bag at the same time. I assume you don't want your courier to be able to read the docs."

"You want forty-five million dollars transmitted before I get the documents? How can I be sure the documents actually exist? And, if they do exist, what's to prevent you from taking the money and not performing?"

"First, they do exist. I'm prepared to provide proof by sending you a couple pages. Second, it's not like we can use a title company to manage this transaction. You know that Mr. Pedace's word is golden. You'll have to count on that."

Rosen remained silent for several seconds. Forsythe filled the void and said, "Let's stop dicking around, Rosen. Your hour's up. It's your move."

"We'll pay the price," Rosen blurted.

Johnny Casale's pulse quickened when he saw Sy Rosen's caller ID on his cell phone. He answered with, "I'm on it, Mr. Rosen. I'm parked outside the broker's office. I—"

"Listen carefully, Casale. This might be our last opportunity. I just got off a call with the broker. I've agreed to buy the documents."

An acid tap seemed to have been turned on inside Casale's stomach. He thought, *If Rosen's got the documents, my fee just flew out the window.*

"You listening?"

"Ye-yes, sir."

"I believe Pedace is about to go into the wind. He can't hang around Redondo Beach because he knows we know he's there."

"If you get the documents, what does it matter where Pedace goes?"

Rosen didn't immediately respond, but Casale could hear the man breathing into the phone.

Rosen finally said, "You want to earn your fee, Casale?"

"Of course, Mr. Rosen."

Rosen shouted, "Then don't ask stupid questions. I got a feeling Forsythe will meet with Pedace. Follow that asshole until he leads you to Pedace." In a voice vibrating with menace, he then said, "I don't want Pedace to ever become a threat to me again. You take care of this problem and you'll get your full fee. Even though you failed to find my documents."

Casale was pissed about Rosen's tone. But he wanted the man's money more than he wanted to vent his anger. But he also saw an opportunity to tweak Rosen's blood pressure.

"I'm sure you're right about Pedace and Forsythe meeting. After all, they've been friends for years."

"What the fuck are you talking about?"

Casale smiled as he said, "The two of them grew up together. Hell, they both worked for your firm, back when Forsythe went by the name Massarino."

"Sonofabitch," Rosen blurted, then hung up.

Casale knew he had only one play. For a six figure finder's fee, he would do whatever it took to finish the mission. He'd watched the Forsythe office building from a coffee shop across the street for the past two hours, observed traffic in and out of the lot, and chuckled at how drivers avoided the black-scarred slot where Forsythe's Audi had burned. He wondered if Forsythe would replace the car today, and he got his answer when a man drove up in an Infiniti sedan with a rental car agency sticker on the door, followed by another guy in a Mercedes convertible sports car. The driver of the Mercedes parked in the company parking lot, went inside the brokerage offices for ten minutes with a clipboard in hand, and then came out and left with the driver of the Infiniti.

At 4:05 p.m., Forsythe exited the building, got behind the wheel of the Mercedes, lowered the convertible top, and sped away.

Five minutes into the drive, Casale figured the guy was on his way to his girlfriend's place on Willoughby. *Probably needs some loving to get over the loss of his luxury car*, Casale thought. The Mustang convertible was already in the driveway when Forsythe arrived. He pulled in behind it. Casale slowly drove by as the young woman greeted Forsythe at the door. No nurse's uniform this time. Just a bathrobe and a big smile.

Casale found a parking place at the curb a few houses down. He walked back to Forsythe's rental car and dropped an envelope on the driver's seat.

It was after 8 p.m. when Forsythe adjusted his tie and then took his suit jacket from his mistress. He folded the jacket over one forearm and hugged her with the other.

She kissed him. "It's awful about the car."

He shrugged and said, "Electrical problem. Hell of a thing with a car that pricey."

She gave him her sweet and innocent smile. "I'm glad I could lower your stress."

He kissed her long and hard. "Thanks, honey." Then he said, "How's day after tomorrow work for you?"

"Can't wait," she answered.

Outside, Forsythe opened the driver's door and spotted something on the seat. *This can't be good*, he thought. He picked up an envelope and opened it. Inside he found a typewritten note that read: *Bruno Pedace or Katherine Wheeler Forsythe? Your choice. You don't provide information that gives me Pedace and the documents, your wife will find out about your little love nest. You've got until 10 tomorrow morning.* There was a telephone number at the end of the note.

Forsythe dropped into the driver's seat and groaned. "You stupid sonofabitch," he muttered.

DAY 13

CHAPTER 21

Roger Briscoe, St. Anne's corporate attorney, looked across the conference room table and said, "Mr. Rosandich, as I understand it, St. Anne's Shelter will receive a wire transfer later this morning in the amount of forty-three million dollars."

Frank Mitchell, St. Anne's Director, and Carol Harper, the organization's board chairman, seated on either side of Briscoe, both looked pale and nervous.

"That's correct. Is there a problem?"

"It's been a long time since I believed in Santa Claus, Mr. Rosandich. I did a search of your name and couldn't find anything. Before we spend a lot of time preparing a gift agreement between you and my client, I want to make certain we're not wasting time."

Rosandich bent to his left and lifted his battered briefcase from the floor. He placed it on the table and popped the clasps. Janet, seated on his right, was the only other person in the room who knew anything about Rosandich's background. When Frank Mitchell gave her a questioning look, she just smiled back. Rosandich riffled through one of the compartments in the briefcase's lid and pulled out a faded-yellow file folder. He dropped the case's lid, placed the file on top of the case, and opened it. He then took out an ID card, a birth certificate, and copies of Google screen shots and slid them across the table to Briscoe.

He announced, "My real name is Bruno Pedace. I've used the

Cecil Rosandich alias for the last nine years." He pointed at the documents. "One of the articles I copied from Google states that the SEC wants to question me about several matters, but there are no charges against me."

Briscoe studied the documents for a couple minutes, then looked up, and said, "Do you want to explain why you've lived under an alias?"

"No. It's not pertinent to this transaction."

The lawyer looked around the room as though to gauge the others' reactions. Then he said, "Well, perhaps we should proceed."

While the final, edited legal documents were being printed, Janet and Bruno moved to her office.

"You sure about this, Cecil? Oops, sorry. Bruno."

"Yes. I've never been surer about anything. It's time I did something that would benefit other people."

Janet felt her face warm. She swallowed hard. "What's going on between you and the former partners you mentioned?" Before Bruno could respond, she added, "Where's the money coming from?"

Bruno shook his head and frowned. "I'm selling something of value to my former partners. The money, when transferred, will be legally mine to donate to St. Anne's. Beyond that, the only thing I want you to understand is that those men in New York City were setting me up to take the fall for a securities scam they orchestrated and that I had nothing to do with."

"Why did you run? Why didn't you just go to the authorities?"

Bruno scoffed. "After they got word that the SEC was investigating the company, I'm sure the partners had records doctored, absolving them of any culpability and making it look as though I had devised and executed the whole thing."

"But wouldn't the truth have come out in an investigation?"

Bruno shrugged. "Yes, perhaps. Perhaps not. But by then it would have been too late. There's no way they would have taken the chance that the SEC investigators would have believed me." He sighed and, after a long moment, said, "My assistant was having an affair with one of the senior partners. One night, after too much wine and sex, he told her about the SEC investigation. He mentioned that I had been behind an illegal scheme to defraud investors. When she asked what would happen to me, he told her I would 'probably never testify.' My assistant and I had worked together for ten years. I guess she knew me better than just about anyone. She knew I would never do anything illegal, and that the partner's comment about me not testifying really frightened her. The poor woman was embarrassed to tell me about the affair, but thank God she came to me. She probably saved my life."

Janet asked, "After the money is transferred, will you be safe?"

Bruno looked at Janet with a soulful expression. "I'll never be safe, Janet. As long as I'm alive, they'll see me as a threat."

Janet's eyes widened and became moist. "What will you do?"

"Leave California."

Janet knew her reaction showed on her face. She slowly shook her head. "I hate to see you go away." Her words had barely been spoken before she realized just how much she would miss him. She had a sudden ache in her stomach and a tightening of her throat. Her eyes flooded with tears. The man had become more important to her than she'd appreciated. Her reaction seemed to embarrass Bruno, who looked down at the briefcase on his lap and played with the brass clasps.

The quiet between them lasted a good sixty seconds, then he said, "It can't be helped. These are dangerous men. There's already been an incident that involved the broker, Charles Forsythe. Someone set his car on fire."

Janet shot him an incredulous look as she dabbed at her eyes with a tissue.

Another fifteen seconds of silence settled between them before Janet said, "Forgive me for asking, but do you have any family?"

"I was married once, but that was a long time ago."

At 7:55 a.m., Briscoe interrupted them. "I need Mr. Pedace to sign this affidavit that he is who he says he is. His driver's license expired a long time ago."

Janet laughed. "If he is who he says he is, good. But if he's not and is a crook, what's to prevent him from lying?"

"Nothing really."

"Then what's the point?"

Briscoe shrugged as he placed the document on her desk in front of Pedace. "Just crossing T's and dotting I's," he said.

Bruno smiled and picked up a pen from her desk. "It's okay, Janet."

"By the way," Briscoe said, "I called Mr. Forsythe and asked him to notify me the minute that the funds are available."

Bruno signed the affidavit and handed it back to the lawyer.

"Mr. Forsythe mentioned that the wire he's expecting is for a total of forty-five million dollars. Did I misunderstand the amount? The documents I prepared reference a gift of forty-three million. Is that still accurate?"

Bruno appeared uncomfortable—his face flushed and he looked away. "The number you put in the documents is the correct one."

Briscoe nodded, shrugged, and left the room.

Charles Forsythe's eyes felt as though they were sunburned. He hadn't slept a minute the night before. He railed at himself as he drove toward Redondo Beach. "How could I be so weak?" he asked himself. *I have a great wife whose father helped stake me years ago. Everything I have is due in no small part to my meeting Katherine Wheeler shortly after I arrived in Los Angeles more than two decades ago. And now I've put everything in jeopardy because my girlfriend makes my blood boil.*

The fact that Forsythe hadn't yet given up Bruno Pedace to the New York private investigator said nothing about a lack of affection for his wife and children. It said everything about his lifelong relationship with Bruno. His loyalties wrestled with one another inside his head and his heart, but, as he exited the I-5 Freeway, he knew what he would do. At the same time, he also knew he would never be able to look at himself in a mirror without feeling miserable. From this point forward, he would be nothing but a characterless shit. A man who'd cheated on his wife and who'd turned on an old friend.

He arrived at St. Anne's at 8:30 a.m. as he'd been asked to do by a lawyer named Briscoe. He was met at the front door by a Frank

Mitchell who led him through to a conference room where he was introduced to Briscoe and Carol Harper. Forsythe shook hands with them and said, "You all look a bit haggard."

Mitchell gave Forsythe a weary smile. "We've been up since 4:00 a.m. preparing documents to confirm Mr. Pedace's gift to St. Anne's."

Forsythe nodded. Just as he was about to take a seat, Bruno entered the room, accompanied by a striking woman who Bruno introduced as Janet Jenkins. When Bruno approached him, Forsythe extended his right hand, but his old friend stepped forward and hugged him. Then Bruno turned to the others and announced, "Mr. Forsythe is like a brother."

Janet watched the two men together and noticed how uncomfortable Forsythe seemed when Bruno hugged him. She thought, *maybe he's too macho to be comfortable hugging another man in the company of strangers.* She brushed the thought aside and took a seat across the table from the broker.

"Thanks for meeting us here and on such short notice," Mitchell said. "I know it's a bit irregular, but Mr. Pedace made it clear that he wanted everything executed as quickly as possible."

Briscoe waved a hand at the stack of documents, "You said that the money would be wired no later than 9:00. We might as well have all of these documents executed in anticipation of the wire coming in. One of the documents we'll give you includes wire transfer instructions from your account to St. Anne's account."

Absent emotion and expression, Forsythe just nodded. He happened to catch the Jenkins woman's raised-eyebrows-look she directed at her boss, Frank Mitchell, who returned her look with a slight hunching of his shoulders.

I'd better be careful, he thought.

It took thirty-five minutes for them to finish their business. Briscoe placed some of the documents in a folio and handed it to Forsythe. "Thanks again for handling this," the lawyer said. He smiled and asked, "When will the funds be transferred to our account?"

Forsythe looked at his wrist watch. "It's almost 9:00. Why don't I call the bank? I'll check to see if the money is in. There should be no reason that the funds aren't in your account before noon today." He dialed a number on his cell and conducted a brief conversation with someone. When he hung up, he announced, "Congratulations. The funds have arrived."

Forsythe thanked the people in the room and then followed Mitchell and Pedace to the front entrance.

"Do you have any idea how important this money is to St. Anne's?" Pedace said.

Forsythe felt his professional mask shatter. His face felt hot and his eyes flitted from Pedace to Mitchell, and back again to Pedace. "St. Anne's is a shelter for abused women. I'm sure there are more demands for its services than there are resources to meet those demands."

"That's right," Mitchell said. "Did you know that more than one in three American women have experienced rape, physical violence, and/or stalking by a domestic partner? Mr. Pedace's gift will make a tremendous difference in St. Anne's being able to expand its mission." Mitchell smiled. "You're doing God's work, Mr. Forsythe."

Forsythe felt as though a golf ball was lodged in his throat and a barbell draped on his shoulders. He had to force himself to put one foot in front of the other as he walked to his car.

An uncomfortable sensation had put Bruno on edge as he'd watched Charlie during the meeting. The sensation was even more intense as his old friend exited the building. He said to Frank Mitchell, "I'll be right back," and rushed after Forsythe.

Outside, Bruno saw Forsythe step into the parking lot, approach a Mercedes sports car, and remotely pop open the vehicle's trunk. He reached the car as Forsythe placed the folio in the trunk and closed the lid.

"You okay, Carlo?"

The use of his birth name seemed to unsettle Forsythe. He wouldn't make eye contact.

"I'd better get to my office to verify wire instructions with the bank, Bruno."

"What's going on, Carlo? Something's bothering you."

"No...no." He showed a weak smile. "Everything's fine."

Bruno continued to stare at Forsythe as he slid into the car. The man cranked the ignition, looked in the rearview mirror, and slipped the shifter into reverse.

"Why didn't you verify the wire instructions for the transfer to the St. Anne's account when you had the bank on the phone?"

He looked straight ahead and spread his arms. "I-I guess I could have. I just wanted to send something official on company stationery."

Before he removed his foot from the brake pedal, Forsythe turned, made eye contact for barely a second, and said, "What will you do now?"

"Find someplace else to live…as soon as you cash out the bonds I still have."

"Oh, yeah. I forgot about them."

Pedace raised his briefcase and asked, "You going to take my bonds with you?"

Forsythe hesitated a moment. "Why don't you hold onto them? Call me tomorrow. We can take care of them then."

"But—"

Before Bruno could finish, Forsythe backed out of his parking spot and roared away.

The sensation that had hit Bruno in the conference room now became even more severe. He felt sick to his stomach. He tried to rationalize Carlo's behavior, but there was only one conclusion that made any sense: Sy Rosen had somehow gotten to his old friend.

But why didn't Carlo take my bonds?

Bruno wheeled around and ran to the building entrance. Janet had just stepped out of the front door as he ran to her.

"What's wrong, Bruno? You look like—"

"We have a problem. Can you drive me somewhere?"

Janet waggled her keys at him. "I was just going out to get a cappuccino to celebrate."

"You'd better put off any celebration."

Charles Forsythe's hands shook as though he had palsy. About to climb the hill up Herondo Street, on the east side of the PCH, he pulled to the curb and took long, steadying breaths. The clock on the dashboard showed 9:25. *Five minutes to contact Casale.*

The phone shook in his hand as he dialed. It took three attempts to punch in the correct number.

"Right at the deadline," Casale answered.

Forsythe swallowed the lump in his throat. "I have the key to the safety deposit box where the documents are."

"Good start. How about Mr. Rosen's cash?"

"It's in my firm's trust account."

"Well, you'd better reverse the wire and send the money back to Mr. Rosen."

Forsythe swallowed hard, but the lump that had formed in his throat seemed lodged there permanently. "I'll take care of it as soon as I get back to my office."

"And what about your old friend Pedace?"

Forsythe felt a pain like a knife in his heart. *How did this guy know he and Bruno were old friends?*

"What about him?"

"I want to know where to find him."

"That isn't going to happen."

"Make a U-turn and cross the PCH. Go down to the old power plant and park at the dead end."

Forsythe twisted in his seat and looked all around. There was a Toyota parked halfway back down Herondo. The driver flashed his lights. "How the hell did you know where I was?"

"You think I was going to trust you? I've been on your ass since you left your house this morning."

Forsythe pulled a U-turn and caught the green light at the PCH.

"Where are we going?" Janet asked.

"Charles Forsythe's office in Beverly Hills."

"To do what?"

"I think Charlie is about to do something very, very wrong."

Janet felt panic as Bruno explained what he thought was going on.

"But the money's already been wired."

Bruno groaned and said, "Yeah, to Charlie's brokerage account. But what if he just reverses the transaction and sends the cash back to Rosen, Rice & Stone?"

"We can sue him and your old partners; we had a deal," Janet said.

Bruno scoffed. "Janet, the documents that my old firm is paying for are in a safety deposit box. I gave the box key to Charlie. If he sends the money back to the Rosen firm, he'll also give them the key. They'll get the docs, destroy them, and be home free. What are we going to do? Sue them all for changing their mind about making a charitable gift to St. Anne's?"

"Forsythe signed the papers. We'll sue him and his firm for fraud...or something."

Bruno just shook his head.

Janet groaned as she went up the PCH.

Past the Redondo Beach arch, Bruno suddenly shouted, "Stop!"

She took a right before Herondo and pulled into a landscape business's parking lot. "What's wrong?"

Bruno pointed off to the left. "That was Charlie in that convertible."

"You're sure?"

"Dammit, I'm sure. Turn around and go after him."

By the time Janet had turned around and crossed the PCH, the Mercedes convertible had parked at the end of the street, down by the closed power plant. A Honda was parked beside it. The driver's side door of each car was open, as were the cars' trunks. Forsythe and another man stood behind the Mercedes. As she drove down the hill, still about one hundred yards away from the men, Bruno ordered, "Pull over." When she did, he exited her car and said, "Wait here. Don't get out under any circumstances."

"But—"

In a loud voice that shocked Janet, he said, "Just do it."

She watched him stride toward the men. She barely heard the two vehicles' motors running over the noise of her own car's engine and PCH traffic behind her. A radio in one of the cars played music. Bruno looked like a different man from the one she had come to know. He moved with confidence and purpose.

Still ten yards away from Forsythe and the other man, Bruno called out, "What the hell's going on, Carlo?"

The two men turned.

Forsythe shouted, "Get out of here, Bruno."

The second man smiled and said, "Well, I'll be damned."

Just a couple feet away from them, Bruno pointed a finger at Forsythe. "What kind of scam are you pulling?"

Forsythe spread his arms. "I'm sorry, Bruno. There was nothing I could do."

The second man, still smiling, said, "If I'd known it was you back in the parking lot of that women's shelter talking to Charlie here, I coulda taken care of business there."

Forsythe yelled, "Bruno, get out of here," as he turned on the other man and pushed him backward. The guy staggered a bit, but quickly righted himself, reached behind his back, produced a pistol, and fired. Forsythe bent forward as he crossed his arms over his chest. A loud burst of air escaped his lungs as he stumbled back a few feet. The man fired again, driving Forsythe to the pavement.

Janet gasped. The man with the gun had shot Forsythe and had now turned the weapon on Bruno. The armed man said something as he stepped forward. Then, Bruno launched himself at the man, swinging his fists, shouting something indiscernible. The man clubbed the side of Bruno's head with the pistol, knocking him down. But Bruno immediately scrambled to get to his feet. The armed man aimed and fired.

Janet shouted, "Bruno," and threw her shifter into drive. She pressed the accelerator to the floor and raced down the street. The gunman had followed Bruno as he crawled backward, toward where Forsythe lay on the street. The man raised his weapon and again fired at Bruno. Then he rushed to where Forsythe lay and pulled something from one of Forsythe's jacket pockets He turned, ran to the Mercedes, and reached into the trunk. He withdrew the folio, went to the Honda, and placed the folio in its trunk. He raised a hand as though to close the lid when he jerked around and stared open-mouthed at the rampaging hunk of metal that was almost on top of him. The front end of the Impala simultaneously smashed into the man and the rear end of the Honda. The noise was deafening. The upper half of the man she'd hit slumped on her hood. She left her car in gear and rushed to Bruno, who lay on his back, just two feet from Forsythe. Two large bloody spots showed on his white shirt. He wheezed; a rumbling sound came from his chest.

"Oh, my God," Janet cried. "Oh, my God. Bruno, can you hear me?"

"Get out...of...here, Ja...net."

"Are you crazy? I'm not going anywhere."

"Get documents. Find key."

"No. I have to—"

"Please."

She ran to the left rear bumper of the Honda and reached into the trunk for the folio. She grasped the top of it and pulled it toward her, but it slipped from her hand. Janet gasped when she saw blood on her hand. She wiped her hand on her skirt, reached again for the folio, and gripped a side of it as tightly as she could. She pulled it from the trunk, ran to her car, and dumped it on the floor in the back. Then she went through the gunman's pockets, found a safety deposit box key in a small red envelope. Janet returned to her car and looked in the front seat for her purse. It had been thrown to the floor, its contents spilled. She bent over, dug through her things, found her cell phone, and called 9-1-1 as she rushed back to Bruno.

After she terminated the call, Janet jerked off her jacket and used it to try to stop Bruno's wounds from bleeding. While she applied pressure to his chest, she looked over at Forsythe. There was a neat hole in the center of the man's forehead. Blood pooled under the back of his head.

PART II
SIX MONTHS LATER

DAY 1

CHAPTER 1

"Are you certain he can be released?" Janet asked Dr. Kanji Bengali, a psychiatrist on St. Anne's staff.

Bengali frowned and said, "Why do you ask?"

"Well...he was shot and nearly died."

"And he's fully recovered and needs to go on with his life. Being a resident here at St. Anne's is neither appropriate for him nor for the institution." When Janet opened her mouth to say something, Bengali raised her hands. "I'm happy we were able to house him in our secure ward since he was released from the hospital. But he can't become a permanent resident."

Janet nodded several times. "He'll probably need a couple days to make other arrangements."

Bengali shrugged. "He's come a long way. You helped him recover."

Janet squinted. "I don't think—"

Bengali stopped her again. "I'm not referring to his physical wounds. You had a lot to do with the psychological changes we've seen in Mr. Pedace. When he was admitted here, he was not only recovering from gunshot wounds, he presented as if he had paranoid delusions because of the years he spent on the run."

"I've seen the same sort of behavior in most of my clients here at the shelter."

"Mr. Pedace suffered from flashbacks of what happened to him in New York. Imagine working at a company for decades, giving your all to that company, thinking your partners are your friends, and then being betrayed by them. Imagine being set up by those people to take a fall for something you had nothing to do with, and then learning that your wife had betrayed you by sleeping with one of the partners." Bengali blew out a loud sigh. "Add to all of that his wife's death and the experience of going underground for nearly a decade, fearing for your life every day, severing your relationships, and then being shot and nearly killed. It's amazing that he isn't completely dysfunctional. But, as I said, you had a lot to do with him recovering."

Janet said, "And, like our clients, Bruno wasn't delusional about his fears, anger, and sense of betrayal. They were real and understandable."

"That's correct. But that doesn't make paranoia any easier to deal with. One worry I have is that the anger that built up in him over years could translate into his acting out in some aggressive, vengeful manner. He'll need support and understanding going forward."

Janet knocked on the door to Bruno's room.

"Come in."

She opened the door, stepped into the efficiency unit, and saw Bruno packing a suitcase.

"You know, you could stay here a couple more days," she said. She'd wanted the statement to come across matter-of-factly, without emotion. Instead, it sounded as though she were pleading with him.

"Thanks, Janet, but these units are intended for battered women and children. Besides, the doctor says I'm healed." He took in a long, slow breath and coughed. "Damn, I'm out of shape."

"More reason to stay here longer."

Bruno smiled. "You've all been great. But it's time for me to leave."

"Where will you go, Bruno? You can't live behind the Pappadopoulos's café like you did before. It's not the most secure place."

"You're correct; I'm not staying there any longer. Wherever I go, I'll have a target on my back. It won't be safe for anyone I'm close to. Sooner or later, Sy Rosen will want to settle things with me." He smiled briefly, then scowled. "He never got the documents. They're still in the box at the bank and I've got the key. And St. Anne's got the money. Thank God Charlie's business partner agreed to sign the transfer of the money from Forsythe's account to your account."

"I know I've asked this before, but you've never given me an acceptable answer. Why not just turn the documents over to the SEC and agree to testify against the firm? It's a government agency, after all. It surely can protect you."

"Maybe I'm being paranoid, but Rosen and his partners have hundreds of millions of dollars in personal and corporate assets. You don't think they can buy off someone? Some cop, some FBI agent, some prosecutor?"

"I can't believe they would still come after you."

"They want to get rid of me because I know everything about the securities scam they carried out. Investors lost billions in those schemes. Even though no one's ever been prosecuted for the sub-prime mortgage deals that Wall Street made, the SEC would have no choice about bringing charges against Rosen, Rice & Stone once I talked. The partners would probably wind up in jail and have to pay hefty fines. You have to take my word for it, those guys will do whatever it takes to avoid that happening."

"You could have gone to the SEC ten years ago and saved yourself years of misery."

"That's true. But I was different back then. I'd never been brave or a fighter. Other people, like Charlie Forsythe, were always there to protect me and to fight my battles. When I learned what my partners were about to do to me, I didn't think going to the SEC was a viable alternative. My instinct was to run. That has always been my first impulse when confronted with danger. And, I believed that Rosen would find a way to kill me. The only way they'd ever feel safe is for me to be eliminated."

"So, what will you do, run away again; hide for the rest of your life?" Before he could answer, she added, "Why not turn the safety deposit box key over to Rosen? Wouldn't that put an end to all of this?"

"As to hiding out for the rest of my life, that was my original plan. But I've now decided all I would be doing is looking over my shoulder, waiting for those bastards to find me. No, I'm not going to run anymore. And I've thought about sending the box key to Rosen. But there are two reasons why I've decided against doing that. The first, is that Rosen will always see me as a potential threat. One way or the other, he'll come after me."

"The second reason?" Janet asked.

"Rosen's responsible for Charlie's death. I can't let him get away with that."

She saw a look in his eyes and in the set of his jaw that she hadn't seen before.

"I've been a coward all my life. Never stood up for myself. No more. Even though Charlie betrayed me, in the end he tried to protect me. That cost him his life. I don't want anyone else hurt because of me. From now on, I fight my own battles."

"What are you planning?"

"Better you don't know." His eyes seemed misty as he smiled at her. "I couldn't have asked for a more caring friend than you. You've made a difference in my life." After a beat, he added, "You should find someone who cares about you. Someone you can love."

Tears rolled from Janet's eyes and dropped on her blouse.

Pedace went to the closet and dragged out his old, brown-leather briefcase. He placed it on the bed, opened it, and removed a small white envelope.

"In there is an unlisted telephone number. In an emergency, and only an emergency, you can reach me at that number. Please don't give it to anyone else."

He then withdrew a large brown envelope. "I'd appreciate it if you would take this to Nikos and Voula Pappadopoulos at their restaurant."

"Sure," she said. "I'll take care of it this afternoon."

Frank Mitchell knocked on the open door and entered. "I see you're about to leave us."

Bruno nodded. "I appreciate everything you and your staff have done for me."

"It was our pleasure. It's the least we could do. Because of you, St. Anne's will be able to serve more people in a very significant way." Mitchell came over and shook Bruno's hand. "If you wouldn't mind, the staff wants to say goodbye. Someone baked a cake."

"Oh my," Bruno said. "I hoped to leave without a fuss."

"You'd hurt a lot of people's feelings if you didn't join them for a couple minutes."

Janet could see how uncomfortable Bruno was with the prospect of being the center of attention, but he agreed to go to the dining room with Mitchell. "I'll be right down," she said, as the two men walked toward the door. She followed them out, but happened to glance back into the room and noticed Bruno had left his briefcase open. She turned and walked to the bed. As she was about to close the case, she saw it was essentially empty, except for a thin folder. She looked back over her shoulder, then opened the folder. Inside were several photographs of the same woman. One was a wedding shot. Another showed Bruno and the woman in swimsuits on a beach. A third showed the two of them at a restaurant table. All but one of the pictures were of the couple together. That one exception was a close-up, full-body shot that gave Janet a terrific view of the woman's features. She was amazingly beautiful, with bright brown eyes, auburn-colored hair, perfectly arched eyebrows, long lashes, a small but straight nose, a sensual mouth, and a swimsuit-model-perfect figure. Janet turned over the photo and read the name there: Paolina. Her throat went dry and she found it difficult to swallow as tears again came to her eyes. She'd always thought, from that first day when she intervened to rescue Bruno from the two teenagers in the Redondo Beach alley, that he must have something of great value in the briefcase. She looked at the photo again and whispered, "I guess he did, after all." Then her tears flowed freely as she thought how Paolina's betrayal must have broken Bruno's heart. And how the presence of the woman's photos was proof that Bruno still loved his former wife.

After Janet watched Bruno leave St. Anne's in a taxi, she drove her two-year-old Chevrolet Trax SUV, which she'd bought after she'd destroyed her Impala, to Pappa's Café. It was 3 p.m. and things were relatively quiet there—only two tables were occupied. She spied a woman wearing an apron seated at a back table, drinking from a cup, and walked over and introduced herself. She asked to speak to Nikos and Voula Pappadopoulos.

"I am Voula. How may I help you?"

"Is Mr. Pappadopoulos here?"

Voula frowned for a second, then smiled. "Where else would he be?"

Janet smiled back. "Bruno Pedace asked me to deliver something to you and Nikos."

"Bruno Pedace?"

"Oh, I'm sorry." Janet suddenly realized her mission here would be more complicated than just delivering an envelope. "The man you knew as Cecil Rosandich is actually Bruno Pedace."

Voula's expression changed to one of worry. "Where is Cecil? We haven't heard from him in six months. He just disappeared. We've been terribly worried."

"You remember that incident in Redondo Beach six months ago? Two men were shot, and a car crashed into the shooter."

"Of course, I remember. We don't have a lot of shootings in Redondo Beach." Then her eyebrows arched, and her hand shot to her mouth. "Janet Jenkins! You're the woman who killed that man."

Janet nodded. "One of the men he shot was Bruno Pedace."

Tears came to Voula's eyes. "Oh my God. That was Cecil he shot?"

"Yes, ma'am." Janet reached across the table and touched Voula's hand. "He's doing fine. I'm sure he would have reached out to you himself, but he was worried that the people who hired the assassin might be a danger to you."

Voula used a corner of her apron to dry her eyes. Then she called out, "Niko, we have a visitor. Come out here."

Nikos wiped his hands on his apron as he came out of the kitchen.

Voula said, "Niko, this is Janet Jenkins, a friend of Cecil's."

Nikos's fleshy, expressive face beamed. He took Janet's hand in his two big mitts, shook it, and said, "Do you know where Cecil is? We haven't—"

Voula tapped his arm. "You ought to let Ms. Jenkins's hand go before you rip it from her arm."

The man blushed. "I'm sorry. Do you know where Cecil is?"

Voula patted the chair next to her. "Ms. Jenkins has something to tell us."

Nikos's face sagged with worry. "Is there bad news about Cecil?"

Janet repeated for Nikos what she'd told Voula. Then she took Bruno's envelope from a folio and handed it to Nikos, who ripped it open. He pulled out a single sheet of paper and read from it aloud:

Dear Niko & Voula:

> *I can't thank you for your kindness over so many years. I apologize for writing to you instead of coming to see you but, for reasons I prefer not to explain, I didn't want to cause you any problems. I will never forget all that you've done for me and will think about you every day of my life.*

> *Enclosed is a key to a safety deposit box at the bank listed below. There is a gift for you in that box. Please accept it with my heartfelt gratitude.*

> *Your friend, Cecil*

"What is this?" Nikos asked as he handed the note to Janet and turned the envelope upside-down. He picked up the key that spilled onto the table.

Janet read the note to herself, then looked across the table at Voula, who now leaned against Nikos's shoulder. Janet turned her gaze on Nikos, gave him a Cheshire cat smile, and shrugged. "He says it's a gift. You'll have to go to the bank to find out what it is."

Nikos looked at Voula, his wide, expressive face confused and sad. "What do I need with a gift?" He stood and huffed back toward the kitchen.

Voula watched her husband walk away, then turned to Janet. "We've both been worried about Cecil. Especially Nikos. He really cared for that poor, lonely man. When he disappeared six months ago, at first he was frightened, then he was angry, and then he became so sad." She glanced back toward the kitchen and smiled. "He's such a sweet man, my Nikos."

Janet and Voula stood and moved away from the table. "I need to get back to work," Janet said. "If I hear from Ce...I mean Bruno, I'll call you."

"That would be very nice." Then Voula stepped forward and

hugged Janet. When she backed away, she said, "You seem like a very nice girl, Janet. I get the feeling you're going to miss…Bruno very much." She giggled. "I can't get used to calling him that. He'll always be Cecil to me."

On the drive back to St. Anne's, Janet was swamped by melancholia. She'd spent time with Bruno every day over the past six months. He hadn't been gone a day and she already missed him.

Back at work, Janet walked to her office and sat down behind her desk. She was about to place her purse in a drawer when she spotted the edge of a white envelope under her blotter. She pulled it out and noticed her name handwritten on it in Bruno's sweeping style. Her throat felt dry and tight as she tapped the envelope against her other palm. She carefully opened it:

Dear Janet:

I can't tell you enough how much I appreciate all you've done for me. From that first day when you bravely saved me from those young thugs, you changed my life. Unfortunately, I changed your life, as well. Whether you believe me or not, I know my old partners will never stop looking for me. And they will stop at nothing to remove the threat I represent to them. That's why I must leave California.

I wish you a bright and happy future and hope you will find someone to love and who will love you as you deserve to be loved. Someone who will keep you safe.

I've left something for you in your middle desk drawer. I hope it will give you the freedom to do what you truly want to do in this life.

It was signed *Bruno.*

Janet's throat now burned. It felt so tight that she found swallowing difficult. She crushed Bruno's note into a ball and threw it across the room. "How dare you presume what's good for me," she shouted. "How dare you!"

She opened her middle desk drawer and pulled out an envelope identical to the one she'd taken to the Pappadopouloses. She slid a letter opener under the flap and dumped the contents—a small note with the name and address of a bank and a key—onto her desk.

Janet stared down at the key, her hands balled into fists. Then she broke down and cried inconsolably. When she could finally speak, she muttered, "Oh, Bruno."

CHAPTER 2

Armed with false ID; thirteen thousand, eight hundred dollars in cash; and one point nine million dollars in cashier's checks he'd received in exchange for the last of the ATC Industries bonds, Bruno felt prepared for the next phase of his life.

The ride from St. Anne's to LAX had been uncomfortable, slouched in the backseat of a taxicab. He thought he'd probably gotten away unnoticed. But he couldn't be certain.

He traveled light. One suitcase, which Janet had loaned him, and his old briefcase. He'd tried to sleep on the plane, but the old paranoia was still alive and well. Bruno guessed Sy Rosen had probably found another hit man since the last one died. Now that he was out in public again, Bruno had a persistent itch between his shoulder blades, as though someone had a rifle aimed at him.

It was gloomy and rainy in New York City when the plane landed at LaGuardia Airport at 10:50 p.m. Once the plane docked at the gate, he retrieved his briefcase from the overhead bin and shook his head at the preposterous airline policy of charging fifty dollars for a piece of checked luggage. A lot of things had changed in the nearly ten years since he'd been on an airplane.

He found his checked bag and lugged it, along with the briefcase, out to the curb and joined the taxi queue. Ten minutes later, he was stuffed into the backseat of a yellow cab that appeared to have been loaned out to the demolition derby circuit before being used as a New York City taxi. It took only a few seconds to discover the vehicle's shocks were shot. The one thing that hadn't changed was the surliness of New York cabbies.

"Where you go?" the Eastern European cabbie asked in a tone that was somewhere between angry and threatening. He wore ear buds, connected to a hardback book-sized radio suspended on a hooked piece of coat hanger punched into the bottom of the dashboard.

Bruno had spent the last six months in a cocoon of affectionate care and friendship, but he hadn't forgotten where he'd come from, who he'd been most of his life, or what had happened to him. He'd resolved to be a different man in the future. He looked at the driver's ID badge on the right visor and saw the name Franco Djokovic.

"Where are you from, Mr. Djokovic?"

"Where you go?" the guy repeated.

"You answer my question and I'll tell you where I want you to take me."

The driver leaned forward and glanced at him in the rearview mirror. "I drive car; no make conversation."

"Okay, Mr. Djokovic. Take me back to LaGuardia. I'll get another cab. After I report you to the New York City Taxi & Limousine Commission."

The driver seemed to think about that for a few seconds. "Okay, okay. I am from Croatia."

"Well, Mr. Djokovic, I'm from New York. So, take me to the corner of Avenue N and East 98th Street in Brooklyn. Do you want me to tell you which route to take, or can you come up with the quickest way all on your own?"

The driver nodded. "I know best way to drive."

"Good. Now you can go back to your music."

The forty-minute drive gave Bruno time to think. He'd had six months to conceive and fine-tune a plan. But he repeatedly tested it for flaws, possible traps, dead-ends. Like a chess player, he tried to anticipate his opponents' moves. Rosen, Rice, and Stone might be assholes, but they were intelligent, unscrupulous assholes.

He exited the cab, walked down 98ᵗʰ Street to a three-story home, and gawked up at the property. It didn't surprise him that it looked about the same as it had when he'd last seen it. For a moment, he was lost in the memories of that day twelve years ago, when he and Paolina had attended a Massarino family function. Even after Carlo had emigrated to California, he and his Paolina were often included in Massarino events. Though he could see his breath and despite the cold drizzle, he felt suddenly warm. Each time he was around the Massarinos it had been like attending a holiday festival. Plenty of great food, too much Italian wine, laughter and arguments, and singing and dancing. And children. The place was always packed with children. It was the children who made him melancholy. He'd wanted kids of his own, but Paolina wanted nothing to do with them.

He climbed the steep steps to the front door, dropped his suitcase on the landing, and reached for the bell. But before he could ring it, a slightly smaller version of Carlo Massarino opened the door.

Louis Massarino had changed a great deal. He appeared to have aged more than the ten years since Bruno last saw him. His hair was completely white and sparser; his skin furrowed. If anything, the man was even thinner than he remembered. The Massarino men had never seemed to be able to gain weight, while their women more than made up the difference.

"*Entra. Benvenuti nella mia casa,*" Massarino said.

"*Grazie, Don* Massarino."

Massarino grabbed Bruno's suitcase from the stoop and led the way inside. He handed off the case to a man waiting in the hallway. "Take this to Mr. Pedace's room, Silvio." Then Massarino turned back to Bruno. "You're probably hungry. We'll get you something to eat; then you can rest."

"That sounds great," Bruno said. "But maybe we can talk a little now."

"If that's what you want."

"If you don't mind," Bruno answered.

"Good. Good."

They moved to a sitting room that was a combination office

and den. It was a man's room, with large leather furniture, heavy built-in bookcases, and an enormous desk. Bruno remembered that the last time he was here, this room had been two rooms—a dining room and a living room.

Seated in two opposing leather chairs, Massarino picked up a crystal bottle from a tray table between them and filled two glasses with a light-brown liquid.

"*Fogolar Riserva*," he said. He smiled and raised his eyebrows. "It helps me sleep."

Bruno picked up a glass. "*Grazie, Don* Massarino. I appreciate—"

"Do me a favor, Bruno, cut out the *Don* Massarino crap. Those days are gone." He chuckled. "Besides, the last thing I need is for the Feds to hear me being referred to as *Don* anything."

Bruno nodded. He sipped from his glass and gave Massarino a wide-eyed look. "Wow. This is exceptional."

Massarino smiled again. "Only the best for my friends."

Silvio returned at that moment with a tray laden with *antipasto*. He placed it in front of Bruno and left the room.

Then Massarino placed his glass on the table, settled back in his chair, crossed one leg over the other, and steepled his fingers. "Now, tell me about my brother's murder."

DAY 2

CHAPTER 3

"This case has it all," Hugo Rosales told John Andrews over lunch at Joe's Crab Shack. "A P.I./hitman, a Wall Street banker, and a Mafia family."

"What are you talking about?" Andrews said. "You're not on that Mafia business again, are you?"

"Charles Forsythe was the son of a Lucchese don. He—"

"Come on, Hugo. That's like saying I'm a cattle rustler just because my great-grandfather stole cows in Wyoming eighty years ago."

Rosales shot Andrews a shocked expression. "Is that true?"

"Yeah, so what?"

"It explains a lot."

"Screw you, Hugo."

Rosales laughed, choked on the food in his mouth, and went into a coughing fit.

"Serves you right," Andrews said, as he bit off a hunk of his sandwich and calmly chewed. After he swallowed, Andrews frowned at his partner, who continued to cough. "God forbid you need someone to do the Heimlich maneuver."

Finally, his coughing jag over, his face still red, Rosales asked, "You think the election coming up next year has anything to do with the D.A. deciding to pursue this case?"

Andrews laughed. "Even if there's no Mafia connection, talking about organized crime will make the D.A. look like the Protector of the People and Crime Fighter Extraordinaire."

"There's that. And imagine the press coverage when Janet Jenkins testifies. I mean, she's like the greatest vigilante killer California has ever seen. She stabs to death the killer Rasif Essam in self-defense after the bastard murdered her mother, and then saves a man from certain death by crushing his would-be killer with her Chevy."

"Maybe some of that press coverage will slough off on us. Could get a promotion out of it."

It was Rosales's turn to laugh. "Don't hold your breath, partner." Rosales checked his watch. "We'd better get over to St. Anne's. It's almost two."

Janet Jenkins had met with the St. Anne's CPA for advice about the one-million-dollar gift from Bruno Pedace. She was shocked to learn that, after taxes, she would be lucky to keep six hundred thousand dollars of her windfall. But it was still more than enough to put a forty percent down-payment on a duplex in Redondo Beach and to pay off her credit card and car loan balances. She planned to rent out one half of the duplex and move into the other side. She felt damned good about being a property owner for the first time in her life, and being a landlord on top of it. She was due to close on the duplex in thirty days.

But she felt empty. She still badly missed her mother, and now she missed Bruno. She looked at the wall in front of St. Anne's whenever she arrived or left the building, hoping that Bruno would be seated there, waiting for her. She grimaced and thought, *those days are over. Even if Bruno returns,* he *won't be sitting on any walls, wearing worn out clothes, and living in the back room of a Greek café.*

After Bruno had recovered from his gunshot wounds, Janet had been amazed at the change that had come over him. In a way, she missed the sad soul of the Cecil Rosandich she'd first encountered in that alley. She chastised herself for thinking that way. She came to the realization she was so used to taking care of people, that she had come to view almost everyone she knew as a victim. *Will Bruno still want to spend time with me,* she wondered, *if he becomes totally independent? But that's all stupid thinking,* she told herself. *Bruno Pedace is long gone.*

A call from the reception desk brought Janet out of her daydreaming.

"Yes, Mary?"

"Detectives Rosales and Andrews are here for you."

"Okay. Put them in the conference room. I'll be right there."

Janet shuddered. Rosales had told her why they needed to meet, but she wasn't looking forward to rehashing the events of six months ago. She took a deep breath outside the conference room and slowly released it. Then she plastered a smile on her face and opened the door.

"My favorite two detectives," she said by way of greeting.

Rosales and Andrews stood on the far side of the table. As Janet took a seat, they sat in chairs across from her.

"How are you?" Rosales asked.

"Pretty good, Hugo. How about you guys?"

Rosales grimaced. "We're not happy about the D.A. reopening this case," Rosales said. "It's all politics."

Andrews said, "Unfortunately, we have no say in the matter." He took a breath and added, "You and Bruno Pedace will be star witnesses for the prosecution."

Janet felt her stomach tighten. "Yeah, I really loved the headline. *Redondo Beach Woman Kills—Again.* What will it be this time? *Jenkins Testifies in Death by Impala Case.*"

"That's not bad," Andrews said.

Rosales gave Andrews a hard look. "The D.A. will want you and Pedace to lay the foundation so he can make the case against the people who hired Casale."

"How in God's name is he going to do that?"

"We just got a copy of Casale's cell phone records. He made and received calls to and from the offices of Rosen, Rice & Stone in New York City. There were also calls between Casale and a guy named Salvatore Trujillo, who turned out to be Casale's brother-in-law. He admitted that Casale called him for information about Pedace and Charles Forsythe. He gave Casale information about the Massarino connection and when Forsythe changed his name. He also told us he knew Rosen, Rice & Stone was a client of Casale's."

"I'm obviously no lawyer, but so what? Unless you've got tapes of conversations between Casale and the Wall Street guys, their lawyers will tear all of that to bits."

Rosales frowned. "Probably right. But think of the press the D.A. will get and the embarrassment that will rain down on Rosen, Rice & Stone."

"And think of the attention that will be placed on Bruno and me." She realized her voice had risen a couple octaves and forced herself to tone it down. "Bruno is a very private person. Bringing attention to him just to give the D.A. press coverage could be damaging to Bruno."

Rosales shrugged. "Look, Janet, I don't know what to tell you. We're talking about murder here. The people who hired Casale need to be punished."

"What if, in the end, they're only embarrassed?"

"That's a form of punishment," Andrews offered.

Janet stared at Andrews and then at Rosales. "And what if Rosen, et al, hire another killer to go after Bruno? What if he's murdered this time?" She could hear her voice rising again, but did nothing this time to modulate it. "Your bullshit case goes down the drain and those Wall Street snakes slither away." After a beat, she added, "And Bruno pays the price."

CHAPTER 4

It would have been difficult to find anyone who looked more like the antithesis of a Brooks Brothers' model than Ryan Flanagan. His clothes never fit properly and were rumpled, his ties were always garish and stained, and his shoes were never polished. His salt and pepper hair was stringy and unkempt, and his body was shaped like a bean bag that had been slept on. But, worst of all, his physical condition was abominable. Even seated, he breathed like an emphysemic who had just run a mile. But, despite all this, Flanagan was the premier criminal defense attorney in all of New York State. There was no question who Sy Rosen would call when the Redondo Beach District Attorney sent him a subpoena for a deposition. The language in the subpoena that had frightened Rosen included words like, 'conspiracy,' 'murder,' and 'attempted murder.'

Rosen entered Flanagan's office and looked at the lawyer seated behind his Olympian desk in his Manhattan agency. He took a chair in front of the desk and forced himself to make eye contact with Flanagan. He thought the man resembled Jabba the Hutt from the *Star Wars* movie. Rosen was disgusted by the man, but made a Herculean effort to not allow his disgust to show. After all, Flanagan might be the only thing between him and prison.

"Can you believe those fuckin' idiots in California, trying to pin a murder on me?" Rosen blurted.

Flanagan eyeballed Rosen and wagged a stogie-sized finger.

"Now, now, Sy, let's not go all indignant." The lawyer wheezed between nearly every two words he uttered. He reached toward a pocket recorder on the middle of his desk pad and pressed a button. "I'm going to record our session so that nothing gets lost in translation. I assume that's okay with you."

Rosen waved at Flanagan. "Of course."

"So, Sy, tell me all about it."

"Tell you all about what? There's nothing to tell. It's a scam cooked up by a former partner of mine. He engineered a mortgage scam that could have ruined my firm. When the SEC came sniffing around, the guy took off. Next thing I know, he pops up in California with two bullet wounds and a fairytale about the shooter working for my firm."

"The shooter didn't work for your firm?"

"Well, he did and he didn't. John Casale did investigative work for us. But he sure as hell wasn't a hit man."

"Uh huh." Flanagan's jowls flapped like a bulldog's as he nodded. "Did you report this partner's activities to the SEC at the time?"

"Of course. They tried to find the partner, but he dropped off the planet. In a way, that was good. A trial would have rained bad publicity down on my firm."

"Imagine the publicity when the media learns that you've been subpoenaed."

Rosen's body was suddenly awash in sweat. "That would be devastating. Absolutely devastating."

"Sy, I'll take you on as a client. I've read the charge sheet and those idiots, as you called them, don't have a thing on you. It's all hearsay and innuendo. But I must tell you, win or lose, you'll come out of this a big loser. What I have to try to control is minimizing the damage. I'll almost guarantee you the Redondo Beach D.A. won't be able to take this to trial. But he's coming up for re-election next year. I'll bet you he'll try to get as much publicity as possible just before election day. He wants your head on his trophy wall because it'll look good to the voters."

"Jeez, you're a ray of sunshine."

"You're paying me to tell you the truth, not to blow smoke up your ass. The whole thing with the mortgage scam will look bad, as will the fact that your firm had a relationship with Casale." He did a triple-wheeze and then continued, "They've got two witnesses who can do damage to your reputation, even if their testimony doesn't send you to prison. Casale's brother-in-law Salvatore Trujillo, and Bruno Pedace."

"It's all bullshit," Rosen whined. "What are we going to do?"

"I'll do the best I can. Don't lose hope."

"Hope ain't a strategy."

Flanagan responded by wheezing, then devolving into a coughing fit.

Rosen left a fifty thousand dollar retainer check with Flanagan and took the elevator down from the twenty-third floor. Out on Avenue of the Americas, he buttoned his coat and opened his umbrella.

He muttered, "That fuckin' Casale had Pedace and let him slip through his fingers." He looked for his limo at the curb and spotted his driver as the man got out of the front seat of the Lincoln and waved. "Oh, well," he said under his breath. "In for a penny, in for a pound." He raised a hand and signaled to his driver that he would be another minute. He retreated to the building's front door, sheltered under the overhang, pulled out his cell, and dialed the first three digits of a number. But he didn't finish dialing. He fast-walked to his limo and dropped into the backseat. As the driver pulled away, Rosen said, "Sammy, find me a store where I can buy one of those… what are they called? Throwaway phones?"

"Burner phones, boss."

"Yeah, Sammy. Burner phones."

"You got it, Mr. R.; I know just the place."

CHAPTER 5

Two men in overcoats trailed Louis Massarino and Bruno Pedace as they strolled in a light rain around Massarino's Brooklyn neighborhood. Massarino held a golf umbrella.

"I have to do it this way, Bruno, 'cause you never know who might be listening. The family's been legit for fifteen years now, but the Feds are always lookin' for something."

Bruno suspected that Massarino was still *connected*, but he wasn't about to argue the point. "I understand," he said.

"What you told me last night; there's no doubt in your mind?"

"Louis, I swear it. My old employer was responsible for Carlo's murder and for me getting shot. The way I see it, I have two choices. I go to the SEC and blow the whistle on the firm. Tell the Feds that Rosen, Rice & Stone set me up. I've got documents that prove it."

"So, why don't you do it?"

"Because they'll make sure I never testify against them. They've got money and power. You know as well as I do that, especially in this town, money and power are everything. The only real danger to them is me. I know too much."

They walked on for a minute before Bruno said, "As long as those guys have money, they have power. Going to the SEC is no guarantee that I'll win."

"And if you did?"

"They'd slap them with a fine. There's no way the Feds can hit them with a solicitation of murder conviction. The assassin's dead. Who's going to testify against the firm?"

Bruno shrugged. "Hell, the Feds are always fining banks for something. No one gives a shit."

Bruno said, "You have that right. Remember what the government did with those giant firms that sold bad paper backed by subprime mortgages?"

"Nothing. The government did absolutely nothing. Not one of those guys went to jail," Massarino scoffed. "And the Feds bailed them out with huge capital infusions. Talk about RICO violations."

Bruno nodded.

"So, they need to shut you up."

"Exactly. That's what Casale was sent to California to do. That, and to recover the documents I took ten years ago."

"You said you had two choices."

"Right. The second choice is to financially ruin the company and the partners. Take away their wealth and power. Without wealth and power, they are no longer much of a threat to me."

In a voice that suddenly turned gravelly, Massarino said, "That's much too elegant a solution for me, Bruno. I want those guys dead. D-E-A-D. They killed my big brother. That's as personal as it gets."

Bruno had anticipated that Massarino would react as he just had. He took a deep breath, steeled himself for a possible aggressive reaction, and said, "Do me a favor, Louis. Just listen to what I have in mind. If you don't want to go that route, then I'll walk away."

Massarino stopped and looked at Bruno. He appeared to study him for a good ten seconds. "Carlo always said you were brilliant. I'll hear you out. But it better be good."

They walked in the drizzle for twenty minutes. Bruno laid out his plan and Massarino threw questions at him. They'd walked almost two miles by the time they circled back to Massarino's house.

"You done?" Massarino asked.

"Yeah. If you don't buy what I'm selling by now, I'll never make the sale. The only thing I want to say is that for men like Rosen, Rice, and Stone, there could be nothing worse than losing everything they own. Death, on the other hand, even a horrible death, would be too quick. I want them to suffer for a long time."

Massarino nodded. "What do you need from me?"

Bruno smiled. "A lot of patience, time to act, and a place to work."

"Okay, you got it. But if your plan isn't complete in ten days, we'll do it my way."

"Ten days! I can't do it—"

"Ten days, Bruno. No longer."

"Janet Jenkins."

"Janet, it's Hugo. Do you know where we can find Bruno Pedace?"

"No, Hugo. All I know is he left town."

"Why didn't you tell us that when Andrews and I met with you yesterday?"

"You didn't ask."

Janet heard Rosales mutter something that sounded like a curse.

"We need to talk with him, to make sure he'll testify against his old partners."

"I don't know what to tell you. He took off and didn't tell me where he was headed. He could be in Europe, for all I know."

"Oh, jeez. If you had to guess, where would he go?"

Janet didn't really want Rosales to find Bruno. The local D.A. was on a political witch hunt that would do nothing to help Bruno. But Rosales was a friend and she wasn't about to lie to him.

"Hugo, I would guess New York."

"Why the hell would he go there? His former partners want him dead. The closer he is to them, the more dangerous it will be."

"I have no idea. You asked me to guess."

"*Oh, dios mio*. The Chief and the D.A. will be pissed."

"I'm sorry, Hugo."

"If you hear from Pedace, please tell him I want to talk with him."

"Of course. But I don't think I'll hear from him. I think Bruno's gone."

DAY 3

CHAPTER 6

Louis Massarino set up Bruno in a two-bedroom apartment on the top floor of a three-story building in Brooklyn. Bruno equipped the second bedroom with a computer, printer, top-end router, TOR browser, and a proxy server. Massarino was present when all the equipment was delivered.

"Jeez, what is all this stuff?" Massarino asked as he moved around the room, serpentining his way around boxes.

"With this equipment, I'll be able to anonymize myself. No one will have a clue where or who I am."

"I got a feeling I'd get a headache if I asked you to explain what that means."

"Louis, I guarantee you that any headache you ever have will be nothing compared to what my old partners are about to experience."

After Massarino left, Bruno unpacked and set up the equipment. It took almost seven hours to get everything up and running. Seated in a wheeled chrome and leather desk chair, he cracked his knuckles and said, "No time like the present."

The software he'd purchased, along with the equipment, allowed him to anonymously access data all over the world. By 9 p.m., he'd built a folder of twenty-four world class commercial office properties that, in toto, comprised eighteen million square feet, and were worth, in his estimation, approximately three point five billion dollars at current market value. He put each building in a separate electronic file. The files included photographs, addresses, and tenant lists he'd taken from each building's website and from hacked files of lending institutions that had mortgage loans on the buildings.

He shifted his shoulders. He was on a roll and wanted to continue to the next step. But he hadn't eaten since noon and he knew he had many long days ahead. He saved his data, shut down the system, and walked downstairs to the street. Seven doors down was a pizza parlor. He ordered a sausage, onion, and mushroom pizza and two bottles of beer to go. As he waited, he felt a rush of enthusiasm that he hadn't felt in a long time. He'd already accomplished a great deal. His mind switched to the years he'd spent in California and how he'd become a pathetic, lonely man with a victim mentality. But everything had changed when he'd met Janet Jenkins. He conjured up the image of the last time he saw her. Two days ago, in St. Anne's Shelter. *Maybe Janet and I could have become more than friends*, he thought. He waved away the idea with a hand, as though swatting a fly, which earned him the attention of the young man behind the counter. The kid frowned but turned away when Bruno smiled at him.

Back at the apartment, he finished half of the pizza and both bottles of beer, and then considered going back to the computer. But he suddenly felt drained. He barely had strength to undress and brush his teeth. He rolled onto the bed and fell into a deep sleep.

Sy Rosen looked forward to his Friday night rides to his Long Island mansion. Even in winter, the place was a welcome respite from the noise and bustle of the City. He usually napped on the ride from Manhattan, but there was no possibility of that happening today. His visit with the lawyer Ryan Flanagan had undermined any chance for peace. The prospect of the humiliation that would be brought on by publicity around a murder trial in California had unhinged him. The Redondo Beach D.A. had not yet filed charges against him, his partners, or the firm, but once that happened, his and the firm's reputation would be damaged, perhaps irreparably. Flanagan was correct. Win or lose, they would all pay a very heavy price.

Rosen considered trying to bribe the D.A., but immediately discarded the idea. *The man's on a mission to get re-elected. What if he told the press that I tried to bribe him? You can never trust an ambitious politician.*

The last time he'd hired someone to eliminate Pedace, things had not turned out well. Casale's failure had created the problem he now had.

"I need to hire a pro," he muttered. "Not some half-ass P.I."

"Did you say something, Mr. R?" his driver asked.

"Just talking to myself, Sammy."

Rosen patted his shirt pocket and felt the burner phone he'd bought yesterday. He'd aborted several calls he'd begun to make, always second-guessing his decision. But he built his resolve and made up his mind. He had no other choice. He pressed the button on the console by his right arm and raised the glass between him and the driver. Then he dialed a number from memory and waited. After five rings, he was about to terminate the call, when a voice answered.

"I have a job…actually two jobs for you."

"You know what you need to do. I'll contact you if I have any questions. What's your timing on this?"

"Yesterday."

He ended the connection and lowered the glass partition. "Sammy, I gotta put together something at my house that I want you to drop off for me on your way back into the City."

"Sure, boss."

The hum of the elevator motor startled Victoria Nguyen. Then she heard heavy footsteps on the carpeted hallway outside her Manhattan cooperative apartment. She snatched a pistol from her nightstand, padded over to her door, and looked through the peephole. A large man approached the door, then knocked.

"What do you want?" Nguyen said.

"Got a delivery from Sy Rosen."

Nguyen opened the door as far as the chain lock would allow. "Slip it through here," she said.

The man inserted a manila envelope through the space. She

grabbed it and quickly shut the door. Then she watched through the peephole as the man backtracked down the hall.

She carried the envelope to the kitchen table and sliced it open. She dumped the contents—bundles of hundred-dollar bills and a white envelope—on the table, and stacked the currency. She knew she didn't need to count it. Not only did it look like one hundred thousand dollars; no client would consider stiffing her. She picked up the white envelope, opened it, and removed a sheet of paper. Typewritten on the paper were two names: Salvatore Trujillo and Bruno Pedace. She frowned. The second name seemed familiar, but she couldn't place why. There was an address and phone number next to Trujillo's name, but none next to Pedace's. Below the two names was a sentence: *There's a $50,000 bonus if you can finish the job within five days.*

Nguyen powered up her laptop and Googled *Salvatore Trujillo*. "I'll be damned," she said, and then laughed. "The guy's on Facebook." She discovered Trujillo was self-employed. His company was named *Lost & Found*. It appeared he was in some sort of investigations business, doing computer research for clients. "Slam dunk," Nguyen said.

When she Googled Bruno Pedace, her heart did a little flip-flop. There was a treasure trove of information about the guy, dating all the way back to his high school days. He was a genius who'd won all sorts of math and science prizes, and then went to Harvard. When she found that he'd joined Rosen, Rice & Stone after college, Nguyen felt a shiver go down her spine. Then there was an article about the SEC being interested in talking with Pedace. "What the hell is Rosen up to now?" she whispered.

She tried to dredge up in her memory why Pedace's name seemed familiar, but it wouldn't come.

There was a newspaper article on the Internet about Pedace being shot in Redondo Beach six months ago. The shooter was John Casale, a New York City P.I. The article went on to mention a woman named Janet Jenkins, who worked at a battered women's shelter, had saved Pedace's life by running her car into the hit man. "Wow," she said breathily when the article mentioned that Jenkins had killed a home invader with a pistol and a knife shortly before she'd saved Pedace.

Nguyen chuckled. "This Jenkins woman should be in my business."

She searched Casale's name on the net and came up with mundane stuff about his P.I. license, his membership in the Knights of Columbus, and his claim to fame: he was once an all-state high school football player. Nguyen found an obituary on the guy and read through it until she came to the section about his family. A bell rang in her head when she saw that Casale had a sister whose married name was Trujillo.

"Curiouser and curiouser," she said. She did a little forensic thinking and concluded that Sy Rosen might have hired Casale to kill Bruno Pedace. Casale had failed. Now, Rosen wanted her to eliminate Pedace, along with Casale's brother-in-law, who must have some connection to what Casale was hired to do. None of that made one bit of difference to Nguyen. It was just that background information often helped her accomplish her mission. The insight sometimes helped her avoid traps along the way.

DAY 4

CHAPTER 7

Bruno woke at 6 a.m., rested but groggy. He quickly showered and dressed and then put on a pot of coffee. While the coffee brewed, he warmed in the oven the other half of the pizza from the night before. *Glad I've got a cast iron stomach*, he thought.

After breakfast, he opened the spiral notebook in which he'd outlined his plan, and scanned the second phase. He knew this would be one of the most difficult parts of his strategy, and the one that would take the most time. He hoped to accomplish it in no more than one week.

He opened the first property file—a thirty-story office building in San Francisco. It took him an hour to hack into the San Francisco County Courthouse and, from there, to access the recorded documents on the Polk Office Tower. They included the title policy on the property, the ownership entity's incorporation papers, the borrower's loan application, the lender's note and mortgage, the survey, an appraisal, and a myriad of other documents. He created an Excel spreadsheet with column headings that read: Property Address, Age, Appraised Value, Square Feet, Occupancy Rate, Net Income, and Loan/Value. Then he entered "Polk Office Tower" on the first line of the form and scrutinized the documents for the data he needed to fill in the blanks. He finished inputting the data for the property a few minutes before 9 a.m.

The loan documents filed in the courthouse on the property

were dated five years earlier. Bruno researched the commercial real estate appreciation rate in San Francisco over the last five years and estimated that the Polk Office Tower's market value today should be approximately twenty-seven million dollars, which meant that the owners had fifteen million dollars in equity in the property, after subtracting out the twelve-million-dollar mortgage loan balance. Assuming a loan to value ratio of 70% against the twenty-seven-million-dollar value, the owners should be able to refinance the building for eighteen point nine million dollars. That would be the amount of the loan that Bruno's report would show on the property.

He downloaded a copy of the appraisal, loan application, note, mortgage, survey, and title insurance policy and then changed the dates on all the documents to dates no older than three months. He also changed the property valuation and loan amount on all documents. These changes took him another two plus hours.

At 11:10 a.m., he reviewed his work, corrected a couple of minor data points, and then stood and stretched. He felt a small amount of exhilaration having finished with one property, but also was frustrated about having twenty-three more to go, and only ten days in which to finish.

Before he went back to building his files, he called Louis Massarino.

"What can I do for you, Bruno?"

"You remember during our walk that I mentioned I would need the help of someone who's an officer at a financial institution? You know, a bank or an insurance company."

"Yeah, I remember. I think I have just the man for you. How soon do you need him?"

"Right away, Louis. I'll also need a security hacker, someone who can help me breach the defenses of a computer network."

"I thought that was your area of expertise."

"You only gave me ten days, Louis. I need help."

"I know just the guy."

Victoria Nguyen had scripted how she hoped her conversation would go with Janet Jenkins, the only connection she'd been able to come up with to Bruno Pedace. She researched the names of staff writers with *The New York Times*, picked a female name, called St. Anne's Shelter, and asked for Jenkins.

"Janet Jenkins."

"Ms. Jenkins, this is Romy Klein with *The New York Times*. I appreciate you taking my call."

"What can I do for you, Ms. Klein? I have to go into a meeting in a few minutes."

"I've been assigned to write an article about people who've survived violent encounters. Your name came up."

"I'm sure there are plenty of other people you can interview, Ms. Klein. I'd rather not rehash my experiences, and sure don't want to be the subject of an article in a national publication."

"I can understand you feeling that way, Ms. Jenkins, but you'd be an inspiration to other women. I think—"

"Not interested, Ms. Klein. Sorry I can't help you."

"Listen, maybe you *can* help. I would love to talk with Mr. Pedace. You know, get his take on what happened. Would you be able to put me in touch with him?"

"I can't speak for Mr. Pedace, but I suspect he'll be even less likely to want to talk with you. Besides, I have no idea where he is or how to get in touch with him."

"You don't have an email address or telephone number?"

Jenkins hesitated for a beat, which set Nguyen's antennae on edge.

"No, Ms. Klein, I have no way to get in touch with Mr. Pedace. Good luck with your article. I'm sorry I can't be of help."

Nguyen's internal radar was now on alert. She felt that Jenkins had lied to her about not having any way to contact Pedace. *Now, what to do about it?*

On reflection, Janet thought there was something off about Romy Klein. The reporter gave in too easily when Janet rejected an interview with her. She sat behind her desk, stared at the opposite wall for a minute, while wondering if there was a Romy Klein at the *Times*. She pulled up the newspaper's website and went to the link headed Staff Writers. There was a Romy Klein on the roster. When Janet clicked on Klein's picture, she discovered the woman was now eighty years old and on Emeritus status. Janet's heart rate jumped. The woman she'd just talked with was a great deal younger than eighty. Something was up and she had a sudden pang of worry. She took her purse from a desk drawer and removed the slip of paper Bruno had given her before he'd left St. Anne's. She looked at the telephone number on the slip. *Should I call Bruno and warn him?* She wondered. *But warn him about what? I can't even give him the real name of the woman who called.* Then another thought came to her. *When I took the call, my phone screen read: Unknown Number.* She dialed #69 to see if she could get the caller's number, but got a recording that said, "This caller's number is blocked."

Janet checked the time on her desk clock and saw she only had a minute to make her meeting on time. She returned the slip of paper to her purse and placed the purse in the desk drawer. *I'll think about what to do later.*

Louis Massarino's organization was more legitimate than illegitimate. The days of operating on the backs of drugs, prostitution, extortion, illegal gambling, and the like had been destroyed by RICO laws and aggressive U.S. Attorneys like Rudy Giuliani. With the assistance of some of the finest tax attorneys in the country, Massarino had converted earnings from illegitimate activities to legitimate businesses like restaurants, travel agencies, construction companies, and mortgage brokerage firms. But Massarino still ran one of the largest loan sharking operations on the east coast. Bobby Tennucci headed up that business. Massarino met Tennucci at Cucina Rosa in Brooklyn at 1 p.m. They took a table at the back.

"It's good to see you, Bobby. How's the family?"

Tennucci moved his head from side-to-side, then said, "Other than having a sixteen-year-old daughter in the house, all is good."

Massarino laughed. "I remember when my Dolores was sixteen. She and her mother were like two tigers in a small cage. They knew how to push one another's buttons. *Mama mia, che casino!*"

Tennucci wagged his head. "That's how I see it. A mess. It's like perpetual war in my home."

"Maybe a convent would take your daughter."

Tennucci said, "I've actually thought about that, but, after a few days, the nuns would send her back." It was his turn to laugh.

A waiter came over and placed an *antipasto* platter between them.

"I took the liberty of ordering for us. You'll love the *frutti di mare.*"

"*Bene,*" Tennucci said.

While Tennucci selected a few items from the platter, Massarino leaned in and whispered, "You still working with the guy at that insurance company?"

"You mean the one in the real estate investment department in Yonkers?"

Massarino nodded.

"Yeah." Tennucci smiled. "The guy's a degenerate gambler. Spends more time in Atlantic City than he does with his family." A sour look came over Tennucci's face. "I may have to...take action soon. He barely can make the *vig.* He owes ninety-eight large."

"There may be a way to make him even."

"You mean pay off his loan?"

"Exactly. I want you to tell him to meet with a friend of mine. My friend will call him."

"Your friend's name?"

"It's Bruno Pedace. But don't tell the guy. Just tell him to wait for a call."

After Massarino left the restaurant, he had his driver take him to a little store in the middle of a block in Brooklyn that had seen better days. The stores were all "mom and pop" affairs: a bakery, a deli, a grocery store, an insurance agency, and a computer repair shop.

"Drop me off in front of Jesse's place," Massarino told his driver, Silvio. "I'll only be a couple minutes. Just circle the block."

Massarino left the car and entered the computer repair shop. The young man behind the counter sat on a high stool, bent over a computer tower. "I'll be right with you," he said, without looking up.

"What'd I tell you about properly greeting your customers?" Massarino said.

The young man continued to stare into the back of the computer hard drive he worked on and said, "I told you before, Uncle Luigi, we computer types don't understand customer relations."

Massarino laughed. "Jesse, come out from behind there and give your uncle a hug."

Jesse Falco slipped off the stool, came around the counter, and hugged Massarino.

"When are you coming for dinner? Your Aunt Rosa misses you."

"I'm sorry, Uncle Luigi. I been workin' seven days a week." He smiled and added, "The best customer relations is based on quality, timely service."

"I have a job for you, Jesse."

CHAPTER 8

Janet had tried to pay attention to the discussions that occurred during the St. Anne's staff meeting, but all she'd been able to focus on was her conversation with the woman who'd claimed to be a reporter. The more she thought about it, the more convinced she was that the woman's call was only about trying to locate Bruno. She wondered if Bruno's old partners had hired another assassin to come after him. But she thought, *A female assassin? Unlikely.*

Back in her office after the meeting, she removed the slip of paper with Bruno's number from her purse and fingered it. It took her several minutes of reflection to finally decide to make the call. A message machine picked up and directed her to leave her name and number.

She left her office and climbed to the third floor to visit some of the women whose cases she was managing. Her first visit was with a mother of two small children whose husband had been locked up after his most recent assault on her. Janet was thrilled that Judy Smith had finally agreed to testify against the man. The fact that St. Anne's had been able to find the woman a clerical job in a radiology practice and to commit to pay for her to attend a radiology technician's training program had made all the difference in the woman's decision to testify. Judy Smith was a victory among many defeats. *All thanks to Bruno's generosity*, she thought.

Janet talked with Mrs. Smith about her job start date and then moved toward her next client's room. But the *chirp* of her cell phone stopped her. She detoured to a stairwell and answered the call.

"Ms. Jenkins, you left a message."

"I did. Who am I speaking with?"

"That's not important. What do you need?"

"I was told that I could reach a friend through this number."

"Yes, yes, Ms. Jenkins. Is there a problem?"

"I'm not certain. Maybe."

"Okay, Ms. Jenkins, here's how this will work. You'll tell me why you called and I'll pass it on to *your friend*. If he wants to call you back, you'll hear from him."

"But—"

"Why did you call?"

Janet explained about the call she'd received from the woman who'd claimed to be with *The New York Times*.

"Okay, thank you."

Janet stared at her phone as it went to a dial tone.

After Bobby Tennucci told him about the call from Janet Jenkins, Louis Massarino considered for a moment that the Jenkins woman was possibly over-reacting. But Bruno had told him about Jenkins and how much he respected her. Massarino called Bruno and passed on her message.

"Thanks, Louis."

"Are you making progress?"

"Yes, but it's a complicated process. Have you thought about my request for help?"

"Of course. Take down these names and numbers."

"Thanks."

"No problem. The first guy is with an insurance company. The second name I gave you is my nephew. In different ways, they're very motivated to help."

Bruno took a cab to a Walmart store, told the driver to wait, and went inside. He bought a couple of burner phones and returned to the apartment. He put off calling Janet until that evening. He didn't want to talk with her at work. He then used one of the phones to call David Lander, the insurance company man whose name and number Massarino had given him.

"David Lander."

"Mr. Lander, I understand from a mutual friend you were told to expect my call."

"Ye-yes, Mr...."

"My name isn't important. What *is* important is that you do as instructed."

A brief pause, then, "I don't want to get into any trouble."

"Huh. I understand you're already in trouble."

The man made a noise that sounded to Bruno like a moan.

"An envelope will be delivered tomorrow at your home. You need to study its contents and then prepare a plan based on the instructions included. You have three days to develop the plan."

"How do I contact you?"

"You don't."

Bruno then called Jesse Falco, Louis Massarino's nephew.

"Jesse's Computer Repairs."

"Mr. Falco?"

"Yeah, this is Jesse."

"Your uncle told me to call you."

"My uncle told me this is about the people who killed my Uncle Carlo."

"That's correct."

"Okay. Tell me what I need to do."

"A messenger will deliver instructions to you today."

Bruno went back to work on the property files. He finished the second file in shorter time than the first property had taken. The second building was also in San Francisco, so the time to hack into the county court records was abbreviated. The third office building was in San Antonio, Texas. Bruno committed to finishing work on it before he took a break.

Accompanied by a loud groan, Bruno slapped the edge of the computer table. Then he said, "Finally," and saved the file on the San Antonio property to the project folder. It was now 10:10 p.m.; 7:10 p.m. in Redondo Beach. He stood, snatched the second burner phone from the desk, and dialed Janet's number.

"Hello."

"Janet, it's Bruno."

"Oh, Bruno, it's good to hear your voice. How are you?"

"I'm fine. How about you?"

"There's a lot going on around here, thanks to your gift to St. Anne's. It looks like the archdiocese will donate the apartment house to us. The foundation in Omaha has approved our request for matching funds."

"That's terrific, Janet."

"Are you okay?"

"I'm fine. Tell me about this reporter who called you."

"She *said* she was a reporter, but when I checked the woman's name on the *Times'* website, I found she was an eighty-year-old, retired employee. The woman who called me sounded much younger. I think she was just trying to get me to give her your contact information."

"Did she leave a telephone number?"

"No. In fact, when I called pound sixty-nine, I got a recording that the number wasn't available."

"Okay, Janet. Thank you. If she calls again, try to get her number."

"What's going on, Bruno?"

"I can't talk about it. Don't worry; I'm fine." Then he told her, "Take care," and hung up.

Janet felt overwhelming sadness after her conversation with Bruno. She was worried about him and badly missed the conversations they'd had during his convalescence. His story had intrigued her, and his metamorphosis from a shy, introverted, down-and-out man to a confident one who'd donated tens of millions of dollars to St. Anne's had shocked her. She remembered the firmness in his voice and the determination in his eyes when he'd told her he planned to leave California. *A man on a mission.* She thought about his last words before he'd hung up on the call: *'Take care.'* Not, "I'll see you soon," or "I'll be in touch." Or, God forbid, "I miss you."

The feeling that Janet Jenkins had either lied or held something back when they'd talked by phone had continued to niggle away at

Victoria Nguyen's brain. *If she knows how to get in touch with Pedace, then she might contact him,* she thought. She called a computer hacker and had him track down Jenkins's office and home addresses. Then she called an informant at the telephone company and gave her the addresses.

"You have a cell number for her?"

"No," Nguyen said. "But can't you track it down from her home address? Her cell phone bill probably goes there."

"I can do that. What am I looking for?"

"I want the number of every telephone call, text, or email she makes from or receives on her cell and office phones."

"My God, there could be hundreds."

"There could be. I don't care. Just send them to me."

"Over what time period?"

"Start with calls from yesterday and go forward until I tell you to stop."

Nguyen then called another informant, this one at a credit bureau. She gave the man Jenkins's name and home address. "What I want is any activity on her credit cards related to travel. Flights, rental cars, hotel rooms. Like that."

Nguyen made a third call. This time to a friend she'd grown up with in New York City. He'd been a member of a Vietnamese gang in the City and had gone to Los Angeles when his parents decided to separate him from bad influences in New York. But Pham Van Duc quickly affiliated with a gang on the west coast and later became the top guy. Nguyen and Pham had stayed in touch and, periodically, helped one another. Nguyen gave Janet Jenkins's address to Pham and told him what she needed.

DAY 5

CHAPTER 9

David Lander went over the contents of the package delivered to his home. The cover document told him he was to prepare an offering memorandum in his employer's name for the sale of a multi-billion-dollar security backed by mortgages on twenty-four class "AAA" office buildings.

The document went on to state that the commission to the investment bank that underwrote the transaction would be one percent. It also noted that the transaction would be closed through the First Fidelity Philadelphia Title Guaranty Company.

The final instruction: *"The dollar amounts aren't firm yet. What I want you to prepare is the offering memorandum, with all the boiler plate. You will be given final numbers and information about the twenty-four properties within the week."*

Lander thought the transaction made good sense, except for the fact that his employer never sold any of its commercial real estate loans. They always held their loans to maturity. He shuddered. *The involvement of Bobby Tennucci in this thing means it can't be legitimate.*

Jesse Falco read the instructions he'd received. It was all cut and dry: a system hack and the creation of an electronic presence for a company, including a website, email address, and social media. Although he'd told his uncle that he would do whatever it took to avenge his Uncle Carlo's death, and do it at no cost, he found ten thousand dollars in the package with the instructions.

The call to Victoria Nguyen from her contact at the credit bureau was disappointing. There had been no travel-related transactions on Janet Jenkins's credit cards. Then her telephone company contact called her.

"All but one of her outbound calls were made to numbers in the 310, 323, and 424 area codes," the woman at the telephone company said. "All L.A. area codes. The only exception was a call made to a 718-number yesterday."

Sonofagun, Nguyen thought. *That's Brooklyn.*

The informant said, "There was also a call to Janet Jenkins's number that couldn't be identified. I suspect it was from a burner phone."

Nguyen's heart did a little tap dance.

"Did she make the call to the 718-area code before the burner phone call came in?"

"Yeah. How'd you know?"

"Who does the 718-area code number belong to?"

"Hold on. I've got it right here. Ah, here it is. Robert Tennucci."

She thanked the woman and ended the call. The conclusion she came to was that Janet Jenkins had called Pedace or a cutout who forwarded her message. Then Pedace had called her on a burner phone. At least, she hoped that was what had occurred.

Nguyen looked up the name Robert Tennucci on Google and found several news items. They all mentioned that Tennucci had a criminal record. One noted he was possibly connected to the Lucchese Family.

Salvatore Trujillo had to get out of the house. His wife's crying was driving him crazy. Ever since her brother, Giovanni, had been killed in California, she'd been an emotional wreck. *Sure, he was her only sibling, but Casale was a lowlife*, he thought. *How long can a person mourn the death of a man like that? After all, it's been six months.* Trujillo cursed his former brother-in-law as he went down the ten steps from his porch to the sidewalk. "Bastard," he muttered. "Now

I'll never get paid for the work I did for him on Charles Forsythe and Bruno Pedace."

He smacked his lips at the prospect of lunch and a couple—maybe a few—drinks at Rico's Ristoranti. If Francesca was working today, maybe they'd be able to set a date to get together. He conjured up a picture of her in bed, her succulent body eagerly welcoming him, her jet-black hair fanned over the pillow.

A block from the restaurant, his cell phone rang. He clamped his jaws together and felt anger build in him, obliterating his vision of Francesca. "Damn her," he barked, thinking it was his wife calling.

He glanced at the screen and didn't recognize the number.

"Sal Trujillo," he answered.

"Mr. Trujillo, my name is Cindy Le. I understand you specialize in doing contract research."

"That's right, Ms. Le. Who referred you to me?"

"John Casale. He highly recommended you."

Maybe Johnny wasn't such a lowlife, after all, Trujillo thought. "When did he make the referral?"

The woman asked, "Is that important?"

"No, Ms. Le. It's just that Mr. Casale was killed earlier this year in…a car wreck."

"Oh, that's terrible. I hadn't heard. I talked to Mr. Casale over a year ago. He did some investigative work for my company."

"Yeah, it's an awful loss. John was a good client and friend. What kind of work did you want to talk to me about?"

"Perhaps we could meet. Our company is interested in having background research performed—credit history, resume verification, Internet activity, criminal records, that sort of thing—on over fifty prospective employees."

Trujillo's pulse beat faster as he did the mental math on the revenue from fifty background investigations. "When would you like to meet?"

"How's this afternoon work for you? I'm only in town for twenty-four hours and then must fly to Paris. There's a nice little café down the street from my hotel across from Central Park. Parq Place Café. Maybe a late lunch. Say, two o'clock?"

"Perfect," Trujillo said. "How will I recognize you?"

"I'll recognize you. I have your picture from your website."

After the woman hung up, Trujillo thought about taking Francesca on a trip. He'd be able to afford it after he finished Cindy Le's assignment. Maybe to Las Vegas. Francesca always talked about wanting to see Sin City. As he drove to Rico's, he said aloud, "No, Johnny, maybe you weren't a lowlife after all."

Despite only two hours sleep the night before, Bruno felt invigorated. He'd finished the files on four properties and now, at 11:30 a.m., had nearly completed the fifth. He rolled his chair away from the desk and stood. His back ached and his eyes burned, but he felt damned good about his progress. He used the landline to call a delicatessen located a couple blocks away and ordered a roast beef and Swiss cheese sandwich on rye, with extra pickles, a bag of Fritos, and a large cranberry juice. The girl who took his order told him it would be delivered in thirty minutes. Rather than go back to the computer, he called David Lander.

"Any questions?" he asked.

"No," Lander said. "It's all very clear, but…"

"But what?"

"I don't understand why you need me?"

"You don't need to understand, Mr. Lander. But it will all soon become clear. Can you finish your task?"

"No problem. I'll probably get it done by tomorrow."

"Good."

CHAPTER 10

The Parq Place Café had an eclectic clientele that included out-of-town shoppers, business types, and the occasional construction worker from a nearby project. The food was good and reasonably-priced…for New York. Ninety percent of the place's business was take-out. There were only six four-top tables.

Victoria Nguyen had taken special care to look her best for her meeting with Salvatore Trujillo. Her skirt was professionally long, but short enough to show off her legs. She knew they were her best feature. She'd taken extra time with her makeup. Her eyes were small, but exotically green. The lipstick she put on was subdued, but just bright enough to highlight the lushness of her mouth. She wanted Trujillo's hormones to be more active than his brain.

She arrived early and, when a table in the back became available, she sat down and watched the entrance. Fifteen minutes later, she spotted Trujillo jaywalk across West 59th Street, his coat collar up against the brisk fall wind. When he entered, she waved. Trujillo weaved through the tables and stuck out his hand when he reached her.

"Ms. Le?"

"Yes," Nguyen said as she stood and shook his hand. "Thanks for meeting me on such short notice."

"It's all about customer service, Ms. Le," he said as he shucked his overcoat, placed it on the chair to his left, and sat.

"Indeed it is, Mr. Trujillo."

"It sounds as though you have a very busy schedule."

She chuckled. "That's an understatement. The company keeps me on the go. In fact, we need to make this brief." She pointed up at the menu board on the wall behind the counter. "I think I'll order a tuna on rye and an iced tea. How about you?"

Trujillo looked up at the menu board and said, "Actually, that sounds good." He moved to stand and said, "I'll take care of it."

Nguyen put out a hand and touched his arm. "No, no, Mr. Trujillo. It's on me." She smiled and asked, "You take sugar in your tea?"

"One packet, please."

She stood, walked to the counter, placed the orders, then moved down the line to the cash register. After she paid the tab with cash, she picked up their drinks and a placard on a small metal stand that indicated their order number, and moved to a condiments counter. She tossed away the plastic lids from the iced tea containers and picked up a sugar packet. As she ripped off the top of the packet, she flipped open the setting on her ring and poured crystalline contents from the ring's recessed space under the setting into Trujillo's tea, along with the contents of the sugar packet. Then she used a wood stick to stir the tea, and returned to the table.

"Here you go," she said, as she handed the drink to Trujillo. "The sandwiches should be here in a minute."

"Thanks. What sort of business are you in?"

"I'm the Personnel Director of SWT Technologies. We have engineering offices in twelve cities around the world. Our—"

Her telephone chimed, as she'd set it to do. "I'm so sorry," she said as she glanced at the screen, then stood. "That's my boss. I need to take this."

Trujillo waved a hand. "Of course. No problem."

Nguyen slipped on her leather coat, moved to the front door, and stepped outside, under the awning that shaded the front windows. She smiled at Trujillo as she pretended to conduct a conversation. He smiled back at her, picked up his tea, and took a healthy drink. Nguyen paced the sidewalk, continuing her phony conversation. She watched Trujillo take another drink. As he did, she spoke into her dead phone, "That ought to do it."

A couple of seconds went by and then Trujillo fell to the floor, convulsing and frothing at the mouth.

As Nguyen walked to the corner and then turned left to hail a cab, she thought about what else she could do to find Bruno Pedace. Her research had given her information about Pedace's background, including his relationship with the Massarino family. And she'd learned that Robert Tennucci was probably associated with the Luccheses, which, by extension, meant the Massarinos. *Sy Rosen is screwing around with the wrong people*, she thought. *I don't like messing with the mob. But an assignment is an assignment.*

Nguyen called her FBI contact, a married guy named Wayne Evans who she'd sexually co-opted a few years back by doing things with him that he'd never experienced before.

"Hey, girl," Evans answered. "It's been a long time."

"Too long, Wayne. I've missed you."

"I may be crazy, but I'm not stupid. What do you want? The only time you call me is when you need something."

She chuckled. "Are you available tonight?"

Evans said, "I could be."

"Good. Usual place. 6:30."

"You didn't answer my question. What do you want?"

"I just want *you*, Wayne." After a small pause, she added, "Oh, and maybe a tiny bit of information. I need the home address of a Robert Tennucci."

CHAPTER 11

The *whoomp-whoomp-whoomp* sounds of her gloved fists hitting the heavy bag had a cathartic effect on Janet. Despite her hands swelling after each workout, there was something recuperative about coming to J's Gym three times a week. She'd signed up for boxing lessons for self-defense purposes, but she'd discovered the sessions at the gym gave her a sense of confidence, not to mention that she'd muscled up and built stamina. Other than having to ice her hands after each training session, she loved the experience.

"Looking good, girl," Jesse Washington said as he unlaced her gloves.

Janet smiled at eighty-year-old Washington, the owner of the gym and a former welterweight boxer. "Thanks, Jesse," she said, "but you say that to all the women who work out here."

"That I do, girl. I keep hoping that I'll get lucky one of these days."

Janet laughed and kissed his cheek. "You old reprobate."

"What you doin' tonight?"

"Working, Jesse. I've got a lot of homework."

"Tsk, tsk, tsk. Good-lookin' girl like you should be out kickin' up her heels, not workin'."

Janet placed a taped hand on the old man's face and smiled.

After showering and changing, Janet stopped at a Whole Foods

Market, bought a week's worth of food, and made her way home. She carried two bags of groceries inside and placed them on the kitchen table. When she turned to go back outside to retrieve her jacket and purse, there was a knock on her front door.

She moved to the door and checked the peephole. Two Asian men stood on her porch. One was about five feet, ten-inches tall and wore a black suit and tie. The other one was much shorter and dressed more casually, in jeans, a white dress shirt, and a blue blazer. Back at the curb, she spotted a black compact car.

What the heck? Janet thought. She placed the security chain on the door, then cracked it open and asked, "Can I help you?"

In perfectly good Brooklynese, which surprised Janet, the taller man said, "I'd like to talk with you for a minute."

"About what?"

"Bruno Pedace."

"Who are you?"

"Police."

Janet almost laughed. "All right, Mr. Policeman, let's see your badge."

The guy stuck a hand inside his jacket, as though to pull out a cred pack, then slammed a foot against the door. The chain snapped and the door flew open. The edge of the door caught Janet's left arm and caused a huge jolt of pain from her elbow to her shoulder. The man moved aside and made room for his companion, who burst through the doorway. Janet reflexively swung at him with her right hand, aiming for his chin. But the man straightened up and her punch struck his throat. He went down, gasping, fighting for air.

The taller man launched himself at Janet. She attempted to block a strike, but her left arm didn't respond. Bright lights exploded behind her eyes and then all was dark.

"Rosales."

"Hugo, it's Detective Jackie Parrish."

"Hey, Jackie. How's everything in El Segundo?"

"I thought you'd want to know. My partner and I just answered a 9-1-1 call. A neighbor called it in."

"What's that got to do—?"

"It's Janet Jenkins's place."

"Oh, man. Is she all right?"

"She's not here. The place was tossed, but there doesn't appear to be anything missing. I mean, it doesn't look like a robbery. There's blood on the floor. Looks like someone vomited, too."

"You mind if I come by and check out the place?"

"Of course not. That's why I called. I remembered you were friends with Jenkins. We found her purse and jacket in her car."

"What's up, Van?" Victoria said into her cell phone.

"You want the good news first?"

"Stop playing around, Van. I'm busy."

Pham Van Duc laughed. "All business, as usual. Okay, I got her."

Victoria Nguyen breathed out a long, steady breath, inhaled, and said, "Any problems?"

Van chuckled. "The guy with me won't be talking or breathing right for a while. The woman clocked him in the throat. But, other than that, no problems."

"You find anything in her stuff about Bruno Pedace?"

"Nope. Nothing."

"Sonofa—Okay, here's what I want you to do."

Detective Hugo Rosales pulled in behind an El Segundo patrol car. An unmarked Crown Victoria was parked in the driveway behind Janet's vehicle. Flashing lights bounced off nearby residences and lit up the sky. As he opened his door, Detective John Andrews told Rosales, "I'll check with the patrolmen; why don't you go through the house? Talk to the detectives."

Rosales nodded and left the car.

A dull pressure invaded Rosales's chest as he entered the bungalow. The stench of vomit hung in the air. Blood covered part of the wood floor just past the threshold, a few feet away from where Janet's mother's blood had once stained the floor. He shook his head as he slowly moved into the residence. The place was a disaster area. Cushions in chairs and the sofa had been ripped open, stuffing thrown about. Rosales shook his head, remembering Janet had replaced the furniture that Essam had destroyed just about six months ago. Drawers from a desk, a credenza, kitchen cabinets lay scattered; their contents wildly strewn about.

Detective Jackie Parrish told Rosales, "It's more of the same upstairs. Doesn't look like robbery. Nothing of value seems to have been taken."

Rosales noticed that appliances and electronic equipment had been kicked in or thrown to the floor, not stolen. *Parrish is correct*, he thought, *this was no robbery*. Rosales climbed the stairs to the second floor and surveyed the destruction there. Back downstairs, he found Andrews crouched by a pile of debris, picking through it. "Anything?" he asked.

Andrews stood and wagged his head. "Nothing here."

Parrish came over. "The neighbor who called it in got a partial plate number on a black Toyota that took off just as he arrived home."

"What made him do that?"

Parrish grinned. "The Toyota sped off like it was in a drag race. Laid down a nice length of rubber." She gave Rosales a toothy smile. "The driver sideswiped a parked car. We got paint and the Toyota's gotta have body damage."

Rosales nodded.

Andrews spread his arms and asked, "What do you think this is all about?"

Pedace, Rosales thought. *It's gotta have something to do with Bruno Pedace.*

Bruno felt exhausted. It was nearly 11 p.m. But it wasn't just fatigue that made concentrating on the tasks at hand so difficult. Ever since his conversation with Janet the day before, he'd felt badly. He'd been so obsessed with his mission that he hadn't been sensitive to her needs. She'd called to warn him about the woman who'd claimed to be a reporter and asked about him. She was obviously concerned. But he'd treated her coldly. He clenched his jaws and felt heat invade his body. He hadn't meant to react the way he had. It was just the way he was. The way he'd always been. Single-minded when it came to a task or project. It wasn't easy for him to admit that his obsession with work had been a big part of the reason his wife had strayed.

One of the burner phones rang, startling him. He snatched it from the table, rolled back from the computer, and stood. He rubbed a hand over his face as though to clear his mind of extraneous thoughts, and answered the call.

"Bruno, it's Louis. We just got another call from your lady friend in California. She sounded…out of sorts. Wants you to call her back right away."

"She say what she wanted?"

"Nope. But I got the impression it was important. Oh, and she said to call her cell phone at 8 p.m., California time."

Seven minutes from now, Bruno thought.

Bruno paced the apartment while he wondered what was up with Janet. At 11, East Coast time, he called her cell number.

"He-hello?"

For a beat, Bruno thought he might've woken her. She sounded…a little out of it.

"Janet?"

"Oh, Bruno."

"What's wrong? Are you okay?"

"They made me give them the number, Bru—"

A man's voice suddenly came on the line. "If you want to save your friend a lot more pain, you'll tell me where you are, Mr. Pedace."

"Who is this?"

"That's unimportant."

Bruno heard Janet scream, "Don't tell them, Bruno." Then there was a slapping sound.

"What do you want?" Bruno asked.

"All you have to do is give me your location."

"And what will you do with Janet?"

"She'll be free to go."

Bruno knew without even the slightest doubt the man was lying. "Let me talk to her."

There were some fumbling sounds with the phone, then Janet came back on. "I'm sorry, Bruno."

Bruno's throat tightened. He swallowed hard. "You've got nothing to be sorry about. I'm going to get you out of this, Janet.

Don't you worry. Now, put the man back on."

"Yeah?" the man said.

"I'll call you back tomorrow morning at 8 a.m., your time. I'll want to talk to Janet then. If you've hurt her, you'll never find me. Understood?"

Bruno hung up, dropped the phone on the floor, and stomped on it until it was nothing but broken pieces. He then used another burner phone to call Detective Hugo Rosales.

"Where the hell are you, Pedace? We've been—"

"I just talked to Janet. She's in trouble."

"You just talked with her?"

"Yeah. The guy holding her supposedly wants to trade her for information about my location."

"Sonofa—"

"I told him I'd call back at eight tomorrow morning."

"You're going to do just that, Mr. Pedace. But you'll have to keep him on the phone for at least a couple minutes so we can trace the call."

"I'm afraid, Detective, that if we wait to trace the call, it will be too late for Janet."

Bruno couldn't work or sleep. He paced the apartment like a cat on amphetamines. Then an errant thought struck: *Louis Massarino's right. I should let him handle Rosen and his partners. Old world revenge would be a better, safer alternative. And maybe Louis can help me find Janet.*

It was close to 11:30 when he called Massarino.

"Whatsa matter?" Massarino asked.

"I'm sorry to call so late, Louis, but I have a problem."

"Something wrong with your plan?"

"You could say that. Could we meet? Now, if possible?"

Massarino didn't immediately respond. After several seconds, he said, "It's that important?"

"It is."

"You at the apartment?"

"Yes."

"I'll be there in fifteen minutes."

After Massarino arrived, Bruno explained about Janet. By the time he'd finished, he was so jacked up with fear for Janet and guilt over what he'd caused that he was unable to sit or stand still.

Massarino took Bruno's arm and guided him to a chair. "Sit, Bruno." Massarino brought him a bottle of water and ordered him to drink.

"Now, we gotta look at this nice and calm, okay?"

Bruno nodded.

"As much as I wanted to take care of Sy Rosen and the others my way, I think your solution makes more sense."

"But—"

Massarino put up a hand like a traffic cop. "Wait. Let me finish."

Bruno lowered his head and nodded.

"Your plan is *piu elegante*. And it has much less risk. So, we'll continue."

"But what about Janet?"

"The man who has her can't possibly let her go. He gets his hands on you; she dies at the same time. You understand that?"

Bruno nodded. "I already came to that conclusion."

"You called the cops out there. You let them handle it."

Bruno stared at Massarino and noticed his expression suddenly change. He looked worried.

"What is it?"

Massarino shook his head. "Something else is wrong."

"What?"

"I gotta figure it out."

DAY 6

CHAPTER 12

Bruno's adrenaline poured into his nervous system as time seemed to move in slow motion. He had trouble concentrating on building the property files as worries about Janet clouded his brain. Afraid that he would miss Louis Massarino's deadline, he called Jesse Falco and asked him to come to the apartment to help. He was amazed at how quickly the kid picked up on what needed to be done and completed property files while Bruno paced the floor.

Bruno watched the LED clock on the microwave as he moved through the kitchen on his pacing circuit and willed it to speed up. When the clock finally reached 10:55 a.m., he broke out in a cold sweat. He'd learned something during the night: he cared about Janet in a way he'd never cared about anyone. Not even his former wife, Paolina. Janet was much more than a friend. The thought of something happening to her, or worse, losing her, made him feel as though he was lost in a wilderness, alone and hopeless.

He watched the last five minutes tick off and then called Janet's cell number.

"I want to know where the fuck you are, Pedace. Right now. No more games."

"I'll give you that information after I talk with Janet."

"No way, asshole. I told you—"

Bruno steeled himself and took a deep breath. "Put her on the phone or I hang up and never call back."

"Bruno?"

"Yes, Janet, it's me." He knew what he was about to ask was stupid, but he needed to keep the line open. "Are you okay?"

"I'm okay, Bruno. How are you?"

Bruno choked up. He cleared his throat and answered, "I'll be fine when I see you again." He breathed and added, "Say hello to Hugo for me."

Janet seemed to hesitate a second and then said, "Oh."

Then the man was back on the line. "Your location. I know you're in Brooklyn. I want the address."

Bruno glanced at the microwave clock and felt fear flood through him. The clock still read 11. Even if it clicked to 11:01, and even if Rosales's people tracked the signal, it would take a long time for them to find Janet. She could be dead by the time they arrived.

"I give you my location and what happens to Janet?"

"I told you before that we'll release her."

"I want her released first."

The guy laughed. "Not gonna happen."

Bruno knew he was gambling with Janet's life, but he also knew if he disclosed his location, there would be no gamble. Her death would be a sure thing.

"Then go screw yourself." He disconnected the call and tried to settle his breathing. His heart raced and his hands trembled. A quick glance at the clock told him he'd been on the line for ninety seconds. He'd wait until the clock turned to 11:05.

About one mile southeast of the junction of Highway 405 and the 710, Detectives Rosales and Andrews had been parked for three hours just around the corner from a seedy strip mall, near where the car in which Janet Jenkins had been carried away had been spotted by an alert patrolman. It was now 8:03 a.m.

"You know, just because Pham's car was spotted here, doesn't mean he's in the area," Andrews said. "He could have abandoned it."

"I know," Rosales said. "But what choice do we have?" Rosales looked across the intersection at the El Segundo unmarked sedan. The two ESPD detectives there were spearheading the op.

"I gotta pee," Andrews said.

Rosales nodded, but then grabbed Andrews's arm when Rosales's cell chirped.

"Go," Rosales shouted into the phone.

"We got the trace. 1967 Bixby Street. Thuoc's Cleanery."

Andrews pushed open his door and ran around to join Rosales as he raced around the corner to Bixby. The big yellow sign, with red letters in English and Vietnamese, identifying Thuoc's Cleanery, was halfway down the block.

Rosales watched a large, black SWAT vehicle shatter the early morning quiet as it roared up the street. The noise from another large horsepower vehicle sounded from behind him, down the alley behind the row of storefronts.

Bruno waited until the clock turned to 11:05. Then he called Janet's cell. The man picked up after one ring.

"You pull another stunt like that and I'll slit her throat."

The angry timbre of the man's voice told Bruno that the guy would not accept any more delays.

"I'm in Brooklyn."

"I already know that!" The guy screamed, "Give me your location."

"I'm at—"

The sounds of shouting and gunfire stopped Bruno cold. "Oh, my God," he groaned. "Janet." The noise through the phone seemed to get louder and louder. The only distinct words that Bruno heard were, "Put down the knife." Pain erupted in the side of his head as he pressed the burner phone harder against his ear.

Bruno chanted, "Janet, Janet, Janet," as the seconds went by. Then a familiar voice came on the phone and asked, "Pedace? It's Hugo Rosales."

"Yes. Is she okay?"

"She's fine," Rosales answered. "I'll put her on."

"Bruno?"

He realized he was holding his breath. He released the air in his lungs. "Ja…Janet."

In a shaky voice, Janet said, "Bruno, I'm okay."

"I'm so sorry. This is all my fault. I—"

"Now's not the time to talk about blame. I want to know what's going on, what you're doing. And I want to see you. I'm coming to New York."

"Janet, you can't. I don't want you involved."

She scoffed. "Bruno, I'm already involved. The men who kidnapped me said they know you're in the New York City area. I'm catching a flight to LaGuardia tomorrow morning. I expect you to pick me up."

"Wait, Janet, that's not a—"

"Bruno, if you think I'm staying around here and waiting for the next shoe to drop, you're nuts. Call me tonight on my cell. I'll give you my flight arrangements."

Before Bruno could object, Janet cut off the call.

CHAPTER 13

Louis Massarino had had a relaxing lunch with his wife, Rosa. At the front door of his home, he kissed her hand and said, "*Grazie, mi amor,*" as he always did before leaving the house. Now in the back seat of his Lincoln Town Car, he called Bruno.

"Any news about your friend in California?"

"She's fine. The police found her in time."

"*Grazie Dio.*" After inhaling loudly, Massarino said, "And how are things with your plan?"

"Ahead of schedule. Your nephew Jesse's been working on the files for me. We're getting twice as many files done as before. The kid's a wizard."

"Good. You still confident they'll take the hook?"

"Years of working with those bastards gives me confidence they'll take the hook, the line, and the sinker."

"How's the guy that Bobby put you with?"

"Lander? Good. He's done everything I told him to do. I'm about to have him make contact."

"When?'

"Today."

Bruno and Jesse finished the documents for the nineteenth property, and then inputted data into the spreadsheet. Bruno scanned the spreadsheet, searched for errors, and smiled when he found none.

Another five properties and he'd be ready to pull the trigger. He called David Lander.

"It's time we met," Bruno said.

Bruno watched an obviously nervous Lander for ten minutes while the man chain-smoked three cigarettes and circled the flagpole in Staten Island's Clove Lakes Park. When Bruno had satisfied himself that Lander had obeyed orders and come alone, he moved from behind bushes and approached the man, who immediately dropped his cigarette and crushed it underfoot. His eyes narrowed as he stared at Bruno.

Bruno handed Lander a stick drive.

"I'm sure you've already figured out that we're going to issue a commercial mortgage-backed security. There are facts, figures, and photos on that drive that support the offering. There's still some data to be added, but this will give you a jumpstart on preparing the final documents. I'll have everything finalized in another two or three days. In the meantime, I want you to put out a teaser. Try to generate some interest."

"Based on what I've already seen, this is a solid, triple-A CMBS transaction. I don't understa—"

Bruno raised a hand, stopping Lander. "Not relevant."

Lander swallowed hard. "Which investors do you want me to contact? I know every large real estate investor and investment banking firm out there. Foreign and domestic. I can call any—"

Bruno stopped him again. "You'll only contact one firm. Let them think you're shopping the deal. But, in reality, you'll only contact Rosen, Rice & Stone."

Lander groaned. "Those bastards only invest when they can steal something."

Through a smile, Bruno said, "You call their investment desk and tell the guy there your firm is considering the sale of a two point four-billion-dollar loan package, with a sixty-nine percent loan to value ratio, backed by class triple-A office buildings."

"That's a big deal for a firm their size."

"Yeah, you're right. But they'll jump on it when they realize the terms of the deal. And one other thing, Lander. I want you to tell them closing must be no later than November 30th. Tell them your company is over-committed to real estate in its portfolio and the insurance regulators aren't happy. That you're realigning your asset base. Let them think the package can be bought at a discount if closing occurs by the end of this month."

Lander's face reddened and he began to sweat. "I don't want to…insult anyone here. But this is obviously not on the up and up. Otherwise, this deal could go through any investment house in the country. If this deal is a scam, I could land in prison."

"Not if you don't use your real name. Let's say this sale is executed and then turns out badly. Then the buyer raises hell and blames your company for cheating them. They go to the SEC and the Investor Protection & Securities Bureau of New York and claim that…oh, how about Joseph Campbell from your company sold them a bill of goods. What's legal counsel at your company going to say?"

"There's no one named Joseph Campbell at our firm."

"Exactly. And make sure you tell whoever you talk to at the Rosen firm that you'll call them, not the other way around." Bruno handed Lander a burner phone and told him to use it for the first call to the Rosen firm.

Lander's face was now less ruddy. "What about due diligence? Won't the buyer discover that something's wrong?"

"Probably. But only if they dig really deeply. And we're not going to give them enough time to do that. Besides, the terms of the deal are going to be so attractive, they'll cut corners to close it." Bruno smiled again. "Greed always conquers caution. Especially with the guys at the Rosen firm."

Victoria Nguyen had just about concluded that tailing Robert Tennucci was a waste of time. She'd spent a fruitless day following him around three of the five New York City boroughs. Tennucci was always accompanied by a man who looked like WWE material. Tennucci and his companion went in and out of every possible sort of business. He never spent more than fifteen minutes in any one place.

After nine hours, she was about to give up, when Tennucci

walked out of a restaurant with another man who looked familiar. She squinted at the second guy, but it was too dark to make out his features. Then the men shook hands. Tennucci went left, down the street to his car, while the other man walked toward a Lincoln parked under a streetlight. In the cone of light, Victoria recognized Louis Massarino.

"I'll be damned," she rasped, as Massarino got in the back seat of the Lincoln. She watched the car pull away from the curb.

Like most New Yorkers, Nguyen knew all about Massarino. Half the television stations in the area did a story about organized crime every couple years. They always showed Louis Massarino's face and mentioned him as being "a person of interest to law enforcement." Her research had given her a connection between Pedace and Massarino, and now she had a confirmed connection between Massarino and Tennucci. She thought, *maybe Janet Jenkins called Tennucci's telephone number to pass a message through Massarino to Bruno Pedace. Maybe I've been tailing the wrong man.*

CHAPTER 14

Bruno finished adding another two properties to the spreadsheet and then crashed onto his bed. He'd agonized over what had happened to Janet. As much as he wanted to see her, the thought of her coming to New York only elevated his angst. Coming to the City was like entering the lion's den. But, after hours of tension, he decided the best way to protect her was to have her close by and enlist Louis Massarino's help.

He slipped a new burner phone from his shirt pocket and called Janet's cell.

"How are you doing?" Bruno asked.

"I was scared before. Now I'm just pissed off."

Bruno couldn't help but chuckle. "You've had a heck of a year."

"You could say that. But I'm ready to see the end of this business, and hanging around here in California, not knowing when or where the next bad guy looking for Bruno Pedace will pop up is not my preferred way to live."

"I'm so sorry, Janet. I've really screwed things up for you."

She blurted a laugh. "At least I'm not bored." She laughed again and said, "You have a pen and paper?"

"Sure."

"Here's my flight out of LAX to LaGuardia."

Bruno wrote down the flight number and time of arrival.

"You'll pick me up?"

"There'll be a guy named Silvio in baggage claim. He'll meet you."

"How will I know who he is?"

"He'll have a sign with your name on it."

"Then what?"

"I'll see you when you get here."

"I'll be damned," Redondo Beach District Attorney Barry Rath raised his arms in victory after he terminated the call from the head of his intelligence section. He snapped his fingers and said, "Just like that." He then called his good friend, Frances Cassidy, the RBPD Chief of Police, and said, "Guess what, Fran?"

"Come on, Barry, it's too damned late to play twenty questions."

"That tap we put on Janet Jenkins's phone just paid off."

"What are you talking about? That tap was just to track the signal so we could find her and her kidnapper."

"I guess we forgot to terminate it. Jenkins just had a conversation with Bruno Pedace. She leaves tomorrow morning for New York to meet him."

"And?"

"Send a couple detectives to New York to be there when Jenkins and Pedace meet. I want to talk to Pedace about that investment banking firm and Louis Massarino's involvement in all of this."

"What you just learned was via an illegal wiretap, Barry. You can't—"

"Don't tell me what I can't do, Fran. I'm the friggin' D.A."

It was a few minutes shy of 8 p.m. when Hugo Rosales called John Andrews at home. "Pack a bag," he announced, "we're going to New York."

"When?" Andrews asked.

"Tonight, on the red-eye."

"Do I sense a Jets game in my future?"

"Hah. Not a chance. But we might locate Bruno Pedace in The Big Apple."

Only a small glow from a crescent moon showed at the western end of the street as Louis Massarino's Town Car pulled up to his Brooklyn home. Victoria Nguyen watched the vehicle enter the garage and the door come down behind it. She checked her dashboard clock: 10:03 p.m., and drummed her hands on the steering wheel. She felt in her gut that she was close to finding Bruno Pedace.

DAY 7

CHAPTER 15

After arrival at LaGuardia Airport at 7:22 a.m., Hugo Rosales and John Andrews took a shuttle to a Best Western hotel near the airport, where they'd booked two rooms. After four hours sleep, they took the shuttle back to the airport, where they went to the Five Guys Restaurant in the pre-security area food court near Concourse D. After a leisurely lunch, they camped out in the terminal where Janet Jenkins's flight was scheduled to arrive at 3:05 p.m.

"I've never had to tail someone in New York City," Andrews told Rosales. "I hear traffic's a bear."

Rosales laughed. "Can't be worse than L.A."

Andrews shrugged. "I'd hate to come this far and then lose her."

Rosales scowled. "We'd have one pissed off D.A. back in Redondo Beach."

Raw nerves and adrenaline had kept Bruno up most of the night and into the morning. He and Jesse Falco worked on the last properties that would go into the two point four-billion-dollar commercial mortgage-backed security package. Bruno's stomach growled and his head ached by the time they'd doctored the last file and inserted the data into the spreadsheet.

At noon, he beat a riff with his hands on the computer table, then pumped a fist in celebration. He stood and stretched his back. He told Jesse, "Do me a favor and check our work one more time."

As Jesse went over the files, Bruno called David Lander.

"Let's meet again at the same place," Bruno said. "3 p.m."

"You want to hear how my call to the investment house went, or should I hold it for later when we meet?" Lander asked.

"Tell me."

"I talked to the guy on their real estate desk. Told him we were about to market a two point four-billion-dollar mortgage-backed security. He said it might be too big for them. I told him that was too bad because the package would include a one percent underwriting fee and a two percent discount to face value."

"Good," Bruno said. "A twenty-four-million-dollar fee plus forty-eight million in discount points should have the boys at Rosen, Rice & Stone salivating."

"I don't know. He seemed intimidated by the deal's scope."

Bruno chuckled. "Let me tell you what will happen next. Their real estate guy will call one of the senior partners, who will ask a bunch of questions about the package, about why your company wants to sell it, and whether you sounded desperate. I assume you told him the regulators are forcing you to liquidate some of your commercial real estate holdings."

"I did. I also told him his firm has the first right of refusal until ten tomorrow morning. After that, I said we would be making calls to other investment houses. I told him our preference is to work with a privately-held firm like Rosen, Rice & Stone rather than deal with a big bureaucratic house like Goldman or Morgan."

"Don't be surprised that when you call he'll demand a five percent discount."

"Nothing would surprise me about those guys. They're a bunch of pirates. But you can't possibly agree to a five percent haircut on this security. That's—"

Bruno laughed. "For appearance's sake, you'll push back and tell him three percent is as far as you can go. He'll push for four percent, and you'll agree to three and a half."

Lander said, "I don't know."

"Stay calm, Dave. It'll work out. I'll see you in the park."

Victoria Nguyen shifted stiffly in the un-cushioned metal chair and rocked her head from side-to-side to loosen her neck and shoulders. She'd been planted in the little café down the street from Louis Massarino's house since 7:45 a.m. and badly wanted to leave and walk around the block. But she knew she couldn't take the chance of missing Massarino. The one-hundred-dollar bill she'd handed her waitress had ensured that the café staff would leave her alone and keep her coffee cup topped off. At 1:30, she desperately rushed to the restroom. At 1:55 p.m., she spotted Massarino's garage door open and his Town Car pull out into the street. Nguyen bolted smoothly from the café, fast-walked to her car, and followed the Lincoln.

At 2:45 p.m., Silvio Caniglia leaned against an unmanned rental car agency booth in the baggage claim area of D Terminal. Other than being a hard man who'd done just about every imaginable job for the Massarinos, he looked similar to the half-dozen other men in the area who were dressed in black suits and held signs with names handwritten on them.

The electronic sign in the area now showed the woman's flight was at the gate. *Right on time*, Caniglia thought.

He scratched his forehead and adjusted his sunglasses as he again slowly eyeballed the baggage claim area. *Nothing out of the ordinary*, he thought. *Pasty-looking New Yorkers who spend most of their time indoors.*

A couple minutes passed. Then he did another scan of the area, taking eyeball snapshots of every person there. His head on a slow swivel, moving left to right, he did a double-take halfway through the scan. Something was off even before his mind registered what it was. He cocked his head to the side, scanned back to the left, and locked on a tall, blond-haired man in a light-brown suit. *Who the hell wears a light-brown suit in New York in November?* Then he noticed the guy's healthy tan. *Beach Boy. Maybe returning from the Bahamas.* But he scrubbed that thought. *People don't usually travel from the Bahamas in a suit. And the guy isn't moving through the terminal. He's stationary, watching deplaning passengers.*

He continued his scan, going right to left, and spotted another healthy-looking guy a few feet away from Beach Boy. This guy was short, dark-skinned, and powerfully-built. Both men seemed zeroed in on the arrivals corridor. Caniglia didn't need to see their IDs to know they were cops. He removed his cell from his inside jacket pocket and hit speed dial number 1.

"Yeah?" Louis Massarino said.

"There's heat at the airport. They look like California types."

After a few seconds, Massarino said, "I bet they followed the woman because they think she'll lead them to Bruno."

"What do you want me to do?"

"As soon as you find Ms. Jenkins, take her to the car. Once you're certain they're tailing you, take the Jackie Robinson Parkway to the end. Go right on Fulton Street, then left on Bedford. After Bedford, take an immediate right on Pacific."

"Ya got it, boss."

Bruno handed another flash drive to Dave Lander. "The spreadsheet on that drive has final numbers. Can you finish everything tonight?"

"The sooner the better," Lander said.

Bruno shot the man a sympathetic look. "What you're doing will wipe out your gambling markers. You look like a smart guy. You ought to think about not getting in deep again."

Lander nodded. "I can't tell you how many times I've told myself to stop." He shook his head.

"You ever sign up for a program? You know, counseling."

"No." A sour expression came onto his face. "Those programs cost a fortune."

"If I gave you the money for counseling, would you do it?"

Lander's jaw dropped. "Why would you—?"

"Answer my question."

"Yeah, I would."

"If this all goes well, I'll make it happen."

Lander looked at Bruno as though he'd just stepped off a spaceship. He nodded several times and said, "Thank you."

Rosales and Andrews watched a burly man in a dark suit approach Janet, take her suitcase from her hand, and then lead her outside the terminal. After they stood by the curb for a couple minutes, a black Cadillac Escalade pulled beside them and the man and Janet got into the vehicle. Rosales and Andrews raced to the taxi queue forty yards to the right. Rosales flashed his badge and jumped the queue. To the accompaniment of a chorus of shouts and curses, they got into the first cab in line. Rosales yelled, "Follow that Escalade."

The driver looked back at the two men and grinned. "You're kidding, right?"

"No, we're not kidding."

"How much?"

"How much what?" Rosales shouted.

"How much over the meter will you pay?" the driver asked.

"Fifty dollars," Rosales said.

"Make it a 'C' note."

Rosales blew out a loud breath and muttered, "Sonofabitch." Then he told the driver, "Okay."

"And you cover any speeding tickets I might get."

"Okay, okay," Rosales shouted. "Just get going."

The driver turned forward and chuckled as he dropped the shifter into drive and roared away.

Janet leaned her head against the corner of the seat in the back of the Escalade and closed her eyes. She hadn't been able to sleep on the plane and now couldn't keep her eyes open. The movement of the SUV was comforting and she soon drifted off.

She didn't know how much time had passed when something woke her. She pressed her hands against her eyes and said, "Did you say something?"

"Sorry to disturb you, Ms. Jenkins," Silvio said as he turned in the front passenger seat and looked at Janet. "I was on the phone with Mr. Massarino."

Janet noticed that the driver kept looking in his mirrors. "Is there something wrong?" she asked.

"Nothing to worry about. I think there are a couple guys in a cab following us."

Janet twisted in her seat and looked out through the rear window. "Who are they?"

A man's voice came over the Bluetooth speaker, startling Janet. "Ms. Jenkins, this is Louis Massarino. We don't know for sure who they are. Maybe police. But, as Silvio just told you, there's nothing to worry about."

Silvio then said, "Boss, I'll be at the end of the Jackie Robinson Parkway in about five minutes."

"Good," Massarino said.

The driver exited the parkway and made the turns Caniglia told him to make. When he was fifty yards down Pacific, Caniglia spotted the trailing cab turn onto the street behind them. He'd gone almost to the end of the first block, where Pacific crossed Franklin, when he saw two cars pull away from the curb behind him and abruptly stop, forming a barricade in the middle of Pacific. The harsh noise of screeching tires and a car horn sounded.

"What's happening, Silvio?" Massarino asked.

"All's good, boss."

"I'll see you here."

The driver turned left onto Franklin and finger-tapped the top of the steering wheel as he whistled and made his way through the streets of Brooklyn.

CHAPTER 16

Wayne Summers had been with Rosen, Rice & Stone for seven years, having joined the firm right out of Wharton Business School. He'd worked his way up to Chief of Acquisitions in the firm's real estate department and had just bought a two-million-dollar co-op apartment unit on Central Park East, and was considering the purchase of a weekend/summer place on the Jersey shore. His salary was three hundred thousand dollars a year, but his bonus had averaged two million dollars over the past two years. He'd already calculated the amount of his bonus for this year if the deal brought to him by Joseph Campbell at Sunrise Casualty Insurance closed.

"Seventy-two million dollars in fees and discount points," he muttered as he walked to the elevator lobby on the seventh floor. "Ten percent bonus on seventy-two million dollars in fees. Holy shit!" *But what if I can negotiate the discount to, say, three percent, instead of two percent?* He thought, as he tallied the numbers in his head. "Holy shit!"

The ride to the twenty-third floor seemed to last forever. He mumbled to himself the pitch he would make to Richard Stone. He thought he had it nailed when he stepped out of the car and forced himself to stand straight, shoulders back. Breathing deeply, he stopped in front of the receptionist at the entrance to the executive suites and announced himself.

"Please have a seat, Mr. Summers," the receptionist said. "Mr.

Stone will be right with you."

Right with you turned out to be twenty-five minutes. By the time Stone's secretary came out to get him, Summers was bathed in sweat and had to pee so badly he'd paced the floor for the past five minutes. As she led him toward the double doors to the executive suites, he peeled off and raced into a restroom. He was in such a rush that he dribbled on the front of his pants and splashed water from the sink on his suit jacket. When he tried to dry his pants and jacket with a paper towel, bits of paper lint stuck to the dark blue material. "Oh no," he groaned. He checked his hair in the mirror and told himself to calm down. He knew Richard Stone wanted his employees to always appear to be under control. He tightened the knot in his tie, buttoned his suit jacket, and tried to hand-brush away, with limited success, paper towel bits that clung to his suit. "Here goes," he muttered. File in hand, he walked back out to the hallway.

The receptionist eyeballed him, gave him a sour look, and slowly shook her head as he stepped forward. She pointed down the thickly-carpeted corridor. "He's ready for you."

The walk to Stone's office seemed interminable. He picked at the lint on his jacket as he moved to the corner office. He lightly knocked once on the office door.

"Come in," Stone shouted, sounding impatient.

Summers opened the door, took one step into the office, and stopped. Stone's desk backed up to a bank of windows that looked down on Wall Street. The man was seated, back to the windows, phone to his ear. Stone waved him forward.

The distance from the entrance to the desk was at least fifteen yards. Summers felt as though he walked a plank as he approached the partner. He badly wanted to sit down, to make himself as small as possible, to hide the damage he'd done to his suit. But he knew he should wait until Stone told him to sit. Thankfully, Stone waved his free hand, directing him to a chair.

Summers removed from his file the report he'd prepared, placed it on the front of Stone's desk, and held the file folder like a shield against his chest.

Stone suddenly ended his conversation, slammed down the

receiver, and glared.

"You've got five minutes," the man said as he picked up the report. "Make the most of them."

Summers cleared his throat, babbled for a couple seconds, then launched into his presentation. "Sunrise Casualty Insurance has given us first right of refusal on a two point four-billion-dollar commercial mortgage-backed security, collateralized by three point five billion dollars' worth of triple-A office buildings. That's about a sixty-nine percent loan to value ratio. The leases in the buildings are seasoned and ninety percent of the tenants are national credits. Average remaining lease terms are eleven years."

"Why is Sunrise doing us this *big favor*?" Stone demanded.

Summers had anticipated the question. "They're under pressure from the New York State insurance regulator and the rating agencies. Their real estate exposure is too high, according to industry standards. My contact didn't say so, but he inferred they're being forced to liquidate some of the real estate assets in their portfolio."

"Why us?"

"Because, if they put the deal out on the open market, they'll effectively tell the world they have a problem. That could negatively impact their stock and bond values. Also, they prefer working with a privately-owned firm like us."

Stone scanned Summers's report, then suddenly popped his head up. His piggy eyes wide, his jowls shaking, he stared and said, "Is this correct? They'll pay us a twenty-four million dollar underwriting fee and sell the security at a two percent discount?"

"That's right."

Stone's expression turned predatory. "You realize this means they'll probably agree to a larger discount, if they're under as much pressure as you think."

Summers felt a chill and shrugged. *Stone's going to get greedy and kill this deal*, he thought.

Stone turned to the report's next page. "What the—? They've got to be kidding. They want to close by the end of the month. That's three days."

"They want the security off their books before their next

Department of Insurance examination in early December."

"Ha," Stone blurted. His fingers moved like octopus tentacles as he said, "Come to papa." He showed his predatory expression again. "Summers, here's what I want you to do. Tell your guy at Sunrise we'll do the deal for a five percent discount."

Summers' heart seemed to drop into his stomach. He visualized his bonus flying out Stone's window and scattering like ashes onto Wall Street. "I don't think—"

Stone raised a hand. "Listen closely. You'll tell him we want five percent. He'll go from two percent to three percent. You'll counter at four and finally agree to three-and-a-quarter, maybe three-and-a-half."

Summers didn't think it would work. He'd thought a three percent discount would be almost impossible. Anything higher would be a miracle. But he couldn't help himself as he rode the elevator back to his floor. He whispered over and over, "Three-and-a-half percent plus one percent underwriting fee is one hundred and eight million dollars. A ten million, eight hundred thousand dollar bonus. Holy shit!"

As he walked across the executive suite to Sy Rosen's office, Stone wondered why Wayne Summers's pants and suit jacket had been covered in lint. But he put it out of his mind as he opened Rosen's door. "You got a minute?"

"Sure. What's up?"

"We should get Karl in here."

Rosen's brow furrowed. "You seem excited."

"Oh, yeah."

Rosen buzzed his secretary and told her to find Karl Rice.

Rice showed up a couple minutes later. "Everything okay?" he asked as he took a seat across from Rosen and next to Stone.

"More than okay," Stone said. After he described the Sunrise deal, he sat back in his chair and waited.

Rosen's face flushed. He picked up his letter opener and tapped a furious beat with it on his desk blotter. "That's a deal of a lifetime," he said. "But can we get the securities laid off? We have enough cash to cover one-and-a-half billion of the deal. But we'll need another seven hundred million, after deducting the underwriting fee and a three point five percent discount. By the time we package the deal for our investors, it could be mid-December. We'd be hanging out for over two weeks with no cash and a massive short-term loan at the bank."

"Whoa, guys," Rice interjected. "One billion of that one-and-a-half billion in cash you just mentioned is client money in our trust accounts. We can't—"

"Bullshit," Rosen said. "We can do whatever we want. Besides, we'll pay the clients two percent interest on the money we use. That's more than they get at a bank."

Stone said, "We've had that line of credit at the bank for years; been paying a commitment fee to those bastards and never used it. The risk/reward ratio on this deal is hugely in our favor."

Rice wagged his head, "I don't know, guys."

"Grow some balls," Rosen said. "How often do we get a chance to make over one hundred million dollars to underwrite a deal? Like, never."

"I hear you," Rice said. "But, what if we can't lay off the bonds to investors? Our firm will be in jeopardy. Our entire capital base could be wiped out. We'd be bankrupt."

"Whoa, Karl, what's with you?" Stone said. "Our capital won't be at risk. The worst case is that we can't offload the Sunrise security at face value. We'd wind up selling it for what we paid—maybe for even more than we paid—but keep the twenty-four million dollar underwriting fee. We put the billion back in our clients' accounts and pay off the seven hundred-million-dollar loan at the bank. Our own half-a-billion would be back in our capital account." He glared at Rice and added, "Remember that Sunrise is no fly-by-night operation. They're a legitimate firm that's been in business for over one hundred years. They have a triple-A rating from Fitch, S&P, and A.M. Best. We'll make a fortune off this deal."

"But three days to close is crazy," Rice said. "There's no way we can do our due diligence in that short a time."

"What did I just say about Sunrise? They're one of the top insurance companies in the country. The due diligence will be pro forma. We'll get it done after we close."

Rice looked from Stone to Rosen. "Okay. I guess you're right."

Rosen smiled. "I'll call the bank and arrange for the draw against our line. Richard, you personally shepherd this thing through our underwriting department. Make sure everything's copacetic. Karl, you make calls to investors to drum up interest in the deal. I don't want that bank line hanging over our heads any longer than necessary." He smiled. "Boys, it's going to be a good year."

After Stone and Rice left his office, Rosen fumbled in his desk drawer and pulled out a burner phone. He called Victoria Nguyen's number and told her, "You'd better have good news for me."

CHAPTER 17

After trailing Massarino's Town Car around Brooklyn for a couple hours, Victoria Nguyen was frustrated and angry. Massarino had stopped at a coffee shop, where he'd spent an hour. After he left the shop, he stopped at a bakery, came out ten minutes later with a couple white paper bags, then cruised around Brooklyn as though he was on a sight-seeing tour. Then, finally, his driver brought him back home. She had nothing to show for the time she'd spent that day, and she knew from the call she'd received from Sy Rosen that he was already pissed off. Back in the café down the street from Massarino's home, she ordered a meal and watched the residence. The waitress had just served her order when an SUV pulled up in front of the house. A man jumped from behind the wheel, ran around to the right rear door, and helped someone out. The big vehicle screened Nguyen's view, so it wasn't until the passenger approached the bottom of the steps up to the Massarino front door that she was able to get a clear view. Nguyen's heart seemed to skip a beat when she recognized Janet Jenkins from her photograph. "I'll be damned," she whispered. She hadn't heard from Pham Van Duc in over twenty-four hours. Her calls to him had gone unanswered. It suddenly felt as though an acid drip had been turned on in her stomach. *If Jenkins is here, she escaped Pham. That could have happened only if the cops had found him.*

Nguyen knew Pham was a tough nut. The cops would not easily

crack him. But that possibility made her shudder.

"Welcome to my home, Ms. Jenkins. You must be tired after your long flight. Would you like to go to your room, freshen up?"

"Thank you, Mr. Massarino. But what I'd really like to do is see Bruno." She paused a moment and added, "Please call me Janet."

Massarino smiled. "And, of course, I'm Louis. I feel like we're old friends. Bruno's told me much about you." His smile broadened. "But he didn't tell me what a beautiful woman you are."

Janet tipped her head at Massarino. Her face felt warm and she tried to smile, but sadness suddenly overwhelmed her. "I'm so sorry about your brother. He was a good friend to Bruno."

Massarino's eyes went hard as he took Janet's hands in his. "Thank you for what you did to Carlo's killer."

Janet lowered her eyes. She didn't feel that saying "It was my pleasure" was appropriate.

Massarino released her hands and turned to Caniglia. "Silvio, please take Ms. Jenkins's suitcase to her room."

"Is there a rental car agency near here?" Rosales asked the cab driver.

"There's a Hertz office a couple blocks away," the cabbie said.

"That'll do."

Rosales looked at Andrews, who had a disgusted expression on his face.

"I guess the guy made us," Rosales said.

"Probably at the airport," Andrews said. "He took us on a joy ride then called in his buddies to block the street."

At the Hertz office, Rosales gave the cab driver four twenties—seventy dollars for the fare, plus a ten dollar tip.

"Hey, how 'bout the hundred extra?" the cabbie yelled as the two detectives got out of his car.

"You lost the Escalade. You didn't earn the hundred," Rosales said.

"Assholes," the cabbie yelled and then peeled away.

Andrews smiled at Rosales and said, "I recall that's what the people in the LaGuardia taxi queue called us when we took that cab."

"Adds a bit of symmetry to the whole experience, don't you think?" Rosales said.

"What now?"

"Considering what we learned about Bruno Pedace's association with Carlo Massarino and, by extension, Carlo's brother, Louis, I think we should go sit on Louis Massarino's house. I'll bet Janet's been in touch with him by now."

CHAPTER 18

It was 6 p.m. when Rosales and Andrews cruised past Massarino's house. They circled the block several times looking for a parking spot, with no luck. They finally pulled into a tiny lot behind a Mexican restaurant, went inside the place, ordered enchiladas, and took turns leaving the restaurant and strolling to the corner of Massarino's block. It was during John Andrews's second shift that he saw the left bay door of Massarino's garage open. Rolling white plumes of exhaust spewed from a black Lincoln Town Car's tailpipe into the cold evening air. He got a brief view of Janet Jenkins slipping into the left rear side of the car. A large man in a black suit closed the door for her and then quickly moved around the vehicle, closing the right-hand-side passenger door behind another man. Then the big man slipped into the "shotgun" seat. The driver backed the car out of the garage into the street, pointing the nose of the car toward Andrews.

Andrews calmly turned around and went past the corner, then sprinted to the restaurant. He opened the front door and waved urgently at Rosales, who leaped from his chair, dropped cash on the table, and raced outside. The two detectives ran to the parking lot, climbed in their Ford Escort rental car—Rosales behind the wheel, and drove out onto the street. They stopped for the red light at Massarino's corner and watched the tinted-windowed Lincoln slowly crawl through the intersection in front of them.

"You're certain Janet was with them?" Rosales asked, tense and worried.

"Of course. Along with three men, one of whom could be Louis Massarino."

Rosales stared at the traffic light that hung overhead and muttered, "Come on, come on," willing it to turn green. He inched his way into the cross street, anticipating the green light, when, just as the light changed, a dark-gray Audi ran the light and sped through the intersection. Rosales's heart did a little tap dance as he braked hard and muttered a curse. He hit the gas and turned left, just behind the Audi.

"You see them?" Rosales demanded.

"Yeah," Andrews answered. "About a block ahead. Don't seem to be in any hurry."

Rosales peered ahead and saw the Lincoln stop at the next light, the Audi immediately behind it.

"Nice car," Andrews said.

"The Audi?"

"Yeah. My landlord drives one just like it. Does a hundred and eighty and costs about the same."

"Nice," Rosales said. "A grand per mile per hour."

Andrews chuckled.

Still four car lengths from the Audi, Rosales saw the light ahead turn green. The Lincoln pulled away. The Audi—a woman behind the wheel—followed. Almost to the end of the next block, the light there turned yellow. But, instead of continuing at a leisurely speed, the driver of the Lincoln sped through the light as it turned red. That didn't particularly surprise Rosales. What did surprise him, however, was that the Audi driver ran the red light, then appeared to slow down after she was through the intersection.

"You see that?"

"Yeah," Andrews said. "Maybe the Lincoln's got a tail. Besides us, I mean."

Janet watched as they passed brownstones and then mom and pop retail stores topped with apartments. Everything looked so old in Brooklyn, compared to what she was used to in California. They'd been in the car for five minutes when Massarino ended a phone call and turned slightly to look at her.

"Bruno tells me you've had one heck of a year."

Janet met his gaze and shrugged.

"How did you and Bruno meet?"

She told him the story about the two kids mugging Bruno for his briefcase.

Massarino shook his head. "Jeez. He didn't tell me *that* story." He smiled at her. "You really *have* had quite a year."

She didn't know how to respond. Every time she thought about the events of the past seven months, she conjured up her mother's sweet face and the bloody scene in her house the day Rasif Essam broke in. She changed the subject. "What's Bruno been up to out here?"

"I'll let him tell you." Massarino looked through his window and added, "We'll be there in a couple—"

"Boss, I think we got a tail," Caniglia announced.

"You recognize anyone?"

Caniglia glanced in his rearview mirror. "No, boss. Just some broad. Uh, sorry, Ms. Jenkins."

"Keep an eye on her," Massarino ordered. "Let's take a Sunday drive."

The driver meandered around Brooklyn streets, seemingly driving aimlessly. He turned down narrow residential streets, drove below the posted speed limit, and stopped for nearly every light. The Audi had turned in at a hotel a block back and hadn't been spotted since.

Caniglia announced, "False alarm, boss. She's gone."

Nguyen pulled into a semi-circular drive fronting a hotel and handed the doorman a twenty-dollar bill and her car keys.

"You checking in?" the man asked.

"Later," she said. "Park it."

Nguyen scooted over to a taxi and climbed inside.

"Where to?" the cabbie asked.

"Just drive. You follow instructions and there'll be a big tip in it for you."

"You're the boss," the driver said.

"What the hell are you doing?" Andrews asked as Rosales parked at the curb in front of the hotel the Audi had pulled into. "You'll lose the Lincoln."

"There's something hinky about the woman in that Audi."

"So what? I thought we were trying to find Pedace."

Rosales gestured with a hand to tell Andrews to be patient. He watched the woman from the Audi rush from her car, say something to a doorman, and then sprint over to a cab parked at the end of a semi-circular drive.

The taxi then drove away.

"Cute trick," Rosales said as he followed the cab. "Very cute."

The cab had barely pulled away from the hotel when it switched lanes, jockeying with other cars.

"What in God's name?" Andrews exclaimed.

"Pretty damned clever," Rosales said. "Massarino musta spotted the Audi and the gal figured that out from the way the Lincoln driver acted."

"She coulda lost the Lincoln while switching vehicles," Andrews said.

"Yeah, she could have. But the way that cab's moving, I suspect she's spotted it."

Nguyen thought she saw the tail end of the Lincoln turn right. "Speed it up," she ordered the cabbie. "I'll cover any tickets you get."

Two blocks down, after making the right turn, she spied the Lincoln as it turned left about fifty yards ahead.

"Take the next left," she said.

Almost as soon as the driver turned left, the Lincoln pulled into a loading zone halfway up the block on the left.

"Drive to the end of the block, then pull over as soon as you can," Nguyen ordered.

After the driver pulled into a handicap space, she exited the vehicle, handed the driver a one-hundred-dollar bill and told him, "There'll be another 'C-Note' for you when I return." She walked to the front door of a pizza joint on the corner and peeked down the street. She watched a large man exit the Lincoln's right front door, look around, and then open the right rear door. Louis Massarino stepped into the street. The driver then got out and opened the left rear door for Janet Jenkins, who joined Massarino. As Massarino, the big man, and Jenkins quickly crossed the street, the driver got back in behind the wheel.

Her eyes on the threesome as they approached a boutique in the middle of the block, Nguyen thought they were headed to the shop. But, instead, they walked past the entrance and stopped at a steel door set into the right front of the building, a few yards from the shop entrance. The big man appeared to use a key to unlock the door. After Massarino and Jenkins went inside, he locked the door behind them and stood guard.

Nguyen's predator instincts were now in hyper drive. Something deep inside told her she'd found Bruno Pedace. *It's all about being patient*, she thought. Nguyen touched the silenced 9mm Beretta automatic in her coat pocket, then withdrew her hand. She guessed Massarino's driver and the man guarding the door would be armed. Massarino could be carrying, as well. The odds were against her taking action then and there. And, if she did, and was successful, she would have to eliminate the taxi driver. *No loose ends*, she thought.

As soon as Rosales turned the corner, he saw the light on the cab's roof down the block on the right. Andrews pointed out the Lincoln parked on the left side of the street, a man in the driver's seat.

"Check out the guy on the right, in front of that shop," Andrews said. "Hands in his coat pockets, eyeing the street and sidewalk."

"Yeah, I see him," Rosales said. "Looks like muscle." He drove past the shop and then turned right at the corner where the cab was parked. He jerked a glance to the right and saw the Asian woman he'd seen get out of the Audi back at the hotel. She now moved from a storefront to the cab. Rosales circled the block and double parked eight car lengths back from the Lincoln. He and Andrews settled in to watch, but less than a minute passed before a loud horn blast startled them. Rosales looked in his rearview mirror and saw the grill of a large truck. "Damn," he muttered. He moved the car forward just as he spotted the taxi pull away.

Rosales asked Andrews, "You get the address where that guy

was standing?"

"Yeah."

"Good. Now let's see where this woman takes us."

Andrews shot a querulous look at Rosales. "What's with you and this woman?"

"Her behavior doesn't bother you?"

"Sure, but she's not the reason we're here."

Rosales shrugged.

CHAPTER 19

Bruno had expected Louis and Janet to arrive thirty minutes earlier. He'd become more agitated with the passage of every minute. When the knock sounded on the apartment door, he leaped from his computer chair, opened the door, and felt a surge of warmth when Janet smiled at him. Bruno reached to take her hand, but she walked forward and hugged him.

"Good to see you, Bruno."

Bruno looked over Janet's shoulder at the mischievous smile on Louis Massarino's face.

The cab deposited the Asian woman back at the hotel where she'd left her Audi. Rosales and Andrews watched the front of the place. Ten minutes later, after a parking valet brought the Audi up from an underground lot, the woman drove away. It was after 8:00 p.m. when they observed her remotely open a gate to an underground parking lot beneath a Manhattan building. The gate closed as soon as she pulled in. Andrews threw open the passenger side door and told Rosales, "I'll be right back." He stepped from the car, slammed the door shut, and ran to the building entrance.

Double parked, Rosales decided to circle the block. When he came back to the front of the building, he picked up Andrews who stood on the curb.

"Talked to the doorman," Andrews said, as Rosales drove off.

"After I flashed my badge, he got real helpful. Told me the only Asian in the building was a good-looking young woman named Victoria Nguyen in Unit 15B. He doesn't know what she does for a living, but said she's in and out at odd times."

"Nguyen is a Vietnamese name." Irony heavy in his voice, Rosales said, "You think there might be a connection between her and the Vietnamese guys who grabbed Janet in El Segundo?"

Andrews scoffed. "Gee, you think?"

Rosales said, "I'm hungry. What say we go back to that street in Brooklyn where the Lincoln was parked and hang around there? There were a couple restaurants on the same block."

"Sounds like a plan."

At 9:00 p.m., Rosales and Andrews took seats at a window table in a pizza parlor up from where the Lincoln Town Car had been parked. Although the car was gone, the big guy in the overcoat was still standing outside. Rosales could just see a sliver of the building where the man stood guard.

"You know Janet may have left," Andrews groused.

"Yeah, I know," Rosales said. "But I'll bet ya five bucks Pedace's in the building where that bruiser is standing guard."

"We have a subpoena for Pedace to appear in court in California. Let's just go knock on the door."

Rosales chuckled. "Whatsa matter, you got a hot date?"

"Shit. I haven't had a date in months. Since I partnered up with you, all I do is work."

"Bitch, bitch, bitch. Just think of all the experience you're—"

"Wonder who the big guy is protecting," Andrews said.

"Let's wait an hour and see if the guy takes off. If he does, we'll go knock on the door."

"And if he doesn't leave?"

"Then we'll go introduce ourselves to him…and then knock on the door."

As he continued to stare down the street, Rosales tucked into a slice of pizza. "This ain't half-bad," he said.

"I was famished," Andrews said.

They finished a large pizza and consumed several cups of coffee.

They'd ordered a couple cannoli just to keep the owner happy, but hadn't touched them.

Bruno and Janet sat on a two-seater couch, ate take-out Chinese food, and talked.

"You really believe your former partners are behind all this?" Janet asked.

"No doubt in my mind," Bruno answered.

"So, why would you endanger yourself by coming to New York?"

"I can't answer that, Janet. The less you know, the better. But take my word that those men will pay for what they've done."

A shiver jolted Janet as fear snaked through her. "What are you up to, Bruno? I don't want anything more to happen to you."

Bruno patted her hand and smiled. "Don't worry about me. Louis is keeping an eye on things. Besides, no one knows where I am." He chuckled. "Ninety-nine percent of the time that I've been back here I've been holed up in this place."

Janet scowled. "It's the one percent that could be a problem."

Bruno took her hand. "It's nice to know you're concerned about me."

Janet scooted toward him and said, "Are you just figuring that out?"

Bruno's face reddened. He looked at his lap and shrugged.

"You really are a klutz sometimes."

Still eyeing his lap, he nodded. "There hasn't been anyone who cared about me in a long time."

"Nonsense," Janet said. "What about Carlo Massarino, Louis, the Pappadopouloses?"

"I meant—"

Janet put a hand under his chin and lifted, turning his head. "Look at me, Bruno." When their eyes met, she said, "I understand. It's been the same for me. Other than my mother and a few people at work, I've been alone for a long time." She leaned toward him and pressed her lips against his. For a moment, he responded to her kiss, but then he suddenly pulled away and clumsily stood and moved away from the couch.

The frightened, lost expression Janet had seen on Bruno's face back in that alley in Redondo Beach had returned. The confidence she'd observed in him of late had disappeared.

"Bruno—"

"I think I'd better call Louis and have him send someone to take you back to his place."

Janet nodded. She felt empty. She'd misread the look Bruno had given her when he'd opened the apartment door earlier. She'd thought their conversations back at St. Anne's had been more than just idle, casual talk. She'd deluded herself into thinking that Bruno felt about her the way she felt about him.

Massarino's driver returned to the apartment at 10:15 p.m. After Janet and Caniglia left with the driver, Bruno repeatedly walked the length of the apartment, talking to himself and maniacally waving his arms, looking like a crazed windmill. The look he'd seen on Janet's face when he'd broken off their kiss had made him feel as though his heart had shattered. He'd wanted so badly to take her in his arms, to tell her how he felt about her. But he couldn't encourage something that might end in disaster. The plan could backfire and he could end up in prison...or dead. Sy Rosen and his partners could accomplish what they'd wanted to do for years— murder him. Until those possibilities were gone, there was no way he could encourage a relationship with Janet. But, as he continued to roam the limits of the apartment, his mutterings became shouts. He screamed at the walls, "Pedace, you're an idiot."

CHAPTER 20

Rosales and Andrews had watched the Lincoln return and then drive away with Janet and the bodyguard. They continued to watch the street for several minutes, but there was no more activity.

"If Pedace's in that building, what do you think the odds are that he's now alone?" Rosales asked.

Andrews answered, "I'd say the odds are pretty damn good. Now would probably be a good time to say hello." Then he added, "Maybe we should call the locals and ask them to serve the subpoena. That would be proper protocol."

"I hate protocol."

"What the hell will we do if someone with malice aforethought shows up armed?" Andrews asked. "Or if Pedace comes to the door with a weapon? In case you forgot, we don't have our pistols."

"Malice aforethought?" Rosales said.

"Yeah. That's what bad guys always come armed with, along with a weapon."

Then a spray of headlights briefly flashed out on the street.

"Somebody coming home from a late date," Rosales said.

"Sonofabitch," Andrews said softly. "Is that the same Audi?"

"I'll be damned," Rosales said. "I think you're right."

They watched the Audi turn right around the corner and disappear.

"I have a bad feeling about this," Rosales said.

"It's that malice aforethought thing."

Rosales grimaced. He stood and walked to the counter where the shop owner was tallying up receipts and intermittently giving him and Andrews the evil eye.

Rosales took out his cred pack and showed it to the man. "You wouldn't happen to have a pistol under the counter?"

The guy scowled. "If you're a real cop, why the hell do you need a pistol from me?"

Good question, Rosales thought. "I left my sidearm at home. I think something's about to go down outside and I'd rather not deal with it empty-handed."

The guy gave him a look that made Rosales feel stupid and incompetent, but he bent down and came up with a dented and scarred Louisville Slugger. "This is all I got. You take care of it. My father passed it down to me."

"I promise," Rosales said.

Bat in hand, Rosales walked back to Andrews and told him to make a 9-1-1 call.

"And tell them what?"

Rosales spread his arms. "Shots fired; officer needs backup."

"You gotta be kidding me."

After Rosales left the pizza place, Andrews placed the 9-1-1 call, gave the operator the boutique's address, and told her he'd heard shots fired and that a police officer was involved. He hung up when she asked him his name. The thought crossed his mind that he and Rosales would be in hot water when the local cops arrived and discovered he'd made a false call. *The 9-1-1 operator probably captured my cell number.* Then he exited the pizza parlor and bumped into a woman dressed from head to toe in black.

"Sorry, ma'am," he blurted. "I didn't see you."

"No problem," the woman said.

"You okay? I mean, it's kinda late."

"Yeah, I'm fine. What's it to you?"

"Jeez, I was just trying to be nice."

She pointed a hand at him. "Go try to be nice somewhere else." With that, she turned and moved down the street.

"Hey, wait a minute," he said, as the distant wail of sirens carried to him. He pulled out his cred pack and held it high. "Stop right there. I'm a cop."

Backed into the recessed area in front of a dress shop's entrance, Rosales heard the exchange between Andrews and the woman and thought, *what the hell are you doing, John?* He moved out to the sidewalk to get a look at what was happening, just as the woman turned around to face his partner. In that moment, he saw her pull something from inside her black jacket and drop into a semi-crouch. Then he heard the *pffft, pffft* sounds of rounds fired by a suppressed pistol. Andrews grunted as he fell to the pavement. Then he shouted, "I've been shot." Rosales charged the woman.

She'd come out of her crouch and turned back toward him, when, in full stride, he swung the baseball bat. Off balance, he didn't connect with the force he'd hoped for, but he made contact with her extended arm as she fired the pistol again. He felt a blow to his chest that took his breath away. His momentum carried him into her, knocking her to the sidewalk. He landed on top of her and heard her emit a loud *oomph*. He thought he heard her head hit the pavement just before all went black.

CHAPTER 21

Bruno heard the sirens but didn't think much of them. After all, this was New York. But, as they became louder, he grew nervous. A minute later, the sirens were directly outside his building. Flashing lights bombarded the apartment's front room. Then he heard voices out on the street and looked through the front window. People had gathered outside. He noticed a couple people lying on the sidewalk. He packed up his laptop, hard files, and the flash drive with copies of his files into two valises. Then he exited through a back door off the kitchen and took the fire escape to the alley behind the building. At the end of the alley, he went left, away from the noise and emergency vehicle lights. One block down, he stacked the two valises against a wall and used a burner phone to call Louis Massarino.

A man answered. "Yeah?"

"It's Bruno. I need to speak with Mr. Massarino."

"Hold on."

"What's the matter?" Massarino said thirty seconds later.

"All hell's breaking loose outside the apartment. There are police cars out front."

"Are you still there?"

"No. I took off."

"Give me an address. I'll have someone pick you up."

Police Officer Timothy Dolan was first on the scene. He found three unconscious persons sprawled on the sidewalk—a man outside a pizza parlor and a second man spread-eagled on top of a woman about twenty yards away. Blood pooled around all three of them. He thought the first man was deceased. The other man and the woman were breathing but, based on the amount of blood on and around them, he didn't have much confidence that they would make it. He found a baseball bat and a pistol mated to a silencer next to them. He used a pen he put through the trigger guard to pick it up and carry it to his vehicle. Dolan called in a situation report and told the dispatcher, "I need three buses here ASAP. Looks like multiple gunshot wounds."

By the time he'd radioed the dispatcher, other units had arrived and officers had cordoned off the scene with yellow crime scene tape. Then ambulances arrived.

When detectives arrived, they pulled Dolan aside.

Detective Rhonda Sparks asked, "You get IDs on any of the victims?"

"No. I was just about to when you arrived."

"You find any weapons?"

"One silenced pistol. It's on the floor on the front passenger side of my cruiser. I didn't want to leave it lying around while I checked the victims. I put my cigarette lighter on the spot where I found the pistol."

"Good thinking," Detective Vince Nicoletti said.

"I also found a baseball bat." He pointed toward the woman's body. "It's there on the sidewalk."

"Where were the bodies when you got here?"

Dolan pointed to where paramedics worked on the man outside the pizza parlor. "That guy was right there." He shifted to look at the second man and the woman, who now lay side by side on the sidewalk, paramedics working on them as well. "The second guy there was lying right on top of the woman. The pistol was next to his left hand."

Sparks looked at Nicoletti. "Why don't you have Dolan show you the pistol? I'll see what I can get from the paramedics."

Sparks moved to where four paramedics attended to the man and woman. "What d'ya got?"

Without looking up, one of the paramedics working on the man said, "Single shot to the upper right side of his chest. Mighta nicked a lung. We gotta get him to the emergency room stat."

"You find ID?"

"Didn't look."

Sparks squatted, patted the man's jacket pockets, and felt something in the left side pocket. She pulled it out and was shocked to find a cred pack with a Redondo Beach Police Department badge and ID. She looked over at the two men working on the woman, who muttered something and appeared to be trying to get up. "What's her story?" she asked.

"No wounds other than a laceration on the back of her head. Maybe a concussion."

Sparks stood and motioned to Dolan. When he joined her, she told him, "Don't let that gal out of your sight. As soon as the paramedics are done with her, cuff her and accompany her to the hospital." Then Sparks moved over to the team with the other male victim, who was now on a stretcher. Before she could ask, one of the paramedics said, "He's gone."

"ID?"

"Yeah." He pointed at a blood-soaked white towel on the sidewalk next to the stretcher. "We found a cred pack in the pool of blood next to the body."

Sparks gingerly lifted a corner of the towel and used the tip of a pen to flip open the ID case. "Detective John Andrews, Redondo Beach P.D.," she whispered. "Huh."

Louis Massarino set up Bruno in a basement apartment in his home. "Bruno, let's close out the deal as fast as possible," he said. "I'm worried about what happened tonight. My guy with the Brooklyn P.D. tells me two cops from California were shot outside your apartment. The local cops took some Asian gal into custody, too. "

"I'm sorry, Louis. I didn't want to bring heat down on you."

Massarino patted Bruno's shoulder. "You got nothing to apologize for. We just need to get this thing done quickly."

Bruno nodded. "Dave Lander's due to call his guy at Rosen, Rice & Stone at ten in the morning."

Janet had just about dozed off at 11:45 p.m. when she heard voices. She got out of bed and listened at her bedroom door. She couldn't make out everything being said, but she was positive she heard someone mention a shooting. She quickly changed into jeans and a T-shirt, slipped on a pair of flats, and left the bedroom. She stopped at the entrance to the living room at the end of a long hall and saw Massarino and Caniglia watching television. Massarino's expression was dour. The look on Caniglia's face was as flat as it always seemed to be.

"Did we wake you?" Massarino asked.

Janet shrugged as she met Massarino's look. "Is something wrong?"

He pointed at the television. "There was a commotion outside the apartment where Bruno was staying. We—"

"Oh my God," Janet exclaimed as photos of Hugo Rosales and John Andrews were shown side by side on the television screen. A female voice in the background said that two Redondo Beach Police Department detectives had been shot outside a pizza parlor in Brooklyn, that one of the officers was dead, while the other was in critical condition. The commentator also mentioned that a woman had been taken into custody. The program didn't show a photo of the woman, but the commentator identified her as Victoria Nguyen.

Janet said, "That could be the woman who followed us when we went to the apartment today."

"I wouldn't bet against it," Massarino said.

Sy Rosen rarely slept more than six hours a night. Since he'd put out a hit on Bruno Pedace, he was lucky to get four hours sleep. *That damned Nguyen had better get the job done soon*, he thought. He shook his head in frustration at the time on the digital clock on his nightstand: 11:57. He got out of bed, slipped on a robe, and quietly left his bedroom so as to not wake his wife. In his first floor home office, he poured a shot of scotch, took a seat opposite the television, and clicked on the set. He sipped the drink and punched in the number of a local news station that streamed news 24/7. When Victoria Nguyen's name scrolled across the bottom of the screen, the liquor went down the wrong way and a violent coughing episode hit him. His eyes watered. The glass fell from his hand and bounced; the scotch spilled and soaked into the antique Persian carpet.

He wiped his eyes and tried to stop coughing as he read the news message that ran across the screen. Victoria Nguyen had been arrested in Brooklyn at a crime scene where two Redondo Beach detectives had been shot.

"Oh fuck," Rosen rasped.

DAY 8

CHAPTER 22

RBPD Police Chief Frances Cassidy was apoplectic with rage. Sure, Barry Rath, the Redondo Beach District Attorney, was a good and long-time friend, but that didn't give Cassidy any comfort. For political reasons, Rath had cajoled her into sending Detectives Rosales and Andrews to New York City to track down Bruno Pedace. Rath wanted to see his name and photo on the front page of every area newspaper trumpeting his finding Pedace and connecting him to New York organized crime and to a financial services firm. But all that had been accomplished was that John Andrews was dead and Hugo Rosales was near death. She did her best to control her anger as she listened to the phone ring. When Rath finally answered, the D.A. sounded as though he was in poor humor.

"Dammit, Fran, it's the middle of the night."

Cassidy took a big breath and let it out slowly. "I know what time it is, Barry. I'm calling to tell you the two detectives you ordered me to send to New York City have been shot."

Rath waited a long beat before responding. "Aw, jeez, Frannie. I'm really sorry to hear that. Do you know if they found Pedace?"

"Are you fuckin' kiddin' me? I tell you that two of my best men have been shot and you don't even ask if they're okay."

"Well, are they?"

"No, Barry, they're *not* okay. Andrews is dead and Rosales is in surgery. They don't think he's going to make it." Cassidy hesitated a couple seconds and added, "And I have no idea if they found Pedace and don't care one way or the other."

Rath groaned.

"You'd better come up with a statement about why you wanted Redondo Beach detectives sent to New York, and it better cover my ass in the process. It wouldn't look good if it became known they were sent to New York to make you look good in the media."

"Now wait a minute, Frannie, I didn't—"

"Don't you *Frannie* me, and don't you dare try to put this on me. I've got the recording of the call you made telling me to send two of my people to New York."

"You recorded our conversation?"

"Fuckin' A, Barry. I always record our conversations."

After a long beat, Rath said, "Okay, Fran. I'll come up with a statement. Keep cool."

"I should never have let you talk me into it. Rosales was my best detective. Andrews was doing really good work for the RBPD. This could cost me my job."

"That's not going to happen as long as I'm the D.A."

"Ha. You won't be D.A. long if word gets out that you're running a cynical political game just so you can get re-elected."

Rath exhaled loudly. Then he asked, "Has the media contacted you yet about the shootings?"

"It's already on the Internet. It'll surely be all over our news in a few hours."

At 1:30 a.m., Brooklyn Detectives Rhonda Sparks and Vince Nicoletti followed a hospital aide as he pushed Victoria Nguyen's gurney from the emergency room into the elevator and then to a room on the fifth floor. They book-ended the sides of Nguyen's hospital bed after a couple aides lifted Nguyen from the gurney. Sparks moved to the top of the bed, handcuffed Nguyen's left wrist to the rail, and looked at the bandage on the back of her head. "Looks like they shaved part of your scalp. Ten stitches and a slight concussion. How're you feeling, Ms. Nguyen?"

Nguyen gave Sparks a hooded-eyed look and raised her arms,

rattling the cuff on her wrist. "What's going on? Why am I being treated like a criminal?"

"You wanta tell us what you were doing in Brooklyn so late at night?" Nicoletti asked.

"So, now it's a crime to go out for pizza after dark?" Nguyen said. "I heard the parlor on that block made great pizza."

"Long way to drive for a pizza."

"They don't deliver outside Brooklyn. And, like I said, I heard their pizza was great."

"What happened when you got to the pizza place?"

"Some guy accosted me outside the joint. Almost knocked me down. I tried to run away and the next thing I know a second guy comes at me with a baseball bat."

"Who shot the two men?" Sparks asked.

Nguyen's eyes turned cold. "I have no idea. Maybe a Good Samaritan."

"The pistol we found at the scene wasn't yours?" Nicoletti said.

"No way. Check out the registration records. I've never owned a gun."

"I guess we won't find your fingerprints on the weapon," Sparks said.

"I told you I've never owned a gun. Besides, I was wearing gloves. It was cold out."

"So, if you didn't fire the pistol, I guess we won't find gunshot residue on your gloves."

Nguyen shook her head a couple times and then swallowed hard.

Sparks gestured at Nicoletti with her head and walked out of the room. Nicoletti followed her down the hall. Near the nurses' station, Sparks stopped and turned to look at her partner.

"What do you think?"

"Just because she isn't in the firearms registry doesn't mean she doesn't own a pistol."

Sparks nodded. "She seem a little off to you? Did you notice her reaction when I mentioned gunshot residue on her gloves?"

Nicoletti compressed his lips and nodded. "Yeah. And she seems more angry than shook up about what happened. Not the usual response we get from the average Jane Doe Citizen vic."

"Any idea when you'll hear back from the call you made to Redondo Beach?"

"Nah. The duty officer told me he'd call the Chief of Police and give her my message."

"Anything on Nguyen?" Sparks asked.

"Nothing in local records. She's as clean as can be. Not even a parking ticket. Still waiting for something from NCIC."

"Maybe she was just in the wrong place at the wrong time."

"Maybe, but I got a feeling about that gal."

Sparks said, "Yeah, me too." Then she smiled at Nicoletti. "I'm gonna collect the clothes from the nursing staff and have the lab run the usual tests, with special emphasis on looking for gunshot residue on the gloves."

CHAPTER 23

Sy Rosen, Karl Rice, and Richard Stone gathered in the executive conference room for their daily early morning meeting. Rice and Stone helped themselves to coffee and bagels, while Rosen sat stiffly in his chair and waited for the others to sit.

"You see on the news what happened last night in Brooklyn?" Karl Rice asked as he moved to his chair.

"Yeah," Stone said. "Awful business."

Rosen swallowed hard. "What are you two talking about?"

"Couple cops from California got shot."

"California?" Rosen said, feigning ignorance. "What were they doing in Brooklyn?"

"No clue," Rice said. "Kinda coincidental they were from the same town—Redondo Beach—where Pedace had been holed up."

Stone said, "They took some Vietnamese woman into custody, but they didn't say who she was or why they took her in."

"You think you guys could focus on something more important?" Rosen interjected angrily. "Like the biggest transaction this firm has ever handled."

Rice met Stone's gaze, shrugged, and spread his hands in a "what gives?" gesture. Then he announced, "I've got all the bonds placed with pension funds." He chuckled. "They were salivating over the coupon rate. Didn't even try to negotiate a discount."

"What about the underwriting of the bonds?" Rosen asked

Stone.

"Our analysts pulled Sunrise's financial statements and their last three insurance examinations from the Internet. They're solid as Gibraltar. The only thing they were surprised at was that they don't seem to be over-weighted in real estate assets."

"When did they put the loans we're buying on their books?" Rosen asked.

Stone answered, "Wayne Summers told me all the loans were booked after their third quarter financials were issued."

"Would another two point four billion in real estate loans have raised their exposure to an unacceptable level?" Rosen asked.

"Maybe."

"When will we finalize the terms?" Rosen said.

Stone said, "Ten o'clock this morning. Summers expects a call from Sunrise then."

David Lander paced his office at Sunrise Casualty Insurance. Each minute that went by seemed like an hour. His desk clock now read 9:57. "Screw it," he said, and took the elevator down three floors to an employee lounge. He waited until two employees left the lounge, then used the wall phone there to call Wayne Summers at the Rosen firm. He knew caller ID would show the Sunrise Insurance name and the lounge's extension on Summers's phone console.

"Wayne Summers."

"It's Joseph Campbell," Lander said. "You sell the deal to your management?"

Summers said, "I'm sorry, Mr. Campbell, but we're going to pass."

Lander's lungs seemed to freeze up. *What the hell?* He took a calming breath and recalled what he'd been told. That the Rosen firm would try to force a bigger discount out of him. *I need to call his bluff,* he thought.

"That's too bad, Wayne. I'll just have to place the security on the market. I should have known this was too big a deal for your firm."

"No, no, that's not it."

Landers brought his breathing under control. "Then what is it?"

"The discount's too small."

"It's a friggin' two percent discount. You gotta be kidding me. How much do you bandits want?"

Summers replied, "Five percent."

"What? Forget it. I'm tired of dealing with your pissant company. I've got twenty other firms who will kiss my ass to do this deal."

"Whoa, wait a minute. There's no way you'll be able to lay off this security to another investment house by November 30th. That's two days from now. We're ready to do it for five percent."

"Three percent."

"Not enough. Make it four and we have a deal."

"We'll go three-and-a-half, but that's it. And I expect closing to take place no later than tomorrow at 10 a.m."

"You told me the end of the month."

"Yeah. I also told you we'd discount the security by two percent. Take it or leave it." Lander held his breath as he sensed the tension coming over the line from Summers. *Probably calculating his commission*, he thought.

Summers apparently couldn't help himself as he whistled a breath through the phone. "We'll take it."

Lander recited the information Summers would need to wire transfer—after deducting the underwriting fee and the discount points—the two billion-plus sum to Sunrise Casualty Insurance.

"I'll need the CUSIP number," Summers said. Then he added, "By the way, all of our real estate transactions are handled through Fortis Title & Guaranty."

Lander's heart seemed to stop. He'd been told that the transaction had to close through a company named First Fidelity Philadelphia Title Guaranty Company. The way these deals usually closed was through a title company which held the money from the buyer in escrow, verified all the documents, ensured the title on the underlying properties, and then disbursed monies to the seller. He figured that one title company was as good as another, and was about to tell Summers that Fortis Title & Guaranty would be fine. But, at the last second, he remembered that Tennucci's man had made it clear that First Fidelity would close the transaction. He took a deep breath, steeled himself, and said, "You know, I really get tired of you guys pushing on every aspect of every deal. We have our own title company which has already issued title binders on all the properties. This will close through First Fidelity Philadelphia or it won't close at all."

"Jeez, you don't have to get your back up," Summers said. "I'm sure your title company will be just fine."

"Good. I'll provide the security's CUSIP number to the title company. They'll send it over with the closing package."

After he ended the call, Lander collapsed into a chair in the employee lounge and tried to calm his breathing. He'd been worried about the CUSIP number from the beginning. Every registered security in the United States had an identifying number that consisted of a combination of nine characters, both letters and numbers, which acted as a sort of DNA for the security, uniquely identifying the company or issuer and the type of security. There was no way he would be able to give Summers a legitimate CUSIP number. The minute Summers tried to verify the CUSIP code, he'd know the Sunrise Casualty Insurance security was bogus.

Lander had barely brought his breathing under control when his burner phone rang. "Lander," he answered.

"Did you have the conversation?"

"Yes. It went just as you said it would. They're on board for a three-and-a-half percent discount."

Bruno laughed. "Greedy bastards, aren't they?"

"Listen, I didn't want Summers to think I was too easy, so I told him they had to close by tomorrow morning at ten."

"Brilliant," Bruno said.

"I was afraid you might be angry."

"Angry? I'm ecstatic."

"He asked about the CUSIP code," Lander said.

"No surprise there. If the money is transferred at ten, everything will be fine."

"But what if they wait to transfer funds until after they receive and verify the CUSIP?"

"That's what they should do. But I don't think they will. Don't worry, Dave. It'll be fine. Anything else?"

"Yes. He wanted to use a title company in New York. I told him that was unacceptable, and gave him the First Fidelity Philadelphia name."

"Good job."

"I gotta tell you, I'm not familiar with that company."

"That's all right. Like I said, everything will be fine."

Wayne Summers felt as though he was floating as he took the elevator to the executive floor. He stopped at Richard Stone's receptionist's desk and was about to tell her he needed to see her boss, but the woman smiled and said, "He's expecting you. Go right in."

Summers felt a comfortable wave of warmth flow through him. This was surely a better reception than the one he'd received when he was last on this level. He tried to whistle as he marched down to Stone's office, but his mouth was too dry. He knocked on Stone's door and waited.

"Come in," boomed from behind the door.

Summers pushed the door open and approached Stone's desk.

"Do we have a deal?" Stone asked.

"Yes, sir," Summers said in a squeaky voice. He cleared his throat and tried again. "Yes, sir. Everything went exactly as you said it would. We got a three-and-a-half percent discount. The only change is that they want to close by 10 a.m. tomorrow."

"Why's that?"

"To save face, I guess. We got everything we demanded. I think my contact didn't want to look like he'd completely caved. Oh, and he wants to use their own title company."

Stone laughed. "No big deal. Any title company underwritten by one of the big insurers will do. And the closing date's not a problem. We already have commitments from investors for the entire two point four billion dollars' worth of bonds. Our money will only be tied up for twenty-four hours."

Stone stood and came around his desk. The dour expression he usually wore was now replaced with a Cheshire cat smile. He stuck out his hand. "Nice work, young man. You just made a name for yourself. In addition to our underwriting fee of twenty-four million, we'll pick up eighty-four million in discount points. A cool one hundred and eight million."

Bruno joined Louis Massarino in his home office and told him the deal was on and closing the next morning.

"Good," Massarino said. "When will the messenger deliver the documents?"

"Nine o'clock sharp."

Bruno and Jesse put the finishing touches on the bond documents, including the signatures of the Sunrise Casualty Insurance President and Chief Financial Officer. Each man's signature had been copied from letters to shareholders in the company's annual reports. The bonds themselves were also fabricated from bond documents they'd clipped from the Internet, including Sunrise's corporate logo and seal. When he was satisfied with document quality, Bruno placed the corporate officers' signatures on the back side of the bonds on the "Transferor" lines, but left the "Transferee" lines blank. Rosen, Rice & Stone could sign there whenever they chose to do so.

CHAPTER 24

Janet found Bruno in Massarino's basement apartment. He was bent over a stack of documents on a desk. "Can I interrupt?" she asked.

Bruno, wide-eyed, jerked upright. "Oh, sorry, I didn't hear you come in."

She waved a hand at the desk where Bruno sat and said, "What's all that?"

"Just…just some paperwork."

She nodded. "Just tell me it has something to do with making bad people pay for doing bad things."

"That I *can* tell you."

"Good."

"Was there something you needed?" Bruno asked.

"I changed my flight to California. I want to go to the hospital to see Hugo Rosales."

"I heard he's in bad shape. It's likely he won't even know you're there."

Janet felt her face go hot. She said, "Yeah, but his wife will. I just called her home and learned from one of their kids she's due at LaGuardia in an hour. I want to be there when she arrives at the hospital."

Bruno looked as though he was about to argue, but then nodded. "I'll ask Louis to have a car take you."

"That's really not necessary. I'm sure—"

"Let's not take any chances."

Detectives Sparks and Nicoletti, having talked with the Chief of Police of Redondo Beach, returned to the hospital where Victoria Nguyen was being held.

"The Brooklyn D.A. wants her released," Nicoletti said as they moved down the corridor to Nguyen's room.

Sparks made a growling sound. "We've got nothing on her."

"I can't believe her gloves weren't in the evidence locker."

Sparks shook her head. She had a sour expression. "Yeah. The paramedics must have stripped them off when they worked on her. Probably tossed them aside and some good citizen walked off with them."

"I'll bet, if we had a little more time, we could tie her in some way to this Bruno Pedace guy who the Redondo Beach Police Chief told us about."

"Maybe." She smiled. "I found it interesting that, according to the Redondo Beach Police Chief, her two detectives were here trying to find Pedace, who she claims has some connection to the Massarinos."

"The shooter could have been sent by Massarino. Nguyen could be totally innocent." After a second, he added, "But I don't think so."

"I've got the same feeling you have, but what choice do we have?"

In Nguyen's room, Sparks took her handcuff key from a jacket pocket and released the woman's left wrist. She said, "We're sorry about what you've had to go through, Ms. Nguyen. The Brooklyn Police Department extends its sympathies about your injuries and regrets having detained you while we investigated the incident last night."

Nguyen rubbed her wrist and moved her gaze from one detective to the other. Sparks thought she was about to rant at her, but Nguyen surprised her when she slowly rolled and sat on the side of the bed, faced her, and said, "I didn't like being handcuffed, but I understand. I hope the wounded officer will be okay."

Sparks shook Nguyen's hand and thanked her for understanding. "The officer is in critical condition and in a medically-induced coma. It's too soon to know if he'll recover. But it doesn't look good."

"I'm sorry to hear that. I'll say a prayer for him and his family."

"It can't hurt," Sparks said, as she looked past Nguyen at the scowl on her partner's face.

Nicoletti came around to Sparks's side of the bed. "Your car was taken to the impound lot here in Brooklyn. We'd be happy to have an officer drive you there. We've already arranged to have your vehicle released. Of course, there won't be any charge."

Nguyen slid down to the floor and spread her arms as though to balance herself. She groaned.

"You okay?" Sparks asked.

"Just a little dizzy. Probably shouldn't have gotten out of bed so quickly."

"You gotta be careful with head injuries."

Nguyen scoffed. "The doctor cleared me to leave as soon as it was okay with you guys. I'll be fine." Then she looked down at her hospital gown, and said, "I hope I don't have to leave wearing this."

Sparks laughed. "Your clothes were covered in blood. They were bagged and stored in Evidence. How about I find a set of surgical scrubs for you?"

Nguyen thanked her.

Sparks left the room while Nicoletti used his cell to call for a police cruiser to take Nguyen to the impound lot. When Sparks returned with scrubs, booties, and a blanket, she was accompanied by a nurse who confirmed that Nguyen had been approved for release. The two detectives left the room while Nguyen changed clothes. Then a medical assistant entered the room and took Nguyen out in a wheelchair.

"The police officer who will take you to the impound lot is waiting outside," Nicoletti told Nguyen as he and Sparks followed her and the medical assistant to the front door of the hospital.

Nguyen's blood seemed to rush through her veins at twice the normal speed. She was pissed off about having been handcuffed, but knew there was no point in showing anger. She also knew she was damned lucky. If that California detective weren't in a coma, he would have been able to identify her as the shooter. She thought, as the young female medical assistant pushed her outside, about praying for the second cop she'd shot. She'd pray the guy croaked before regaining consciousness. If he regained consciousness, he could ruin everything.

Outside, Nguyen wrapped the blanket around her shoulders as she stepped out of the wheelchair. An Arctic-like wind blasted her, almost ripping the blanket from her hands. Nicoletti escorted her to the right rear door of a waiting police cruiser, eased her inside, and closed the door.

Nguyen watched the two detectives walk away from the front of the hospital to an unmarked Crown Victoria parked at the top of the circular driveway. By the time she'd secured her seat belt, the two detectives had pulled away.

"You warm enough, ma'am?" the police officer asked.

"Yeah, I'm fine."

"I heard you had a real bad experience. I hope you don't hold what happened to you against all of us New Yorkers."

She was just about to tell the cop that she lived in the City and that he should keep his eyes on the road, when movement to her left, on the sidewalk near the hospital entrance, distracted her. She glanced at two people—a man and a woman—and felt a sudden rush. She turned in her seat as the cruiser left the driveway and watched Janet Jenkins and Bruno Pedace enter the hospital's front door and disappear inside. A large black SUV with a man behind the wheel was parked twenty feet from the entrance.

"How long will it take to get to the impound lot?" she asked.

"No more than ten minutes. Detective Nicoletti told me to stay with you and make sure there are no delays in getting your car."

Nguyen thought, *I'll be lucky to be back at the hospital in thirty minutes. Ten minutes to the lot, ten minutes to get my car, and ten minutes back to the hospital. If Pedace and Jenkins are at the hospital to check on the wounded detective, surely they won't stay less than half-an-hour.* Then she had a sinking feeling. *What if the California detective wakes up?*

In the hospital's main lobby, Bruno touched Janet's arm and said, "I'll wait here."

Janet took the elevator up to the ICU floor and spotted Carmela Rosales in the waiting area. She rushed over to her. They cried as they held onto one another for support. After almost a minute, Janet stepped back and motioned for Carmela to sit in a chair across from her.

"Any news?" Janet asked.

"They did surgery to stop the bleeding and repair the internal damage. They have him on IV antibiotics to prevent infection, and are watching him closely." She dabbed at tears with a tissue. "They say he's doing as well as can be expected."

"He's tough," Janet said. "If anyone can make it through, it's Hugo."

Janet reached across the small space between them and took Carmela's hands. They sat like that for a couple of minutes. Then Janet said, "Do you know what Hugo and John were doing out here?"

Carmela nodded. "Hugo complained about having to come here. He said it was all political BS. He told me the D.A. wanted to track down a man who could testify against some investment banker. He said the man they were looking for might be connected with organized crime." She shrugged and added, "I think there's a connection to the shooting you were involved with in Redondo Beach last spring." Carmela's mouth turned down as though she'd tasted something awful. "I think Hugo told me they were looking for a man named Pedace."

Janet felt her face go hot.

Carmela continued, "That bastard Barry Rath used John and Hugo to help with his re-election." Her voice got louder when she added, "And look what happened. Rath is responsible for John's death and Hugo's…" Carmela devolved into sobs.

"I can hang around to make sure you get your car," the Brooklyn policeman told Victoria Nguyen when he pulled into the impound lot.

Nguyen squinted at the young man. "That's not necessary. I'm sure you have many more important things to do than babysit me."

The cop blushed. "It would be my pleasure, Ms. Nguyen."

She could sense the cop was coming on to her. She gave him a hard look and said, "How about you just drop me off at the impound office. I'll be okay from there."

"I can do that," the officer said, sounding disappointed.

"By the way," she said, "do you know the name of the detective who was shot last night? The one from California."

The officer answered, "Rosales. Hugo Rosales."

"I hope he'll be okay."

The young man shrugged. "I have no idea. I hope so, too." He pulled up to the office at the front of the impound lot, dropped her off, and drove away.

Inside the office, Nguyen went to the counter and gave her name to a uniformed officer.

"Oh, yes, ma'am," the officer said as he took a file off a desk behind him and opened it on the counter. "I've been expecting you. We have your purse. It's in a locker. We inventoried everything in your vehicle. You'll find it all just as we found it."

A chill hit her spine and her stomach felt suddenly queasy. Her spare pistol—a Beretta—was under the trunk liner, along with two loaded clips.

The cop passed an inventory sheet to her. "Why don't you go over that while I get your purse from the property cage? Then I'll go get your car." He smiled. "Gotta check your ID before I can turn over your car."

By the time the officer had checked Nguyen's ID from her wallet and gone outside to retrieve her Audi, fifteen minutes had passed. She was getting more aggravated by the second, thinking she would miss Pedace at the hospital. Another five minutes went by before the officer returned.

"It's right outside," he said. "I left the motor running and turned the heater all the way up."

"Thanks," Nguyen barked. She signed a release form, scooted outside, jumped behind the wheel of her Audi, and roared away.

Detective Rhonda Sparks balled up the remains of her turkey sandwich in the paper wrapper and stuffed it in the empty paper cup her iced tea had come in. She grimaced at Nicoletti and said,

"Another executive lunch at Subway."

Nicoletti chuckled as he wiped crumbs from his tie and shirt. "You always take me to the best places."

Sparks frowned and said, "They've got the best banana peppers in the world at Subway. That's the reason I come here."

"You serious?"

She laughed and led the way outside. A cold but lazy, anemic breeze that carried the pungent aroma from the McDonald's restaurant on the other side of the street ruffled her short hair and caused her to button up her trench coat.

"You smell that?" Nicoletti said. "Grease in the wind. Nothing like it."

"If I didn't look out for you, you'd eat nothing but cheeseburgers and fries every day."

"Yeah, but what a way to go."

"What say we stop at the hospital and check on Rosales? You can get your blood pressure checked while we're there."

"Ha, ha. You know we could call. Besides, we just left there less than an hour ago."

Sparks compressed her lips and shrugged. "Yeah, we could and we did. But no one will give us information over the phone. And it's on the way back to the station."

"Whatever you want, partner," Nicoletti said.

Sparks laughed. "You know if my ex had learned that phrase we'd probably still be married."

"Nah, that guy was an idiot."

Victoria Nguyen made it to the hospital parking lot in eight minutes, parked in the lot as close to the building as possible, and popped the trunk release. At the rear of the vehicle, she lifted the trunk liner and blew out a loud breath when she saw the automatic and the loaded clips. She shrugged on a parka she kept in the trunk and swapped the surgical slippers for heavy wool socks and ankle-high boots. With the pistol now in the right-hand pocket of the parka, she slammed the trunk closed and moved toward the hospital entrance.

A guard at the front door eyeballed her, smiled, and touched his forehead in a half-assed salute. She guessed the surgical scrubs she wore under her open parka sent the message that she legitimately belonged in the building. Around a corner from the front lobby, she came to an information desk and asked, "Can you give me the number of Hugo Rosales's room?"

CHAPTER 25

The drive from the Subway shop to the hospital took Sparks and Nicoletti ten minutes. The breeze had grown into a gale. The cold blasts caused them to hustle to the front entrance from the visitors' parking lot. As they approached the elevator doors, one sprang open. Inside the car, Nicoletti pressed the button for the ICU.

"You realize this is a waste of time," he said.

"Yeah, probably. But that's what most detective work is anyway. Humor me."

Nicoletti scowled for a couple seconds, then smiled. "No wonder you're no longer married."

"Right," Sparks said. "My divorce was all about me being a pain in the ass, but had nothing to do with my husband sleeping with his secretary."

The door opened on the sixth floor before Nicoletti could respond. As they exited the car, he pointed to the right at a men's room sign. "I need to make a pit stop," he said.

Sparks waved an "Okay" and went left. Twenty-five yards down the hall, she turned right toward the ICU. Except for the interminable beeping of monitors, a deathly quiet hung over the unit. The ICU suite was at the end of the hall—fifteen yards away. A nurses' station was several steps ahead on the right, slightly recessed from the hallway. As Sparks approached the station, a male voice shouted, "What are you doing?" shattering the quiet. Sparks turned into the recessed area just when a metal tray flew past her head and crashed into the glass wall of one of the ICU rooms opposite the nurses' station.

Sparks placed a hand on the service revolver in her hip holster as she tried to make sense of the situation.

A woman with long black hair, dressed in a parka and what appeared to be hospital scrubs, pistol in hand, leaned over the counter. Not believing she had time to pull out and fire her own weapon before the woman found her target, Sparks charged and body-slammed the woman against the counter. The woman gasped, staggered momentarily, and then righted herself. She turned, her gun hand sweeping toward Sparks, who chopped down with her fisted hands on the woman's wrist. The pistol fired, sending shockwaves of sound reverberating off the glass walls. Sparks heard breaking glass as she hit the woman in the side of her face with a solid punch, which backed her up. Then she leaped forward, grabbed the woman's weapon in two hands, and ripped it away. She swung it and connected with the woman's head, dropping her to the floor as though her bones had turned to sawdust. A wide, bloody gash showed on her forehead.

Sparks pocketed the pistol, rolled the woman onto her stomach, and cuffed her wrists. Then she leaned over the counter and saw a man in a white smock and pants huddled behind it.

"You okay?" Sparks asked.

"Jeez," he blurted as he stood. "Yeah, I'm okay, thanks to you. She wanted to know which room Hugo Rosales is in. When I asked her if she was a family member, she went ballistic."

Sparks backed away just as she heard running footsteps behind her. She pulled out her revolver as she whipped around, but quickly lowered her weapon when she saw Vince Nicoletti rush toward her.

"Jesus, Mary, and Joseph," Nicoletti shouted. "What the hell happened?"

She pointed at the woman on the floor. "You recognize her?"

Nicoletti leaned to the side and stared at the unconscious woman. "Victoria Nguyen. What the hell is she doing here?"

At that moment, two women turned the corner up the hall, moved toward the detectives, but then abruptly stopped.

"On my God," one of them yelled, her voice high-pitched, beyond anxious.

Sparks moved in front of Nicoletti, removed her cred pack from a jacket pocket, and held her badge high.

"We're detectives with the Brooklyn P.D.," Sparks said. "Who are you?"

The woman who'd spoken stepped forward. "I'm Carmela Rosales." She pointed at one of the ICU rooms. "That's my husband in there. What happened?"

Sparks said, "My best guess is that woman over there was trying to get to your husband. Why, I don't know."

Carmela turned to the woman with her. "This is my friend, Janet Jenkins."

Sparks said, "Maybe you should both come down to the station. We'll need to get statements. Maybe you can shed light on what went on here." Sparks handed Carmela a card.

"We'll meet you there," Carmela said.

"Make it an hour from now," Sparks said. "We'll have to process our prisoner."

Detective Nicoletti watched the male nurse patch up the wound on Victoria Nguyen's forehead. "I'm no doctor, but won't that thing need stitches?"

"Absolutely," the nurse said. "But if we wait a while, the scar will be larger and more visible."

Nicoletti smiled. "You must be Italian."

"Nope. I'm Lithuanian. Italians aren't the only ones who are into revenge."

The lobby and the circular drive in front of the hospital entrance had turned into a circus. Police vehicles with flashing lights had taken over the area outside, while uniformed cops guarded the entrance, the elevator doors, and the entrances to stairwells. On her way through the lobby, Janet, who had left Carmela Rosales on the ICU floor, spotted Bruno standing outside the gift shop. She waved at him to follow her, and quickly left the building.

"Do you know what's going on?" Bruno asked, when he caught

up to her. "The police checked my ID and searched me for weapons. It's like a war zone."

"Wait until we're in the car."

Back in the SUV, as Massarino's man, Silvio, drove them away, Janet told Bruno what had happened.

Bruno cleared his throat. "I have to believe the woman they arrested was hired to kill me. Detectives Andrews and Rosales were in the wrong place at the wrong time."

Janet felt her temperature rise. "And she came to the hospital to kill Hugo because he might have seen her face last night."

Bruno nodded. "Probably right."

"Carmela Rosales gave my name to two detectives in the hospital," Janet said. "They want us to come to the police station to make statements. When I don't show up, they'll surely check my name and find information regarding Giovanni Casale and Charles Forsythe's deaths."

Bruno nodded. "And then they'll tie me in, as well."

Janet said, "You can't go on hiding for the rest of your life."

"I know, Janet. I think I'll be able to come out of the dark pretty soon…if all goes as planned."

"You want to tell me about it?"

Bruno smiled at her. "Not a chance. The less you know, the better off you are."

DAY 9

CHAPTER 26

Bobby Tennucci carried three boxes of documents into a messenger service office in Brooklyn at 8 a.m. He filled out a transmittal slip, paid cash for the delivery charge, and handed the desk clerk four one-hundred-dollar bills.

"Two of the hundreds are for you and the others are for your delivery guy. I want these boxes delivered at 9 a.m. sharp. You got that?"

The clerk said, "Yes, sir. They'll be the first off the truck."

Tennucci gave the man a piercing look. "If they're dropped off late, I'll be back to have a conversation with you."

The man visibly swallowed. "You can depend on us, sir."

"Oh, I'm counting on it."

"I hope this works," Massarino said.

Bruno exhaled a nervous little laugh and nodded.

"What about the...what did you call them? You know, the codes."

"CUSIP," Bruno said. "Yeah. If they check the codes I put on the securities before they wire the funds, we're screwed." He closed his eyes and thought, *and if someone calls Sunrise and asks for Joseph Campbell with a last-minute question, we're also screwed.*

Massarino collapsed in the roller chair beside Bruno and rubbed his hands together as though they were cold.

Bruno breathed out a long sigh.

Wayne Summers hovered in the Rosen firm's lobby like an expectant father outside a delivery room. The receptionist had told him three times that she would call him the second the documents from Sunrise Casualty Insurance arrived. But he preferred to wait in the lobby. At 9 a.m., a messenger came inside pushing a hand truck stacked with three boxes. Summers rushed over, looked at the label on the top box, signed for the delivery, lifted the box, and shouted at the guard at the front door to grab the remaining two. With the guard in tow, Summers fast-walked to an elevator and rode a car up to the partners' floor. They walked to the conference room and placed the boxes on the table. After he dismissed the guard, Summers called his secretary on the intercom.

"Barbara, the documents are here."

Summers sliced open the boxes and stacked the contents on the table, organized by property. From the third box, he removed the securities documents that were collateralized by the properties. When his secretary arrived, he ordered her to check the property docs against the list they'd prepared yesterday. "Make sure everything's in order."

Checklist in hand, Barbara moved to the other side of the table and took an inventory of the documents. By 9:20 a.m., she'd verified that all twenty-four property files were there.

"You want me to match the property IDs against the information on the securities?" Barbara asked.

"Yes, please," Summers said.

It was 9:58 when she finished. She had just announced that everything was in order when Richard Stone entered, followed by Karl Rice and Sy Rosen.

"Cutting it close," Stone said.

Summers exhaled loudly as he glanced at the wall clock.

"Everything okay?" Rosen asked.

"Yes, sir," Summers answered. "We just need to verify the CUSIP numbers and then we can order the title company to wire funds."

Stone glanced at the clock. "That'll take too long. It's already ten. You can authenticate the numbers after the wire goes out. We don't want to screw up this transaction."

"But—"

Stone shot a grim smile at Summers. "Don't worry, Wayne. Sunrise Insurance is as solid as they come. I'm sure everything's in order. Besides, we already received the title binders from the title company. We know the property titles are correct and that the loans on each are exactly as Sunrise stated they are."

"That's not usual procedure, sir," Summers said. "It won't take too long to verify the codes."

Rosen interjected, "We blow this deal because we're late transferring funds and I'll see that you don't get another job on Wall Street."

Summers felt his temperature rise and his heartbeat accelerate. He visualized his bonus flying away. "Yes, sir."

Rosen slapped two documents on the corner of the table. "Here are the wire transfer authorizations. Better get them transmitted right away."

Wayne Summers looked over the shoulder of the clerk processing the wire transfer instructions. He'd already verified that the seven hundred million from the company's bank line had been deposited into the company's bank account, as had one billion dollars from Rosen, Rice & Stone client trust accounts and five hundred ninety-two million from the company's senior partners' capital accounts. *Two billion, two hundred ninety-two million dollars, net of fees and discount points. Big bucks*, he thought. But he knew the firm already had investors lined up to purchase the securities. He mentally went through the sequence of events that would follow. *We'll close with the investors tomorrow, pay off the bank line, replenish client trust accounts, and restore the money into the partners' accounts. It will only cost the firm one day's worth of interest on the bank line and the client trust accounts.*

Summers's body trembled with excitement. *Once the line of credit is paid off and the trust funds repaid, the final part of the deal will be complete, and my bonus will have been earned. Almost eleven million dollars.* Not for the first time did he think about taking the bonus, paying his taxes, and moving back to his hometown of Las

Cruces, New Mexico. *I'll be a hotshot in Las Cruces with that kind of money.*

The wire instructions to the company's bank went out at 10:05, a few minutes past the time Joseph Campbell had demanded. Summers held his breath, worried for a moment that Campbell might call and cancel the deal. He held his breath as the wire clerk sent closing instructions to the title company. Then Summers returned to the partners' floor with hard copies of the wire transmittals.

Bruno Pedace and Louis Massarino sat side-by-side in roller chairs, their eyes fixed on the computer screen on the desk in front of them. Bruno's fingers twitched as they hovered over the keyboard. Seconds ticked by and turned into minutes. It was now 10:07 a.m.

"What the hell's going on, Bruno? I thought everything would be done by ten."

Bruno felt his stomach cramp. He swallowed hard and looked at Massarino. "I'm sure the instructions went through. I expect them any second now."

Massarino pushed his chair back, stood, and paced.

Eyes still glued to the screen, Bruno tried to be calm, but he was just about to pace along with Massarino when the computer chimed and a message from the Mercantile Savings Bank of Brooklyn, addressed to *Wire Department, First Fidelity Philadelphia Guaranty Company*, popped up.

Massarino rushed over behind Bruno, stared at the screen for a few seconds, pointed, and said, "What the hell is that?"

"That, my friend," Bruno said, "is the beginning of the end for Rosen, Rice & Stone." He read the message aloud: "*$2,292,000,000 transferred from Rosen, Rice & Stone Investment Bankers account #715-690-4503 at Mercantile Savings Bank of Brooklyn to First Fidelity Philadelphia Guaranty Company account #870-215-8999 at Roxborough Bank & Trust.*"

"How will you get the funds out of the title company's bank account?"

Bruno's fingers fairly danced over the keyboard as he said, "That won't be a problem, Louis. *I'm* the First Fidelity Philadelphia

Guaranty Company. *I* opened the account at the Roxborough Bank & Trust."

Bruno then sent wire instructions to the Roxborough Bank & Trust: *Transfer $592,000,000 to Forsythe Capital account # A-45979211 at Antigua Victoria Bank.* After providing the bank's code number, he hit SEND.

"It's done," Bruno announced.

"Sonofabitch," Massarino exclaimed. "Hot damn. What will you do with the money?"

Bruno braced his head in his hands, elbows on the desk. He suddenly felt exhausted. Just wanted to go to bed and sleep for days. "Louis, based on the financial information I found on the Internet, there's no way the Rosen firm could have come up with the entire two point two plus billion out of their own reserves. They would have had to borrow all but about six hundred million. I'll return whatever they borrowed. I'll keep whatever came out of the partners' capital accounts. But I have to transfer the money without leaving a trail. Remember, even though the Rosen firm is a corrupt organization, *I* just committed several kinds of fraud. The company may go down, but so will I if the Feds sniff out my involvement." He took a calming breath, shook his head, and then slowly stood.

"But it's pretty much over?"

"Almost."

Massarino placed a hand on Bruno's shoulder. "Good job."

"Rosen and his buddies are going down, Louis. I hope that gives you some satisfaction."

Massarino nodded. "Yeah, Bruno. I'm feeling pretty good about that." He slapped Bruno on the back and left the basement.

Two floors up, Massarino called Bobby Tennucci and told him he wanted to meet.

"I can be there in twenty minutes, boss."

"Better we meet in the park by Frankie's place. Thirty minutes."

CHAPTER 27

"So, why don't you clear up my confusion?" Detective Rhonda Sparks said. "You were in the hospital ICU because…?"

Victoria Nguyen stared back with a dead-eyed, blank expression across the interrogation room table.

Sparks pointed at the bandage on Nguyen's forehead. "You attacked the nurse there because he was rude?"

The same blank stare.

"Do you always pull a pistol and shoot at people who are rude to you?"

Nguyen threw her head back, tossing her long black hair off her left shoulder. Her handcuffs rattled. When her gaze reconnected with Sparks's, the detective involuntarily shuddered. The coldness she saw in the woman's eyes momentarily unsettled her.

"What's your game here, Ms. Nguyen? Why were you on the street outside that pizza joint the other night? Why did you shoot Detectives Rosales and Andrews?"

Sparks glared at Nguyen and waited a few seconds. When there was no response, she said, "Someone paid you to kill the detectives; isn't that right? Give me the name of your employer and I'll talk to the D.A. Maybe she'll offer you a deal."

Still no response.

Sparks took a guess and said, "We know you went to the hospital to murder Detective Rosales because he was the only living witness to you killing Detective Andrews."

Nguyen's frozen mask finally cracked. She grinned at Sparks, but still didn't speak.

Sparks left the room and stood next to Vince Nicoletti who stared into the one-way window. "What do you think of the ice princess?"

While he continued to stare at Nguyen, Nicoletti pinched his lips and said, "Did you see her reaction when you mentioned her coming to the hospital to kill Rosales?"

Sparks grunted a reply.

"That little grin told me she thinks she's got us fooled."

"What do you mean?"

"Maybe she wasn't at the hospital to murder Rosales. Or, maybe she was there to kill him *and* someone else." He shook his head in frustration. He grimaced at Sparks. "I don't know, partner. I just got this feeling we're missing something."

Sparks turned as though she was about to return to the interrogation room, but she pirouetted back to face Nicoletti. "You know Carmela Rosales's friend, Janet Jenkins, didn't come to the station with her."

Nicoletti scrunched up his face. "I was about to mention that. That's kind of strange. I mean, it seemed like she wanted to cooperate."

"I'll start again on Nguyen. Why don't you meet with Mrs. Rosales? And, on a lark, maybe you should run the friend, Janet Jenkins, through the system."

Janet felt a deep unease as she thought about what Bruno had gotten into. She badly wanted to question him about his activities, but he hadn't been receptive when she'd broached the subject before. She felt confined and impotent. *I need to get out of here*, she told herself. Her boss, Frank Mitchell, had called "to check in." But she knew what he really wanted to know was when she would return to work.

She went to the closet, removed her suitcase, and tossed it on the bed. "To hell with it," she muttered.

"David Lander."

"Dave, it's Bobby's friend," Bruno said.

"Yeah, I recognized your voice. What's the problem?"

"Calm down, Dave. It's almost over."

"I'm never placing another bet."

"I'm glad to hear that, Dave. Don't forget the treatment program I promised to pay for. You tell me where and when you want to go and I'll wire the fee to them."

"I sure appreciate that. But you said it's *almost* over. What do I have to do now?"

"It's simple. You're going to be a hero at Sunrise Casualty Insurance."

The creation of an electronic presence for First Fidelity Philadelphia Guaranty Company had been relatively simple and had taken Jesse Falco a mere four hours. But the hack into Rosen, Rice & Stone's computer system had taken Falco almost twenty-four hours. When he'd finally broken through the company's firewall, he jumped to his feet and whooped like a ball player who'd just hit a game-winning home run. "I'm in," he'd shouted.

Falco called Bruno Pedace.

"Yeah?"

"It's Jesse. You told me to call when I finished."

Bruno coughed a tired laugh. "Great work, Jesse. You're amazing."

Falco breathlessly asked, "What do I do now?"

"I'll messenger a flash drive to you at your shop. Load the files on it into the company's server."

The kid said with undisguised exuberance, "I can do that."

"There won't be any footprint?"

"Of course not."

"Never a doubt in my mind, Jesse."

Bruno made a call at 4:30 p.m. on a burner phone to the investment department of Eastern Teachers Retirement Fund, one of Rosen, Rice & Stone's largest institutional investors. He guessed that ETRF would have been one of the first organizations the Rosen firm called to invest in the real estate deal.

"Bess Katz, Investment Department."

"Ms. Katz, is Eastern Teachers about to invest in a CMBS underwritten by Rosen, Rice & Stone?"

"Who is this?"

"You don't need my name. But I warn you that if you don't listen to me, your organization will be very sorry."

"Are you threatening me?"

"Quite the opposite, Ms. Katz. I'm trying to save you a huge amount of embarrassment."

"You've got one minute and then I'm hanging up."

"That's more than enough time," Bruno said. "Assuming you're participating in the syndication I referred to, you're about to be scammed. The entire thing is smoke and mirrors. The mortgage loans in the deal aren't owned by Sunrise Casualty Insurance Company. Sunrise has no idea their name is being associated with a bogus transaction. It's unaware that Rosen, Rice & Stone has bundled fictitious loans into a security collateralized by real estate supposedly securing Sunrise loans."

"That's impossible," Katz said. "The CUSIP system would never—"

"Have you checked the CUSIP registry?"

"Well, not yet. We wouldn't wire funds until we had."

"Do yourself a favor. Call the real estate investment department at Sunrise and ask them if they're divesting of any of their commercial mortgage loans."

Bruno cut off the call and waited.

David Lander hadn't been able to sit down for the past fifteen minutes. He compulsively checked his iPhone clock. Bobby Tennucci's friend had told him he should receive a call shortly after 4:30. From whom and about what, he had no idea.

When his desk phone rang at 4:48, Lander dropped into his desk chair so hard that the chair rolled back against the wall with a loud *thud*. He rolled forward, picked up the receiver, and, in too loud a voice, said, "David Lander."

"Mr. Lander, this is Bess Katz at Eastern Teachers Retirement Fund. I wonder if you could answer a question for me."

At 5:00 p.m., Bruno called Lander and asked, "Did you receive a call?"

"You bet. And I can tell you there's one very angry woman over at Eastern Teachers Retirement Fund."

"Well done, Dave. I'll be in touch next week. I hope you'll have the name of the counseling center by then."

As he terminated the call, movement to his left caused him to jerk in that direction.

"Sorry to disturb you, Bruno," Janet said. "I want to say goodbye before I leave."

"What! You're leaving?"

Janet squinted at Bruno. "I've been here long enough. And now that the Nguyen woman has been arrested, there's no reason for me to hide out any longer."

Bruno stepped closer to her. "Whoever hired Nguyen can hire another killer. I don't think you're safe just yet."

She waved her hands in a dismissive manner. "I'm just a hanger-on here. Besides, I need to get back to work."

"Give it another day, Janet. Please."

Janet stiffened her back and jabbed a hand at Bruno. "I've had enough of this, Bruno. I think I'm in more danger here than I was in California. I know you're into something that's more than likely dangerous, probably illegal. But I have no idea what it is, since you refuse to tell me. I—"

"It's for your own safety. That's why—"

"Let me finish. I lied to the police about going to their station to meet with them. I figure it's only a matter of a day or two before those detectives try to find me. Hell, they've probably already asked Carmela Rosales about me. I'm getting out of here."

"Would it help if I told you what's going on?"

She spread her arms but didn't immediately respond. After a few seconds, she said, "At this point, I'm not sure I want to know."

"One day, Janet. That's all I ask. Wait until tomorrow morning."

"Not if I can catch a flight out tonight." She spun around and left the basement.

Perhaps it was stress, or fatigue, or worry about Janet leaving, or all those things that made Bruno go weak. He sagged as though boneless into a nearby chair. The clock on the desk showed it was 5:59 p.m. He tiredly reached for the television remote on the side of the desk and clicked the POWER button. When the screen came to life, he turned to a local news channel. At 6:00, the lead-in music and graphics for the news show came up; a flashy blonde in a black dress welcomed the audience and, in a dramatic voice, announced, "We have breaking news that a New York-based investment house may have attempted to defraud a group of institutional investors in the amount of billions of dollars." She frowned and added, "Yes, you heard me correctly. I said *billions*. We're looking into the allegations and will have more to report at ten."

Bruno felt newly energized. It was almost done.

Then one of his burner phones rang. He saw Jesse Falco's number on the screen.

"What's up, Jesse?"

"The job's done."

"Good. Now I want you to destroy the flash drive and *BleachBit* any code that might remain on all devices you used."

Louis Massarino returned to his home at 6:05 p.m. after meeting with Bobby Tennucci. He hugged and kissed his wife, Rosa, and told her, "I'll join you for dinner in an hour, but first I need to talk with Bruno."

"You okay?" Rosa asked.

"Getting there, *mia cara*."

"I hope your troubles over Carlo's death will soon be behind you."

He kissed her again. "Soon. Very soon."

CHAPTER 28

Sy Rosen usually left his office early on Fridays. But on this Friday, he was too wired to make the ride to his Long Island estate and then put up with his wife's grousing about the shitty service at the country club or their daughter-in-law's bitchy mother. He was both concerned and exhilarated. He hadn't heard from Victoria Nguyen for a couple days. That worried him greatly. But not enough to suppress his excitement over the closing of the real estate mortgage deal with Sunrise Casualty Insurance. All in all, this was a night for celebration. It had been a long time since he'd spent a night with Sylvie. He felt a sudden flush as he thought about how the young woman made him feel. *It'll be worth every penny of her two-thousand-dollar fee*, he thought.

He checked his Rolex and smiled: 6:15. Rosen put away the papers on his desk and moved toward his private bathroom. He brushed his teeth and slapped on a little cologne. As he moved back toward his desk, his office door flew open.

"What the hell?" he blurted.

Richard Stone, trailed by Wayne Summers, burst in. The look on Stone's face caused Rosen's stomach to flip. "Jesus, Richard, you look like the Grim Reaper. What's wrong?"

"We have a problem."

Rosen scoffed. "Jeez, that much I already figured out. Someone screw up a customer order?"

Stone shuffled to a chair and collapsed into it. Summers remained halfway between the office door and Rosen's desk, his eyes wide and his skin grayish.

"Come on, spill it," Rosen growled. "What is it?"

Stone opened his mouth, but nothing came out. He gaped like a beached fish.

Rosen turned toward Summers, pointed at the chair next to Stone, and barked, "Sit."

After he sat, Summers cleared his throat, sounding like a toad with emphysema. He coughed, then said, "I received a call from a guy at Sunrise Insurance about our deal. He—"

"Joseph Campbell?" Rosen asked.

"What?"

"Joseph Campbell. The guy at Sunrise who you worked with on the deal."

Summers shook his head as though he was having an epileptic fit. He made the toad sound again and then, in a raspy voice, said, "No, it was another man named David Lander."

"What do you mean, 'another man'?" Rosen asked as he moved his gaze onto Stone, who'd slumped almost prone in his chair. "Who's this guy, Lander?"

His head bent, Summers replied, "My usual contact in the company's real estate investment department." Summers gulped and added, "Anyway, Lander called me a few minutes ago and wanted to know about the deal. I told him I'd been working with Joseph Campbell. He...he told me there was no one named Joseph Campbell at Sunrise." Summers whimpered. "Lander said he got a call from one of our investors in the deal wanting to verify they were selling part of their commercial real estate mortgage portfolio. When he told her he didn't know what she was talking about, she went ballistic."

Rosen felt a stabbing pain in his chest. He didn't know what the hell was going on, but he knew that whatever it was, it was very, very bad. In fact, it was god-awful. He stared at Summers as though he were something sub-human. He turned back to Stone and wondered if the man was having a stroke. His mind whirled as he thought about what to ask next when his desk phone rang. The screen on the console read: *Helen James, The Wall Street Journal.* He snatched the receiver from its cradle and, with forced calm, said, "Hey, Helen, working late?"

"Glad I caught you, Sy. I'm following up on a rumor that you guys are involved in a fraudulent transaction involving billions of dollars. You wanna clarify the rumor?"

Rosen blurted a small laugh. "What the heck are you talking about, Helen? Rosen, Rice & Stone is one of the most reputable firms on the Street. We would never be involved in any kind of tainted transaction."

"That isn't going to fly, Sy. I've had three calls in the last thirty minutes from investors who claim you attempted to sell them a phony mortgage-backed security deal. I just got off the phone with an officer at Sunrise Casualty Insurance who refused to comment beyond telling me that Sunrise has never sold a real estate-backed loan security before its maturity. What's going on, Sy?"

"I have absolutely no idea what you're talking about."

"Are you telling me that you aren't in a transaction with Sunrise?"

When Rosen didn't respond, James said, "One of the people who called me said the CUSIP code on the security you created is fictitious."

A cold hand reached inside Rosen and gripped his chest. He jerked open a desk drawer and pulled out a bottle of antacid. "Helen," he said, "I already told you I don't know what you're talking about. How 'bout I get back to you after I check into it?"

"I'll be here at my desk, Sy."

Rosen hung up and looked at Stone and Summers. "What the fuck have you two done?"

"I told you I wanted to check the CUSIP codes but—"

Rosen's icy stare cut Summers off.

Sergeant Michael Hallinan had been an honest cop in Brooklyn for eighteen years. That changed four years ago when his wife was diagnosed with cancer and her treatments were determined to be experimental and not covered by insurance. The medical bills had almost ruined them and they were in the process of having to sell their house when Hallinan was approached by a neighbor, Bobby

Tennucci, who wanted information about a police investigation. Tennucci had offered him twenty thousand dollars.

Hallinan rationalized the transaction by telling himself it was only information. It wasn't as if he was taking drug money or stealing something. And the money he'd received from Tennucci for the past four years for other information had saved his wife's life and allowed them to keep their home. He now knew the neighbor worked for the Massarino Family...and couldn't have cared less. When Hallinan heard that Detectives Sparks and Nicoletti had brought in a Vietnamese woman suspected of being a hired killer, he, along with several other cops, strolled into the interrogation area to get a glimpse of her through the one way glass. After all, female assassins were a rare breed. It wasn't until hours later that Hallinan heard a rumor that the woman had finally struck a deal with the D.A. In return for disclosing the identity of her employer and her targets, she would be given a reduced sentence. The rumor also included information about the woman's client and her intended target. The names Sy Rosen and Janet Jenkins meant nothing to Hallinan, but the name Bruno Pedace rang all kinds of bells in the cop's memory bank.

Hallinan recalled Bruno Pedace's name coming up about a decade ago concerning some Wall Street scandal. The Pedace name was not an easy one to forget. He also recalled news reports about Pedace being from Brooklyn and going to school with one of the Massarinos. *Maybe the Massarino Family would like to know about this assassin*, Hallinan thought. He called Tennucci at 9:16 p.m., passed on the information, and then went back to work.

Bobby Tennucci called his boss as soon as he got off the phone with Hallinan.

"Very interesting," Massarino said. "Thanks, Bobby. Make sure the Irish cop is properly thanked."

"Of course, boss. I assume you still want me to go forward."

"Oh yeah, Bobby. Even more so now."

"You certain about the news media?"

"It's already begun, Bobby."

"You know, these guys won't do well in prison. Someone will

265

punk them out five minutes after they hit a cellblock."

"Yeah, but they'll be alive. That's a luxury my brother Carlo no longer has."

Massarino went down to the basement apartment and found Bruno asleep in a chair, an empty beer bottle in his hand, the television on. He padded over, carefully picked up the television remote, and muted the sound. Bruno startled awake.

"Sorry, Bruno," Massarino said. "I didn't mean to wake you."

Bruno placed the empty bottle on the table next to him and rubbed his face. He glanced at a wall clock and said, "I'm glad you did. I want to watch the late news."

Massarino asked, "Your old partners go broke, lose everything, maybe go to jail; that'll be enough for you?"

"It'll have to be, Louis. What else can I do?"

Massarino nodded. "I understand." He sat in a chair and looked at the clock. "Almost time for the news." He turned the sound back up on the television. The end of a sitcom segued to a local news channel. A blow-dried news anchor with supernaturally-white teeth and a spray-on tan welcomed the audience and then immediately announced that New York State and Federal authorities were investigating possible fraudulent securities transactions at the Wall Street firm of Rosen, Rice & Stone Investments. The anchor went on to state that very little information was available, but the station had learned that a scheme involving forged documents and billions of dollars of loans on commercial real estate properties across the United States were involved. He finished the story with, "All attempts to contact the company have been unsuccessful."

"What'll happen next?" Massarino asked.

"Investigators from the U.S. Attorney's office, the SEC, the FBI, and the State of New York will probably storm the company's offices and take control of all their files and computers. They may have already done that, despite it being Friday night. The investigators will try to find a whistleblower among the partner ranks who'll rat out the others about every petty indiscretion that might ever have occurred."

"You certain there's no way the Feds can track anything back to you?"

"Absolutely. Your nephew, Jesse, is a genius."

"What will you do now?"

"I'll call the SEC and tell them how the firm set me up a decade ago."

"What about the documents you took?"

"They'll just make my case. I'll turn them over to the investigators." Bruno chuckled. "With the three partners locked up, I'll feel safe again."

"So, you do that; then what?"

"I'm not sure."

Massarino frowned. "Are you really that oblivious?"

"Oblivious? About what?"

"That lady upstairs is nuts about you. Don't you have any feelings for her?"

"Sure. She's a good…friend. But nuts about me? What are you talking about?"

Massarino laughed. "You're not just oblivious; you're obtuse. She thinks you've kept what you've been doing here from her because you don't trust her."

"That's crazy. I've kept her out of it to protect—"

Massarino held up his hands. "I know that, Bruno. But *she* doesn't because *she* has no clue how you feel about her. She told me she wants to go back to California. She would have been gone if there'd been a flight out tonight at a reasonable hour." Massarino smiled. "You're a fool if you let that gal leave here not knowing your feelings."

"Until Rosen, Rice, and Stone are behind bars, there's still a risk. She doesn't need to be—"

Massarino stood and waved a hand at Bruno. "You're hopeless," he said as he went to the staircase.

After thinking about what Louis had said, Bruno mounted the stairs from the basement to the second floor. He felt conflicted. He wanted to see Janet, talk with her, but he knew that he couldn't tell her what he'd done. What he still planned to do. He tiptoed down the hall and clenched his jaw when the wood floor creaked underfoot. Still ten feet from her room, he saw the door was open. After taking in a large breath and letting it out slowly, he stepped to the doorway and knocked on the doorframe.

Her back to the door, Janet turned and shot Bruno a sour look.

"What's up?" she asked, her tone impatient with a tint of anger.

Bruno took a hesitant half-step into the room, then stopped and backed up. He felt his face go hot as he stammered, "I-I thought I'd…."

Janet turned around and placed clothing into an open suitcase on the bed.

"Can I come in?" Bruno asked.

"I can hear you from there."

"Listen, Janet, I want to apologize for keeping you in the dark, and for getting you involved in all of this. I mean…you could have been killed by that gang in California and by that Nguyen woman here in New York. It seems to me I've done nothing but put you in jeopardy since you intervened with those two teenaged thugs in that alley in Redondo Beach."

Janet whipped around, her hands full of clothes, and glared. "People don't complain when their friends need them. They step up and do whatever's necessary."

Bruno opened his mouth as though to respond, but she held up a handful of blouses to stop him. She momentarily closed her eyes and slowly shook her head. She turned back to the bed and dropped the clothes into the suitcase. When she turned again, there were tears in her eyes.

Bruno took a step into the room and then froze, not knowing what to do next.

"I think you've been hiding out too long, Bruno. You've been a recluse for so many years that you've lost the ability to connect with people. Or maybe you were always that way. You have a generous nature, but you have no clue when it comes to relationships and sharing your feelings." She sighed and then moved toward him. She planted a hand in the middle of his chest and lightly pushed him backward, out into the hall. "I hope whatever you're doing brings you peace and happiness, Bruno." With that, she closed the door.

Sy Rosen had told Richard Stone and Wayne Summers to go home and to neither answer their phones nor respond to email or text messages. "I'll take care of this," he assured them. Then he called the firm's five junior partners and told them the same things he'd told Stone and Summers. When those calls had been made, he called Wallace Becker, his personal attorney, at his Central Park West condominium and told him he needed to see him right away.

"It's late, Sy. Can't we do this on Monday?"

"Wallace, you've got thirty minutes to be here before I fire you and hire another lawyer who will kiss my ass for the millions I spend in legal fees every year."

It was fifteen minutes shy of midnight when Rosen and Becker finalized a strategy for dealing with the fallout they anticipated was about to rain down on Rosen, Rice & Stone. Two minutes later, Rosen received a call on his cell phone from the SEC. He shuddered. *This is worse than I thought if the SEC is on this matter late on a Friday.*

"I've been expecting your call," Rosen said, as Becker smiled and nodded at him from the other side of the desk. "Of course, we will fully cooperate with any investigation." Rosen listened for a few seconds and then said, "Yes, I'm in my office right now. I'll meet you at the front door. One hour."

"Okay," the lawyer said. "I'm going to take a walk while you clean up things."

At first, Rosen was confused by his lawyer's statement, but then he realized that Becker was giving him time to delete files and correspondence relating to the Sunrise deal.

"What's the point of getting rid of the computers? Whatever's on them will be on the servers."

"That's true. But by the time they look at the servers, you'll have a deal with the Feds."

"Aah," Rosen said.

DAY 10

CHAPTER 29

Louis Massarino and Bobby Tennucci sat in the backseat of Massarino's Town Car. Silvio Caniglia was behind the wheel. The radio volume was cranked up high enough to overwhelm any listening device that might be on the vehicle. Caniglia swept the Town Car daily with a bug, phone tap, GPS and spy-cam detector, but Massarino was paranoid about his privacy.

"It's almost three o'clock," Massarino said. "Is everything set?"

"Yeah, boss," Tennucci said. "At least for two of them."

Massarino kept his gaze straight ahead, on the back of Caniglia's head. "What's the problem?"

"The SEC's all over Rosen's building. They've been there with Rosen since around midnight."

"You talk to our SEC guy?"

"Cyril Kalinov? You bet. Rosen and his lawyer have agreed to turn over everything they've got to the Feds in return for blanket immunity."

"So, Rosen'll work a deal that leaves his partners holding the bag."

"That's what Kalinov told me."

"What's Kalinov say will happen to the firm?"

"It's going down. They borrowed a ton of money from their bank and took a billion dollars from client trust accounts. It's likely the bank will take over the company." Tennucci chuckled.

"Our friend, Bruno, says he's going to make the bank and the firm's customers whole. He's going to wait a couple weeks so that a shit storm rains down on those bastards. Then he'll wire their money to the SEC."

Tennucci gave Massarino a bug-eyed look. "What is he, crazy?"

Massarino smiled. "He's a good man, Bobby."

"Hell, he's a saint. But I still think he's nuts."

Massarino nodded. "At least he's keeping the partners' money. Over half-a-billion. Without that money, the company will have no capital. You're right. It's going down."

"*Santa madre di Dio.* How much is he going to share with you?"

"I'm not in this for the money, Bobby."

"*Occhio per un occhio.*"

"That's right. An eye for an eye."

"The partners are all gonna be broke?"

"The partners—at least the three senior guys—probably have tens of millions squirreled away. I'd bet you five thousand dollars to a doughnut they have bank accounts and homes in extradition-free countries."

"Like where?"

"Most of those countries wouldn't be much better than prison. You know, places like Afghanistan and Iran. But there are a few places that wouldn't be too bad."

"Why would Rosen need to leave the U.S.? I mean, if he's got a deal with the Feds."

"Because the Feds probably won't give immunity to Rosen unless he turns over all his assets. He won't have a dime left here in the States. He has to run to maintain his lifestyle." Massarino rubbed his chin and huffed. Then he turned to Tennucci. "I just thought of something. Call Kalinov and ask him to check Rosen's passport records. Find out where he's traveled to over the last five years, or so. Business and leisure travel."

"We might still be able to get to him here."

"Nah, not likely. The Feds will keep him under lock and key until he testifies in court against his partners." Massarino patted Tennucci's arm. "It's okay, Bobby. Just take care of business with the other two. I'll deal with Rosen."

After Massarino dropped him at his home at 4 a.m., Tennucci pulled out his cell phone and punched in a number while he walked up the front steps to the porch.

"Yeah?"

"It's a go," Tennucci said, then disconnected the call. He made a second identical call.

An hour later, the first man Tennucci had called jimmied the door to the pool house that was attached to the rear of Richard Stone's house. Inside the pool house, he stared up at the star-lit sky and quietly hummed a couple bars of *Figaro's Aria* from the *Barber of Seville*. The humidity in the pool house was oppressive. His shirt and underwear stuck to his body. The balaclava he wore was miserably hot. He'd wanted to shuck it but he knew that would have been dumb, considering the security cameras on the property.

He knew the old rock mansion on Long Island was alarmed, but even in this upscale neighborhood, he'd be in and out of the house well before the police could respond. He placed a suction cup on a pane of glass in the back door, then used a cutter to take out a circle of glass around the suction cup. He stuck a hand through the hole he'd made and unlocked the deadbolt. As he slowly opened the door, the alarm kicked in with a steady *beep-beep-beep*. He propped the door open with a vase from the kitchen counter, slipped quickly through the house to the staircase leading to the second floor, and withdrew his silenced pistol from his jacket pocket as he climbed the stairs. Careful to put his weight on the sides of the steps, he raced to the second floor and turned left. The east side of the house had the best view of the ocean. He guessed the master bedroom would be there.

The door to the room was open. Two lumps showed under the covers. As the intruder glided into the room, the alarm siren went off and the two lumps shifted. The man immediately saw the bleached curls on the head of the lump on the right side of the bed, and moved to the left. The man on the left groaned and shouted, "Damn alarm." He sat up and reached for the black sleep mask covering his eyes. The intruder waited until the man removed the mask and had the time to realize a stranger had invaded his home. Then he placed the end of the pistol two inches from Richard Stone's head, pulled the trigger twice, reversed direction, and exited the house to the blaring sounds of the home alarm and a woman's screams.

The second man whom Tennucci had called jimmied the lock on a door to the basement of a high-rise condominium building on Central Park East. Inside the basement, knapsack on his back, he found a desk and a box on the wall with dozens of keys. He took a key for unit 28-B and walked to the service elevator. He rode the car to the twenty-eighth floor, moved to unit 28-B, unlocked the door with the stolen key, but found a security chain in place. He'd anticipated this and shrugged off the knapsack, took out a pair of bolt cutters, and snapped the chain. After replacing the cutters in the sack, he removed a pistol from his shoulder rig and took a sound suppressor from his jacket pocket.

After he screwed the silencer onto the pistol's muzzle, he entered the condo and oriented himself. The living room was directly ahead, the lights of the City visible through large windows. A half-wall separated a dining room from a living room. A hallway led off to the right and the left. The *hum* of what could have been a refrigerator came from the right. He went left down the hallway, passed three closed doors—one on the left and two on the right. At the end of the hall, he detected a small glow under another closed door and moved toward it. He slowly pressed down on the lever handle, opened the door a couple inches, and looked in on a palatial bedroom. A man sat up in a king-sized bed, a reader of some sort in his lap. The intruder pushed the door open until he could slip through. He'd taken two steps into the room before the man in the bed startled and released a choked scream.

The armed man quickly stepped to the foot of the bed, raised his pistol, and aimed at Karl Rice, who raised his iPad as though it would stop a bullet. The intruder fired three silenced shots, the first of which went through the reader and entered Rice's right eye. The second bullet was also a headshot. The third struck center mass.

CHAPTER 30

The morning television news programs single-mindedly reported on the SEC raid of the Rosen, Rice & Stone offices and the murders of two of the firm's senior partners. Because no official statements had been made by any law enforcement agency, the media couldn't report on the facts, so it reported on inane possibilities and worthless suppositions, and brought in experts who expounded on those possibilities and suppositions.

Bruno Pedace tried unsuccessfully to reach Louis Massarino after he learned about Richard Stone and Karl Rice's deaths. Rosa Massarino told him that her husband was out. Bruno paced in Massarino's basement apartment while he stared at the television set, anticipating that a report would come out at any moment about Sy Rosen's murder.

"Dammit, Louis," he blurted. "We had a deal."

"What's that, Bruno?"

Bruno jerked around and saw Massarino enter the room. "I can't believe you killed those guys, Louis. Wasn't taking down their firm enough for you?"

Massarino shrugged. "I've never killed anyone. Not my style, Bruno."

"Don't play semantics with me. Maybe you didn't pull the trigger, but I'll bet you know who did. I just wanted those men humiliated. I never wanted to be involved with murder."

Another shrug.

"What about Rosen? Is he still alive?"

"As far as I know."

Bruno scrunched his face and asked, "Why would you leave Rosen alive and kill the other two?"

Massarino shook his head. "You're not listening, Bruno. I told you I've never killed a soul."

"Dammit, Louis. I—"

"You talk to Janet?"

"Don't change the subject. I—"

Massarino ended the conversation by exiting the room.

Wayne Summers wanted to cry. The woman from the SEC's Investigations Division had grilled him for three hours. He told himself he should have hired an attorney before talking with her, but he knew he had done nothing wrong. Now, it was too late. He felt as though he'd been cooked through and forked when done.

"You claim some guy named Joseph Campbell was your contact at Sunrise Insurance."

"I don't *claim* he was my contact. He *was* my contact."

A sinister little sneer came over the woman's face. "You never questioned the name?"

"Why would I question a name like Joseph Campbell?"

"You never heard that name before?"

"Sure. The writer Joseph Campbell."

The sneer again. Then she smiled. "There's a Campbell quote I remember from a class in college. 'We must be willing to get rid of the life we've planned, so as to have the life that is waiting for us.' The life waiting for you, Mr. Summers, will not be pleasant. Securities fraud is a serious crime."

"What the hell are you talking about? I didn't do a damn thing."

"That's not what Sy Rosen tells us. He says you and his partners were behind the entire scheme."

Summers felt his stomach lurch. Bile burned the back of his throat. He looked around the company conference room in search of a wastebasket. He swallowed the bile and grabbed the glass of water in front of him. After sipping from the glass, he meekly announced, "I want a lawyer."

The woman chuckled. "That's the first smart thing you've said." She chuckled again. "You should have asked for a lawyer hours ago."

Sy Rosen and his attorney, Wallace Becker, sat across the desk from two SEC officers. Becker smiled, pushed the documents that Rosen had signed across the table, and asked, "Are we done?"

One of the SEC officers pushed the documents back at Becker. "Are you kidding me?" the officer said.

The supercilious smile on Becker's face dissolved. "I don't understand. We agreed—"

"We agreed to grant immunity to Mr. Rosen as long as he flipped on his two partners. Now that they're dead, the only senior partner we've got left to charge is your client."

"Wait a minute. There are junior partners. And don't forget Wayne Summers. He's the one who brought the Sunrise deal to the firm."

"Oh, come on, Becker. Summers is a convenient dupe. The junior partners were completely in the dark about the transaction. The files we found on the company's server make it clear the three senior partners were fully cognizant of the transaction and the scheme. Your client's going down."

"What files? What scheme?"

"Don't play dumb with me, Counselor. We found emails between the senior partners that prove all three of them fabricated this scam starting back almost twelve months ago."

Becker jerked a look at Rosen, as though to say, "I thought you erased all the files."

"Bullshit," Rosen screamed. "How could we have fabricated a scam a year ago when Sunrise came to us less than a week ago?"

The SEC officer just smiled smugly.

Becker said, "This makes no sense at all. If my client was behind the scam, he would have known that he would be found out as soon as the CUSIP numbers were checked. He would have known his reputation would be destroyed. Whatever he stole would have been confiscated almost immediately." Becker took a deep breath and then added, "Besides, why would he have left an electronic trail?"

The SEC officer stared at Rosen and said, "Maybe your client planned to skip the country. Maybe he thought he had this weekend to go on the run."

"Oh, come on." Becker threw up his hands. "We'll fight this thing for as long as it takes."

The second SEC officer shot a poisonous look at the attorney. "That's exactly what we want. Our names will be in the papers and on TV for years. It'll be great for our careers. Your client will spend millions of dollars fighting us. Hell, even if he wins, he'll have nothing left. No reputation, no property, no cash." The man laughed. "We've already put a freeze on all of his assets."

"What do you want?" Rosen said.

The second man offered up the same poisonous expression for a couple seconds, which then transformed into a gleeful smile. "Why, that should be obvious. A confession, of course." He glanced at his co-worker. "We can probably get approval of a five-year sentence… if you make restitution to your clients and the bank. Otherwise, you'll die in prison."

The first SEC man looked at Becker and said, "Tell your client to take the deal."

"Where the hell will I get one point seven billion dollars? I've told you ten times I'm the one who was defrauded. I'm innocent."

The two SEC men laughed. One of them said, "Yeah. Yeah. Yeah. We hear that all the time."

CHAPTER 31

Michael King was a six foot, three-inch-tall, seventy-five-year-old who'd worked for the Massarino Family for three decades. King had been raised tough on the streets of Brooklyn, had served three tours of duty in the Vietnam War with the U.S. Army, and then earned an undergraduate degree in two-and-a-half years and a law degree thereafter. At first, he'd handled small legal matters. But, lately, he was the man who Louis Massarino called when he had a serious legal issue.

Ramrod-straight and grim-faced, King was an imposing presence. Nothing about his posture or his expression changed when Victoria Nguyen entered the interview room at the Brooklyn jail, dressed in an orange jumpsuit, white slippers, and handcuffs.

"Who are you?" she asked.

"My name's Michael King. I'm your attorney as of this moment."

"The court appointed *you* to represent me?"

"Not exactly. Now, how 'bout you sit there, keep your mouth shut, and listen."

Nguyen opened her mouth as though to respond, but then clamped her teeth together and compressed her lips.

"Good," King said. "Okay, here's the situation. You've been charged with one count of murder, with special circumstances because the man you killed was a cop."

"I didn't kill any—"

"Ms. Nguyen, you know you murdered that California detective, and I know it, too. Don't waste my time." King waited a couple seconds. When he was convinced she wouldn't interrupt him again, he said, "You've also been charged with two counts of attempted murder, again with special circumstances in one of those cases. Since no one's been executed in New York in decades, you're looking at spending the rest of your life in prison. How's that sound?"

"Shitty. But I suspect you're about to tell me there might be an alternative."

King nodded. *Smart lady*, he thought.

"I had a talk with the D.A. He's willing to reduce the charges and get you a twenty-year prison sentence in return for telling him who hired you to commit murder and mayhem. He'll even agree to bail pending trial."

"Bullshit. Since when do people charged with murder get bail?"

King smiled. "The bail will be set at one million dollars. The D.A. doesn't believe you can raise it."

Nguyen lowered her head for a moment, then looked up at King. "Tell the D.A. to go fuck himself."

King grinned. He moved his chair forward, lowered his voice, and said, "Take the deal, Ms. Nguyen. I guarantee you'll never spend another day in prison."

"You have twenty-four hours to agree to the SEC's plea deal before they throw you in prison," Wallace Becker said.

Rosen shook the ice cubes in the bottom of his glass and placed the glass on his home office desk. Then, as an after-thought, he picked up the glass and threw it at the opposite wall.

"Sonofabitch," he shouted. "I didn't do a damn thing. We were suckered. Someone had it in for us and set the whole thing up."

"Who, Sy?"

"*Arrgh*," Rosen yelled. "I have no idea. But I'll tell you, it has to be someone who knows the securities business and has a grudge against me the size of the Empire State Building."

"Any names come to mind?"

"Yeah, a couple." He put his hands on the back of his head and stared at the pieces of broken glass on the floor. "Hell, I don't know."

Becker asked, "Any former employees or partners?"

"Hmm. Sure, there's always that possibility. But I can't think of anyone I fucked over that badly who would go to this kind of trouble for payback."

"What about that Bruno guy who you sicced the SEC on a decade ago?"

Rosen scoffed. "Shit, Wally, that was a long time ago and, besides, Pedace's a wimp. He doesn't have what it takes to fight. And orchestrating something like this would expose him to the SEC all over again. After all, whoever was behind this Sunrise transaction committed fraud. They took a shitload of money from my company, my clients, and our bank."

"Sy, what are you going to do?"

"You said I've got twenty-four hours. I plan to take every second of that time. I'll come by your office at three tomorrow afternoon."

"You know you can fight this thing. In the end, you'd probably win."

"After spending seven years in court and having my name dragged through the mud like some criminal. That doesn't sound very appealing."

"No, I guess it doesn't."

Bobby Tennucci, seated next to Louis Massarino in the backseat of Massarino's Town Car, ended a phone call and turned to his boss. "One of my guys is parked outside Rosen's Manhattan condo. He says there's a team of Feds watching the place."

"Rosen's no dummy. He's gotta know the Feds will cover him like white on rice. He'll find a way to sneak out of there. You sure about the information our guy at the SEC gave you?"

"Oh, yeah, boss. Over the last five years, Rosen traveled there three times. Always on private jets. He's set up a charitable foundation over there and has given away millions to various causes. He must have a solid relationship with the country's leaders."

"Any property over there?"

"Not that Kalinov was able to find. But he'll continue looking."

"Okay," Massarino said. "You know that guy, Rosen, is responsible for my brother's death? He's the one I really want."

"Yeah, boss. I know." After a beat, Tennucci said, "It'd be a lot cheaper to do it here."

"But a lot more dangerous with the Feds watching his ass."

The Brooklyn District Attorney was so excited that his hands shook. He took the signed statement from Victoria Nguyen, witnessed it, and then turned to Attorney Michael King.

"Okay, Counselor, your client's free on bail." He glanced at Nguyen and then back at King. "But if she doesn't come to my office on Monday as we agreed, all bets are off and I'll put her away for the rest of her life."

"I get it," King said. He shook hands with the D.A. and then told Nguyen, "Let's get you home."

As soon as King and Nguyen left, the D.A. called his counterpart in Manhattan and asked for a favor. Fifteen minutes later, NYPD detectives and uniformed officers armed with an arrest warrant drove to Sy Rosen's Manhattan condominium building.

Sy Rosen looked at his Rolex and saw he had five minutes. He hefted the two suitcases he'd earlier placed in the foyer, opened the door, and calmly walked to the end of his floor to the maintenance elevator. He took it to the underground garage and smiled at the line of five identical black Lexus sedans. He handed the bags to the driver of the fourth car, who put them in the trunk, while Rosen sat in the backseat.

Back behind the wheel, the driver said, "Where to, boss?"

"Teterboro Airport, Sammy. Your friends know what to do?"

Sammy laughed. "You can count on them, Mr. Rosen."

"Good. Then let's do it."

Sammy honked the horn twice. The first Lexus in line immediately took off, tires squealing, and headed up the ramp to the street. Then the second car took off. In less than ten seconds, the five identical vehicles roared out of the garage. Two went left, three went right, and they all turned again within a couple blocks of the condo building.

From his spot on the floor in the back, Rosen asked, "How's it going, Sammy?"

"Perfect, boss. Absolutely perfect."

CHAPTER 32

Michael King stared across his desk at Louis Massarino and asked, "How'd you know, Louis?"

"Hah. Instinct, I guess. Rosen's a survivor. Guys like him always have a scapegoat and an escape route. Once his partners were killed, his scapegoats were no longer available. He had to get out of the country before the Feds confiscated his passport."

"You sure about his destination?"

Massarino shrugged. "We'll see. His pilot filed a flight plan from Teterboro to Mexico City. I've got eyes down there who'll let us know where he goes next." He stood and asked, "Where's the girl?"

King tipped his head toward a door. "In the conference room."

"Thanks, Mike. I'll take it from here."

Massarino opened the conference room door and looked at Victoria Nguyen who stood by a large window, appearing to stare out at the street. She didn't turn when he moved to the table and took a seat.

After he watched the woman continue to stare outside for a few seconds, Massarino said, "Twenty years is a long time, especially for a young woman."

Nguyen finally turned around, her eyes wide and her mouth open when she looked at Massarino. "I'll be damned," she said. She moved to the chair across from Massarino and cocked her head. "That lawyer out there told me I'd never have to serve a day."

Massarino nodded. "That's true, as long as you leave the country and go somewhere that doesn't have an extradition treaty with the U.S."

Her mouth opened again, then she exhaled a loud breath. "I shoulda figured there'd be a catch."

Massarino folded his hands together on the tabletop and bent forward. "You know, I could have used someone like you in my organization." He shook his head. "But I guess it's too late for that."

"What do you want from me?"

"I have a proposition for you that will keep you out of prison and stake you to a damned good life…at least for a few years until you can make it on your own."

"I'm listening."

"You have to understand something. You don't ever get to return to the U.S."

"And…?"

Massarino smiled again. "Clever girl, aren't you?" After a beat, he added, "How's your Vietnamese?"

Bruno had never been one to lose control, but from his florid complexion and the fire in his eyes, Massarino thought his old friend was about to explode.

"You've got to be kidding. Rosen got out of the country? He's free as a bird?"

Massarino leaned back in his chair, arms crossed. "What can I say, Bruno? The guy did a runner. You're not the only person pissed off about it. The SEC, the FBI, and the local D.A. are going crazy. The media is making them all look like dolts."

"I don't care about the authorities. I want Rosen broke, humiliated, *and* in prison."

"Listen, Bruno, no matter what you did to Rosen, he was never going to be broke. He's too smart for that. He's gotta have millions hidden away. As far as his being humiliated, the guy's a sociopath. He couldn't care less what people think of him. And, if he fought the charges against him, sooner or later he would have been exonerated. I mean, the Feds would try to follow the money trail. Once they discovered that Rosen didn't make a dime off the

Sunrise transaction, they would have started looking elsewhere."

"So now there's no prison, either. Zero for three. I should have let you kill Rosen like you wanted to." He threw up his hands as he paced the Massarino living room. "It was all for nothing. Rosen's probably lying on a beach somewhere."

Massarino scoffed. "You took a lot of money from those bastards. That's not *nothing*."

"I wasn't in it for the money."

"I know that. But you can do a lot of good with that much money. Have you thought about that?"

"A bit. As I told you before, I'll send one point seven billion to the SEC to pay back the bank and the client trust accounts."

"That still leaves five hundred and ninety-two million."

Bruno nodded.

"Maybe you should talk to Janet. She might have some good ideas."

Bruno shook his head. "I'm the last person she wants to talk to."

"Bruno, you're clueless."

TWO WEEKS LATER
DAY 24

CHAPTER 33

Victoria Nguyen had been skeptical that she would have enough money to maintain a decent lifestyle in Ho Chi Minh City, the former Saigon. After all, the city was a huge metropolis where living had to be expensive. But she soon discovered that the quarter-of-a-million Louis Massarino had promised her, on top of the half-million she'd saved from doing jobs for clients, put her in the top financial echelon of Vietnamese society. The villa she rented three blocks from the old *Cercle Sportif Saigonnais* in Tao Dan Park was a mansion compared to her two-bedroom apartment in New York City. She figured the money she had would last a very long time in Vietnam.

Ho Chi Minh City was nothing like New York. She knew there was no place on earth like The Big Apple. *But it's a whole lot better than prison,* she thought. Seated at an outside table in a café on *Nguyen Du* Street, in *Ben Thanh* Ward, across from the Vietnam Immigration Department in the Ministry of Public Security, Nguyen nursed an orange drink while she watched the front of the government building for the target to appear. He was like an automaton. Arrived at work at 7:30 a.m. and left for home at 5 p.m. Every day.

Do Van Khiem exited the front door of the Ministry of Public Security, leather folio tucked under his left arm, umbrella in his right hand.

The man exudes the essence of uptight, scrubbed-clean bureaucrat, Nguyen thought. She followed his progress as he waited for the traffic light to change, crossed the street, and turned right toward the café. When he was a few steps away, she stood, feigned losing her balance, staggered into Do Van Khiem, and grabbed his arm to steady herself.

"*Toi xin loi, thu'a ban,*" she apologized in a respectful, mousey tone.

"Quite all right," he responded in Vietnamese. "Are you okay?"

"A bit dizzy," she said. She gave him a sweet smile and saw him blush. "I need to cross over to the government building. Would you mind walking with me to the corner?"

"Of course not," he answered. "But the offices are closed now."

Nguyen wearily returned to her chair and sighed. "What a mess," she said. "I was supposed to get some information for my mother in the United States about a long-time friend of hers."

"Do you mind if I sit down?" Do Van Khiem asked.

"Please," Nguyen answered.

He sat and said, "You're from the United States?"

"Yes."

"I thought I detected something in your accent."

"Oh, is my Vietnamese poor?"

"Oh, no. I apologize if I gave you that impression." He seemed flustered. His eyes bounced around like ping pong balls and his complexion had turned even redder. He waved a hand around as though it had a mind of its own and asked, "Are you visiting?"

"Actually, I moved here permanently. I wanted to return to my roots, as we say in the United States. It was as though I never felt like I belonged in America. Like something was missing."

Do nodded. "I hear that quite often from people who have come back to the motherland."

"I've only been here two weeks." She offered him a self-deprecating smile. "I am quite lonely. I have no family and people here don't seem to accept me."

Do smiled. "Perhaps you intimidate people."

She showed a quizzical look.

"Excuse me for being forward, but beautiful, sophisticated

women can put people off their game."

Nguyen dropped her eyes, feigning embarrassment. When she looked back at Do, she said, "You are quite the gentleman."

Do's face reddened again. Quickly changing the subject, he said, "Perhaps I can assist you with the information for your mother."

Nguyen looked confused. "How would you do that?"

"If you're feeling up to it, we can cross to the government building."

"Oh, do you know someone there?"

He smiled and said, "Something like that, my dear. After we find the information you want, perhaps we can have dinner together."

"Oh, that would be very nice," she said.

CHAPTER 34

"Is everything okay, Janet?" Frank Mitchell said.

Her boss's question surprised her. She frowned for a second. "Sure, Frank. Everything's fine. Why do you ask?"

Mitchell shrugged. "It's just that you've been kinda…I don't… mopey for the past couple weeks. Ever since you returned from New York."

Janet forced a smile. "Oh, I get depressed occasionally. I guess it's what we do around here. Our clients, you know?"

"Uh huh," Mitchell answered, not sounding convinced. "Well, if you need someone to talk to."

"Thanks, Frank. I'll keep that in mind."

She looked at her watch after Mitchell left her office and saw it was almost noon. She took her purse from a desk drawer, stood, and went left into the hall, in the direction of the exit to the parking lot. But then she stopped, turned around, and walked toward the building's front entrance. Outside, she glanced in the direction of the wall, hoping, almost expecting to see Bruno seated there. But she was once again disappointed.

No calls, no emails, no letters, no nothing, she thought. Janet sucked in a deep breath as she turned down the walkway to the parking lot. As she vented the air in her lungs, she concluded that she would never see Bruno again.

"Bruno, you gonna hang around here for the rest of your life?" Massarino asked.

Bruno's face seemed to droop when he looked back. "I'm sorry, Louis. I know I've abused your hospitality. I'll pack up today."

"You misunderstand me, my friend. You can stay here for as long as you like. Hell, you can live in this basement forever, for all I care. But it wouldn't be much of a life. I was just wondering if you've thought about what you'll do in the future."

"I've been waiting to hear something about Sy Rosen. I hoped the Feds would have tracked him down by now."

"Hah. Hope and wishes are like Santa Claus and the Easter Bunny. Besides, the Feds have bigger fish to fry than Rosen. Keep in mind that, in the end, he didn't take any investor money. You saw to that when you wired one point seven billion dollars to the SEC to repay the firm's clients and their bank. The Feds pretty much lost interest in him after that." Massarino laughed. "The Feds are probably more interested in tracking down whoever was behind the counterfeit securities deal that brought down Rosen, Rice & Stone."

"You know I spent four hours with the SEC investigators this morning and they didn't ask me one question about it. They were a little shocked when I walked in unannounced."

"I'll bet. Are they going after you for what happened ten years ago?"

"At first, things were a bit tense. Although there was no one there that remembered the securities fraud of a decade ago, once they pulled the file, the investigators acted as though they'd found a prosecutorial pot of gold. I thought they might handcuff me and throw me in a cell right then and there. But once I gave them the old files I'd taken and explained how my former partners had set me up and sent a hit man after me, and how they'd ruined my marriage and the last ten years of my life, they backed off. After the recent happenings at the Rosen firm, they were more than willing to accept my story." After a couple seconds, Bruno said, "I think you might be wrong about the Feds not going after Rosen. Putting him on trial for securities fraud and solicitation of murder would be a prosecutor's dream. Hell, if the Feds could get that Vietnamese woman to testify—"

"Did ya see the article in *The Wall Street Journal* today about the bank that took over Rosen, Rice & Stone?"

"Yes, I did," Bruno answered. "The new owner kicked out all the junior partners and a bunch of the employees in the real estate investment and legal departments. Thirty-three people. I guess they're tainted, as far as the bank's concerned. Those people will have a tough time finding jobs. I know a lot of them from when I was with the firm. They're talented and honest. It's too bad. Unintended collateral damage."

Massarino waved at Bruno. "I gotta go uptown for a couple hours. I'll see ya later." He moved to the bottom of the staircase, but stopped. "As I said before, you can stay here as long as you want. But if you're hanging around, hoping Rosen turns up or that Vietnamese gal testifies against him, you're wasting your time."

"Why do you say that?"

Massarino shrugged. "Just a feeling."

DAY 25

CHAPTER 35

A flight from Ho Chi Minh City to Phu Quoc Island would have taken a few minutes more than an hour. But the risks associated with her name being in the airline's computer system were too great. Instead, Nguyen, dressed like a peasant—black pants, white blouse, sandals, and a bamboo coolie hat—boarded a bus at 5 a.m. She carried a tin of soup, two bottles of water, a box of crackers, and a thick wad of Vietnam Dong inside a mesh bag. Also in the bag, wrapped in a towel, was a combat knife with an eight-inch blade.

Ten hours later, the bus pulled into Hà Tiên on the west coast of the mainland, near the Cambodian border. She made her way to the docks where dozens of small fishing boats bobbed against one another. Most of the boats had been abandoned for the day. One improbably frail looking fisherman—he couldn't have weighed more than ninety pounds—with a sun-leathered face chattered like an angry bird at a young man who helped him store fishing nets. She could see that his teeth were stained black from chewing betel nuts.

"How much to take me to Phu Quoc?" Nguyen asked.

The weary old fisherman scoffed while the young man leered at Nguyen. The old man looked her over and, apparently thinking she couldn't afford to pay him enough to sail to Phu Quoc after he'd already spent a dozen hours fishing, waved a dismissive hand. "The first ferry boat leaves at 8:30 in the morning. It'll only cost you two hundred thirty thousand Dong."

Nguyen did a quick mental calculation. *Between eleven and twelve dollars*, she thought. "My mother is very sick. I need to get to her tonight."

The old man waved her away again.

The younger man laughed, then cursed and spat at the ground. "Go away, woman. We're tired."

"How much to take me to Phu Quoc and back tonight?"

The old man threw his hands into the air and shouted, "*Hai triệu đồng*." He turned back to his nets.

"Okay," Nguyen said. "Two million *Dong*. Half now and half when you bring me back to *Hà Tiên*."

She sensed the old man's mental wheels turning. One hundred dollars was probably much more than he made in a full day of fishing. Both men stopped what they were doing.

"Let me see your money first," the old man said.

Nguyen reached into her sack and held up a wad of *Dong*.

They stared open-mouthed for a second and then quickly loaded the nets onto the boat. The elderly man cranked the motor in the wheezy fourteen-foot craft, while the younger man hauled in the anchor with a manual crank.

"How long will it take?" Nguyen asked.

"Where on the island?"

"The Five Oceans Restaurant."

"Good," the young one said. "That's on the eastern side of Phu Quoc. Seven hours if we use the sails."

"What about the motor?" Nguyen asked.

"Gasoline is expensive."

"I'll give you another two million *Dong* if you run the motor there and back."

The young man smiled.

It had been a very long and tiring day, but Nguyen didn't dare doze off. The look she'd seen on the young man's face was warning enough to remain alert. When the boat docked on the eastern side of Phu Quoc Island, it was after 11:00 p.m. She climbed onto a rickety wooden dock that terminated on a sandy beach, fifty yards from a restaurant with a sign that read: Five Oceans Restaurant, in

English, French, and Vietnamese. Her real destination was an estate two kilometers to the north, on the edge of the Phu Quoc National Forest. She held up a finger and said to the old fisherman, "*Tôi sẽ trở lại trong không quá một giờ.*"

The man answered, "Okay. Two hours. But if you are not back by then, we will leave. But you must give me the other one million *Dong* now. The two million for the fuel, we get when we return to *Hà Tiên.*"

She handed over the one million Dong. "Two hours," she repeated, and turned toward the restaurant. She skirted the side of the building, fast-walked between half-a-dozen cars parked on the other side of the building, and then ran to the dirt road on the far side of the lot. The forest was barely one hundred yards on the right. She moved up the road and entered the tree line. The thick, lush canopy screened out light from the quarter-moon. It became so dark she couldn't see her feet in front of her.

Despite not being used to running in sandals, Nguyen settled into a twelve-minute-per-kilometer pace. When lights from the right side of the road shone through to the road ahead, she abruptly stopped and checked her cell phone. Twenty-two minutes had gone by since she'd left the fishing boat.

That must be the place, she thought as she stared at light leaking through the trees on the right side of the road.

She stayed close to the right tree line as she cautiously moved forward. After a dozen steps, she spotted a chain link fence that paralleled the road. After another two hundred meters, past a slight bend in the road, she noticed a guard shack in the beam of a security light mounted on a twelve-foot-high post. She removed the knife from the mesh bag, then stowed the bag beside a tree. She slowly, quietly approached the guard shack. Still ten feet away, she froze when the door to the little building popped open. Nguyen held her breath, took a half-step to her right, and pressed against a tree trunk. She watched a man dressed all in black—fatigues, boots, and baseball cap, flashlight in hand, walk across the road into the tree line. He stuck the flashlight into a back pants pocket. Then she heard the distinctive sound of a zipper and then the man urinating.

She stepped out of her sandals and moved across the forty feet that separated her from the guard. She covered the man's mouth with one hand and drove the knife blade into his right kidney. Then she withdrew the knife and slit his throat. After cleaning the knife blade on the man's shirt and removing a pistol from his hip holster, she dragged him further into the trees, returned to the road, retrieved her sandals, and checked the guard shack. Empty.

Only one guard, she thought. *Not smart.*

She moved to a personnel gate next to a locked vehicle gate and slowly pushed it open. Then she made her way up a serpentine driveway that had to be at least two hundred meters long. At the end of the driveway was a magnificent, three-story, French colonial building. The sounds of waves lapping the shore behind the house carried to her. She crept to the front door and tried the lock. No luck. As she tip-toed around the left side of the house, the sound of the waves became louder, masking the noise of her footsteps on the crushed sea shell-covered ground. She padded around to the back and saw the chain link fence extended there and separated the house and a backyard from the beach and ocean. Security lights came on as she rounded the back corner of the house.

Shit. Motion detectors. Anyone inside must now be alerted.

Nguyen rushed to the back of the house, to the middle set of three ten-foot-high French doors. She reached for the door handle, when movement to her left startled her. She whipped around, her knife-hand extended, and felt a surge of fear-induced adrenaline. A giant, snarling dog stared back at her.

Unable to breathe, she backed against the door, reached around behind her for the door handle, and pushed down on it. She released the air in her lungs when the door opened. Then she quickly shut the door as the animal snarled and slammed into it.

She heard an angry shout from upstairs somewhere. The shout came again. "Sonofabitch. God damn dog."

Then the sound of a door opening and a man yelling again.

Nguyen ran across a large, marble floor. Again, she slipped out of her sandals, leaving them at the bottom of the staircase. She took the steps two at a time and followed the noise of the man's shouted curses. She took a right turn down a hall, then abruptly stopped at the second door on the left. Her ear to the door, she heard a man grumbling. Then she heard what sounded like mattress springs groaning. She carefully, slowly depressed the handle and pushed the door open onto a spacious bedroom. A king-size bed sat twenty-five feet away, against the back wall. The occupant of the bed, still grumbling, was turned on his side, facing toward the open French doors.

The thick carpet felt good under Nguyen's feet. She pressed her toes into the fabric as she moved cat-like around the foot of the bed to the far side. Still a few feet away from her target, the motion detector lights outside went out, momentarily startling her. The only illumination in the room now came from a small slice of moonlight that shone through the open balcony door, bathing the man's face in an eerie glow. Nguyen raised her double-bladed knife. In the fraction of a second it took her to plunge her hand downward, Sy Rosen's eyes popped open and his mouth gaped. Whatever he tried to say was drowned by a gasp of pain.

On the boat ride back toward Hà Tiên, Nguyen watched the two men navigate the dark, murky waterway. She scrutinized every movement—how they handled the wheel; how they controlled the craft's speed; how they kept alert for debris or other craft. When the old man pointed out the lights of Hà Tiên as barely a blush of illumination, Nguyen attracted the younger man's attention. She waved at him, smiled, and said, "Can we talk for a moment?" Without waiting for an answer, she moved to the boat's stern and looked out at the sea.

"What can I do for you?" the young man asked as he placed a hand on the small of her back.

"You stink of fish and sweat," she said as she turned to face him. She smiled as she stuck her knife into the soft spot below his ribs and covered his mouth with her other hand. She drove the blade upward, causing him to rise on his toes, his eyes wide, his nostrils flared. It took little effort to push him over the rail. Then she made her way toward the old man.

TWO WEEKS LATER
DAY 39

CHAPTER 36

"How long do you plan to keep me hanging out to dry, Mr. Williams?" Bruno Pedace growled at the SEC administrator.

"I don't know what you're referring to, Mr. Pedace," Williams responded. "We haven't brought any charges against you."

Attorney Michael King placed a hand on Bruno's arm and said to the SEC flack, "And you haven't officially dropped the investigation either. I thought this was all behind us a couple weeks ago. Now, you've got my client twisting in the wind. It's been ten years since Rosen, Rice & Stone set up my client. We've agreed to cooperate with the SEC, which seems to me to be especially valuable considering that Rice and Stone are dead and no one knows where Sy Rosen is. But if he ever shows up, my client will be the best witness you could have to testify about the games that bastard has played for years." King stood and motioned for Bruno to stand. "You've ruined my client's Christmas. What do you want to do, ruin New Year's, too? You've got 'til the end of the day." He looked at his watch. "Five hours from now. We don't have a letter from you stating that Mr. Pedace is no longer part of any investigation into the Rosen, Rice & Stone operation, my client will no longer cooperate with you. Oh, and one other thing, we want a positive reference from you personally. Mr. Pedace may want to join a company regulated by the SEC at some point, and we want no obstacles to keep that from happening."

King moved toward the conference room door. Bruno followed.

In the elevator on the way down to the lobby, Bruno asked, "You think bullying the SEC will work?"

King chuckled. "They've got nothing on you. Despite that, they're preventing you from doing anything related to the securities and investment industries. They don't realize that you've already told them everything you know about Rosen and his partners." He chuckled again. "I'll give you ten to one odds we get a letter from them in less than three hours. Then you can go on with your life."

Bruno cocked an eyebrow. "I wish I was as confident as you. You really think they'll give me a reference?"

"You gonna take my odds?"

Bruno smiled. "Okay. Ten bucks says they don't get us a letter within three hours."

"Ten bucks, my ass," King blurted. "Make it a grand."

Two-and-a-half hours later, Bruno peeled off ten one hundred-dollar bills and placed them in Michael King's hand. "Best bet I ever lost in my life," he said.

King pocketed the bills and shook Bruno's hand. "Good luck, my friend. I hope your business does well."

"Thanks, Mike."

"You come up with a name yet?"

"I'm going to keep the Forsythe name."

"You still set on California?"

"That's where the company's offices are."

"When are you going there?"

"Not long. First I have to take a trip out of the country."

DAY 40

CHAPTER 37

The balmy, flower-scented air kissed Bruno's face as he stepped down the movable airplane stairs to the tarmac of the Antigua International Airport. He moved toward the terminal building and spotted a black gentleman in a white suit and matching Panama hat waving at him. Bruno diverted away from the stream of disembarking passengers and extended his hand.

"Mr. Blake?" he asked.

"No, no, I am Ambrose Downing, Mr. Blake's assistant." The man spoke with a distinct British accent, with a pleasing Caribbean lilt. "Mr. Blake is waiting for you at the bank."

On the way to the city of St. Johns, Downing pointed out the temporary housing that had been constructed to accommodate the refugees from Barbuda who had fled the devastation of Hurricane Irma in 2017. "It will be years before these displaced people will be able to return to Barbuda. Nearly every building on the island was destroyed."

The drive to the Antigua Victoria Bank took fifteen minutes. The building was a three-story affair, with a white marble front and an imposing, highly polished brass door. Inside, Bruno followed Downing across the cool, gray marble lobby to an elevator, which they took to the third level.

Blake and Bruno shook hands as Downing excused himself and left.

"Please take a seat, Mr. Pedace. It is an honor to have you here."

"Thank you for taking time out of your busy schedule to meet with me, Mr. Blake."

Blake scoffed. "You are a valued customer of my bank, sir. My time is your time."

Bruno nodded his thanks.

Blake cleared his throat. "I have to say that, with all of the international bank offices here in Antigua, I was pleasantly surprised that you chose Antigua Victoria Bank."

Bruno smiled. "Ah, but Mr. Blake, you being the sole stockholder of Antigua Victoria Bank offers advantages the big banks can't offer."

Blake briefly smiled, but then his expression turned serious. "In what way, Mr. Pedace?"

"I need a partner in an investment banking firm I wish to buy. I will put up one hundred percent of the capital, but I need an offshore partner interested in fronting ownership of the company."

Blake's expression became severe. "We are very…protective, Mr. Pedace, of our reputation."

Bruno chuckled. "Despite my Italian name, I am not part of some…illegal enterprise. I assure you the money I deposited did not come from drug dealing or any other such criminal activity. But, for reasons of my own, I do not want my name on United States ownership documents or business licenses. The company I want to purchase is a small investment banking firm in Los Angeles named Forsythe Investments. My proposal is that your bank will own one hundred percent of the company's stock, but will hire my management firm to run the company. My management firm will receive ninety-five percent of profits and Antigua Victoria Bank will receive the remaining five percent. I plan to capitalize the company with five hundred million dollars."

"How long will this arrangement run?"

"Details, Mr. Blake. We can hash those out in the contract." Bruno opened his briefcase and passed over a folio. "In there is a business plan, including pro forma financial statements, and references. My plane leaves tomorrow at 10 a.m. I expect to hear from you before then. If I don't, then I will have to make other arrangements. You can reach me at the Blue Waters Antigua."

Edward Blake ordered his investment department to do research on the Forsythe Investment firm. He personally called the people listed in Bruno Pedace's list of references. A senior officer at the SEC told Blake that Pedace was a solid citizen who had assisted the commission in "bringing down a corrupt enterprise." The administrator of an organization in California that helped battered women told him that Pedace had donated a substantial sum of money to them.

Just before 5 p.m., Blake called the Blue Waters Antigua Resort and was put through to Pedace's room.

"Hello."

"Mr. Pedace, it's Edward Blake. I think we should sit down in the morning and discuss our future business relationship. Perhaps you could change your travel plans. I think we might need an extra day or two to finalize an agreement."

"Of course, Mr. Blake. Would 10 a.m. be good for you?"

"Perfect, Mr. Pedace."

10 DAYS LATER
DAY 50

CHAPTER 38

Janet Jenkins no longer even glanced at the wall in front of St. Anne's Shelter. She'd long ago given up on the hope that Bruno might show up. She'd tried to nurture anger at him, for not confiding in her about his plans, for not communicating with her since she'd left New York, and for having his former wife's photo in his suitcase. It was a new year and she knew she needed to get on with her life. She tiredly half-shuffled, half-walked from her office to the building's side door to the parking lot. It had been a long, tiring day, with two visits to badly beaten women in hospitals and half-a-dozen sessions with women housed at St. Anne's. All but one of the six women at St. Anne's planned to return to their abusive husbands because the men had promised to change. *God, how many times have I heard that sorry tune?* she thought. *Too many times to count.*

The thirty steps to her car seemed like three hundred. *Maybe it's time to do something different*, she thought.

Behind the wheel of her car, she checked the rearview mirror and shifted into reverse, but hit the brakes when a large black limousine stopped directly behind her. She watched the vehicle for a few seconds, waiting for it to drive off. But, when it didn't move, she exited her car and spread her arms at the driver in a "what gives?" gesture.

The left rear door of the limo opened and a man got out and smiled.

"Hugo," Janet cried. She rushed forward and hugged her old friend. "It's so wonderful to see you again. Where have you been? Are you okay? How's Carmela? What are—?"

Hugo Rosales laughed and held Janet at arm's length. "Whoa, girl, one question at a time." He laughed again and said, "I'm the new head of security for an investment firm. RBPD forced me to retire on full disability. We should get together for coffee some time and get caught up." He waited a beat and then pointed at the car. "My new boss wants to talk with you."

The right rear door of the car opened. Bruno Pedace stepped out and came around to where Janet stood.

Janet was shocked to see him. She was also surprised by his appearance. He wore an immaculately-tailored blue pinstripe suit, a white shirt, and a power-red tie. He looked ten years younger than the last time she'd seen him.

"You look...different."

Bruno smiled and spread his hands. "I guess it's the suit."

She nodded. "More than that."

"I'm healthier than I've been in a very long time."

Janet pressed her lips into a thin slash and said, "That's good to hear, Bruno. Now, you want to have your driver move that land barge so I can go home?"

"Please, Janet. Give me a minute."

Janet shrugged and waited.

"I know you're angry with me, Janet. I—"

"No, I'm not—"

He held up a finger and pleaded, "Please let me finish."

She glared.

"I kept things from you because I didn't want you implicated. I wanted to tell you what I was doing, but I just didn't know how. *And* I didn't want to put you in jeopardy." He sighed. "I've missed you terribly. You're the most important person in my life. I don't want that to change."

"*Everything's* changed, Bruno. I've followed the news. People have been murdered. People who hadn't done anything wrong lost their jobs when Rosen, Rice & Stone was taken over by their bank. I don't have to be a financial genius to figure out you had a hand in all that."

Bruno raised his hands. "I had nothing to do with anyone getting killed and every one of the people who was fired has been offered a job at a company I took over."

Janet met Bruno's gaze and thought, *He's telling the truth.*

"I made a lot of mistakes. But, if I had to do it all over again, I would still not share my plans with you. The danger to you would have been tremendous. As it was, I put you in danger." He waved his arms around and added, "My God, look what happened with that Vietnamese gang. You could have been killed."

Janet continued to stare, momentarily at a loss for words.

"Have dinner with me tonight."

She shook her head. "Too much has happened, Bruno." She swallowed and then said, "It's been months and you didn't call me even once. I didn't know if you were dead. And now you just show up here and want to go to dinner. Besides, I have no interest in spending time with a man who's still in love with a woman who betrayed him." She half-turned toward her open car door.

"Janet, you have to believe me. Paolina means absolutely nothing to me. The man who carried around her picture no longer exists. That man was a professional victim. Holding onto that photo was weak and stupid. I'm not that man anymore. I don't need a protector and I don't need a crutch. What I need is a friend."

Janet turned back to look at him.

He said, "I'll be here in this parking lot at 5 p.m. every night until you agree to have dinner with me."

Janet shrugged, did an about-face, and sat down behind the wheel of her car. Before she closed her door, she looked in her rearview mirror, smiled, and thought, *We'll see if he shows up tomorrow.*

*

READ OTHER BOOKS IN JOSEPH BADAL'S *CURTIS CHRONICLES* SERIES:

"THE MOTIVE"
THE CURTIS CHRONICLES (#1)

In "The Motive," the first book in *The Curtis Chronicles*, Joseph Badal delivers the same sort of action and suspense that readers have come to expect and enjoy from all his novels.

Confronted with suspicious information relating to his sister Susan's supposed suicide in Honolulu, Albuquerque surgeon Matt Curtis questions whether his sister really killed herself. With the help of his sister's best friend, Renee Drummond, and his former Special Forces comrade, Esteban Maldonado, Matt investigates Susan's death. But Lonnie Jackson, the head of organized crime in Hawaii, afraid that Matt has gotten too close to the truth, sends killers after him.

This is an artfully written book that will appeal to readers who like thrillers with fully developed characters, a big plot, and plenty of action, seasoned with friendship and romance.

" 'The Motive' is a nail biter I couldn't put down. Joseph Badal knows how to make his legion of readers sweat to the very last paragraph. He has mastered the art of writing—and suspense. Bravo!"
—Parris Afton Bonds, Award-Winning Author of "Dream Time"

http://a.co/gAt7BtZ

"OBSESSED"
THE CURTIS CHRONICLES (#2)

"Obsessed" brings back Matt Curtis and Renee Drummond and their villainous nemesis, Lonnie Jackson. This second installment in Joseph Badal's *The Curtis Chronicles* takes the reader from Rio de Janeiro to the mountains of New Mexico to the Mexico/United States border, following a crazed Jackson on his single-minded quest for revenge against the two people he blames for the deaths of his mother and brother and for the destruction of his criminal empire in Hawaii.

"Obsessed" is another master stroke of fiction from this Amazon #1 Best-Selling Author, two-time winner of the Tony Hillerman Award for Best Fiction Book of the Year, Eric Hoffer Award Winner, International Book Awards Finalist, and three-time Military Writers Society of America Gold Medal Winner.

"Joseph Badal's characters play on a world stage—and that world is a dark and dangerous place, seen through the pen of a master storyteller."

—Steven F. Havill, Award-Winning Author of "Easy Errors"

https://amzn.to/2VCFwPL

"JUSTICE"
THE CURTIS CHRONICLES (#3)

Amazon #1 Best-selling author, Joseph Badal, delivers "Justice," the third in his *Curtis Chronicles* series, with the same relentless tension that is a trademark of his award-winning suspense novels.

In "Justice," Matt and Renee Curtis return, along with their maniacal tormentor, Lonnie Jackson. On a trip to Costa Rica with their friends Esteban and Alani Maldonado, Matt and Renee believe they are beyond Jackson's reach. They soon find out how wrong they are, however, when Jackson orchestrates the kidnapping of Renee and Alani and transports them to his human trafficking headquarters located in Nicaragua.

Matt and Esteban recruit former special operations soldiers living in Costa Rica to help them rescue their wives, sending readers on an action-packed journey.

As with all of Badal's novels, "Justice" is a bold and complex thriller. It weaves an intricate plot involving multiple international locations, a human trafficking organization, the CIA, Special Operations, corrupt politicians, Bulgarian organized crime figures, Swiss bankers, and a compelling cast of engaging, inspiring, and diabolical characters.

The Curtis Chronicles is an epic series that delves into the age-old conflict between good and pure evil, where each book leaves you begging for more.

" 'Justice,' the 3rd in the *Curtis Chronicles*, whips around the world at breakneck speed and dives into the dark world of human trafficking. Wonderful characters, a rapid-fire plot, and action that will make you sweat. Highly recommended."
—D.P. Lyle, Award-Winning Author of the *Jake Longly* and *Cain/ Harper* Thriller Series

https://amzn.to/2RjxJXc

"EVIL DEEDS"
DANFORTH SAGA (#1)

"Evil Deeds" is the first book in the *Danforth Saga* series. The story begins on a sunny spring day in 1971 in a quiet Athenian suburb. After breakfast together and a bit of roughhousing with their two year old son, Michael, Bob leaves for his U.S. Army unit. Then the nightmare begins: Michael is kidnapped. So begins a journey that takes the Danforth family from Michael's kidnapping and Bob and Liz's efforts to rescue him, to Bob's forced separation from the Army because of his unauthorized entry into Communist Bulgaria, to his recruitment by the CIA, to Michael's commissioning in the Army, to Michael's capture by a Serb SPETSNAZ team in Macedonia, and to Michael's eventual marriage to the daughter of the man who kidnapped him as a child. The reader experiences CIA espionage during the Balkans War, attempted assassinations in the United States, and the grisly exploits of a psychopathic killer.

"Another tightly plotted, deftly executed page turner from a master of suspense and international intrigue. Joseph Badal writes timely stories with authority and compassion. Highly recommended."
—Sheldon Siegel, *New York Times* Bestselling Author of "Hot Shot"

https://amzn.to/31Fka6b

"TERROR CELL"
DANFORTH SAGA (#2)

"Terror Cell" pits Bob Danforth, a CIA Special Ops Officer, against Greek Spring, a vicious terrorist group that has operated in Athens, Greece for three decades. Danforth's mission in the summer of 2004 is to identify the terrorists in order to bring them to justice for the assassination of the CIA's Chief of Station in Athens. What Danforth does not know is that Greek Spring plans a catastrophic attack against the 2004 Summer Olympic Games.

Danforth's mission becomes even more difficult when he is targeted for assassination after an informant in the Greek government tells the terrorists of Danforth's presence in Greece.

"Joe Badal takes us into a tangled puzzle of intrigue and terrorism, giving readers a tense, well-told tale and a page-turning mystery."
—Tony Hillerman, *New York Times* Bestselling Author

https://amzn.to/2MJesfz

"THE NOSTRADAMUS SECRET"
DANFORTH SAGA (#3)

This third historical thriller in the *Bob Danforth* series builds on Nostradamus's "lost" 58 quatrains and segues to present day. These lost quatrains have surfaced in the hands of a wealthy Iranian megalomaniac who believes his rise to world power is preordained by Nostradamus. But he sees the United States as the principal obstacle to the achievement of his goals, and attempts to destabilize the United States through a vicious series of terrorist attacks and assassinations.

"The Nostradamus Secret" presents non-stop action in a contemporary context that will make you wonder whether the story is fact or fiction, history or prophesy.

" 'The Nostradamus Secret' is a gripping, fast-paced story filled with truly fanatical, frightening villains bent on the destruction of the USA and the modern world. Badal's characters and the situations they find themselves in are hair-raising and believable. I couldn't put the book down. Bring on the sequel!"
—Catherine Coulter, *New York Times* Bestselling Author of "Double Take"

https://amzn.to/31JwD8R

"THE LONE WOLF AGENDA"
DANFORTH SAGA (#4)

With "The Lone Wolf Agenda," Joseph Badal returns to the world of international espionage and military action thrillers, crafting a story that is as close to the real world of spies and soldiers as a reader can find. This fourth book in the *Danforth Saga* brings Bob Danforth out of retirement to hunt down lone wolf terrorists hell bent on destroying America's oil infrastructure. Badal weaves just enough technology into his story to wow even the most a-technical reader.

"The Lone Wolf Agenda" pairs Danforth with his son Michael, a senior DELTA Force officer, as they combat an OPEC-supported terrorist group allied with a Mexican drug cartel. This story is an epic adventure that will chill readers as they discover that nothing, no matter how diabolical, is impossible.

"A real page-turner in every good sense of the term. 'The Lone Wolf Agenda' came alive for me. It is utterly believable, and as tense as any spy thriller I've read in a long time."
—Michael Palmer, *New York Times* Bestselling Author of
"Political Suicide"

https://amzn.to/2qDT9U0

"DEATH SHIP"
DANFORTH SAGA (#5)

"Death Ship," the fifth book in the *Danforth Saga*, introduces Robbie Danforth, the 15-year-old son of Michael and Miriana Danforth, and the grandson of Bob and Liz Danforth.

A leisurely cruise in the Ionian Sea turns into a nightmare when terrorists hijack a yacht with Bob, Liz, Miriana, and Robbie aboard. Although the boat's crew, with Bob and Robbie's help, eliminate the hijackers, there is evidence that something more significant may be in the works.

The CIA and the U.S. military must identify what that might be and who is behind the threat, and must operate within a politically corrupt environment in Washington, D.C.

Michael Danforth and a team of DELTA operatives are deployed from Afghanistan to Greece to assist in identifying and thwarting the threat.

"Terror doesn't take a vacation in 'Death Ship'; instead, Joseph Badal masterfully takes us on a cruise to an all too frightening, yet all too real destination. Once you step on board, you are hooked."
—Tom Avitabile, #1 Bestselling Author of "The Eighth Day" and "The Devil's Quota"

https://amzn.com/B016APTJAU

"SINS OF THE FATHERS"
DANFORTH SAGA (#6)

The Danforth family returns in this sixth edition of the *Danforth Saga*. "Sins of the Fathers" takes the reader on a tension-filled journey from a kidnapping of Michael and Robbie Danforth in Colorado, to America's worst terrorist-sponsored attacks, to Special Ops operations in Mexico, Greece, Turkey, and Syria. This epic tale includes political intrigue, CIA and military operations, terrorist sleeper cells, drug cartels, and action scenes that will keep you pinned to the edge of your seat.

This is fiction as close to reality as you will ever find.

"Outstanding! Joseph Badal combines insider knowledge with taut writing and a propulsive plot to create a stellar thriller in a terrific series. Well-written, intense, timely and, at times, terrifying. Highly recommended."
—Sheldon Siegel, *New York Times* Bestselling Author of the *Mike Daley/Rosie Fernandez* Novels

http://a.co/eZTFJlO

"BORDERLINE"
THE LASSITER/MARTINEZ CASE FILES (#1)

In "Borderline," Joseph Badal delivers his first mystery novel with the same punch and non-stop action found in his acclaimed thrillers.

Barbara Lassiter and Susan Martinez, two New Mexico homicide detectives, are assigned to investigate the murder of a wealthy Albuquerque socialite. They soon discover that the victim, a narcissistic borderline personality, played a lifetime game of destroying people's lives. As a result, the list of suspects in her murder is extensive.

The detectives find themselves enmeshed in a helix of possible perpetrators with opportunity, means, and motive—and soon question giving their best efforts to solve the case the more they learn about the victim's hideous past.

"Borderline" presents a fascinating cast of characters, including two heroic female detective-protagonists and a diabolical villain.

"Think Cagney and Lacey. Think Thelma and Louise. Think murder and mayhem—and you are in the death grip of a mystery that won't let you go until it has choked the last breath of suspense from you."
—Parris Afton Bonds, Author of "Tamed the Wildest Heart" and Co-founder of Romance Writers of America and Co-founder of Southwest Writers Workshop

https://amzn.com/B00YZSAHI8
Now Available at Audible.com: http://adbl.co/1Y4WC5H

"DARK ANGEL"
THE LASSITER/MARTINEZ CASE FILES (#2)

In "Dark Angel," the second in *The Lassiter/Martinez Case Files* series, Detectives Barbara Lassiter and Susan Martinez are assigned to investigate a brutal murder. They discover that their suspect is much more than a one-off killer. In fact, the murderer appears to be a vigilante hell-bent on taking revenge against career criminals who the criminal justice system has failed to punish.

But Lassiter and Martinez are soon caught up in the middle of an FBI investigation of a monstrous home invasion gang that has murdered dozens of innocent victims across the United States. When they discover a link between their vigilante killer and the home invasion crew, they come into conflict with powerful men in the FBI who are motivated more by career self-preservation than by bringing justice to innocent victims.

"Badal delivers a nice tight mystery and two wonderful female detectives you'll be cheering for."
—Catherine Coulter, *New York Times* Bestselling Author of "Nemesis"

http://a.co/5fFx9vs

"NATURAL CAUSES"
THE LASSITER/MARTINEZ CASE FILES (#3)

Homicide detective partners Barbara Lassiter and Susan Martinez return in this third edition of The Lassiter/Martinez Case Files series.

Called in to investigate a mysterious death in a retirement home, Lassiter and Martinez find themselves entangled in a case that might very well involve multiple murders committed by a psychopathic killer. The deeper they go into their investigation, the more complex and dangerous the case becomes, threatening them and their loved ones. Political and bureaucratic machinations within the detectives' department and the involvement of organized crime only make their jobs more difficult.

" 'Natural Causes' by Joseph Badal is a first-rate thriller, a powerhouse of a story that will keep you turning the pages into the wee hours. The pacing is relentless, with a sense of menace that grows almost unbearable. Lassiter and Martinez are two homicide detectives for the ages. I loved it!"
—Douglas Preston, #1 Bestselling Co-author of the Famed *Pendergast* Series

https://amzn.to/2MKYRe8

"THE PYTHAGOREAN SOLUTION"
STAND-ALONE THRILLER

When American John Hammond arrives on the Aegean island of Samos, he is unaware of events that happened decades earlier that will embroil him in death and violence and will change his life forever.

Late one night, Hammond finds Petros Vangelos lying mortally wounded in an alley. Vangelos hands off a coded map, making Hammond the link to a Turkish tramp steamer that carried a fortune in gold and jewels and sank in a storm in 1945.

On board this ship, in a waterproof safe, are documents that implicate a German SS Officer in the theft of valuables from Holocaust victims and the laundering of those valuables by the Nazi's Swiss banker partner.

"Crisp writing, masterful pacing, and characters to genuinely care about. This is what top-notch is all about."
—Michael Palmer, *New York Times* Bestselling Author of "Political Suicide"

https://amzn.to/2pMTSl8

"ULTIMATE BETRAYAL"
STAND-ALONE THRILLER

Inspired by actual events, "Ultimate Betrayal" is a thriller that takes the reader from the streets of South Philadelphia, through the Afghanistan War, to Mafia drug smuggling, to the halls of power at the CIA and the White House.

David Hood comes from the streets of South Philadelphia, is a decorated Afghanistan War hero, builds a successful business, marries the woman of his dreams, and has two children he adores. But there are two ghosts in David's past. One is the guilt he carries over the death of his brother. The other is a specter that will do anything to murder him.

David has long lost the belief that good will triumph over evil. The deaths of his wife and children only reinforce that cynicism, and leave him with nothing but a bone-chilling, all-consuming need for revenge.

" 'Ultimate Betrayal' provides the ultimate in riveting reading entertainment that's as well thought out as it is thought provoking. Both a stand-out thriller and modern-day morality tale. Mined from the familial territory of Harlan Coben, with the seasoned action plotting of James Rollins or Steve Berry, this is fiction of the highest order. Poignant and unrelentingly powerful."
—Jon Land, Bestselling and Award-Winning Author of "The Tenth Circle"

https://amzn.to/2PbbHVS

"SHELL GAME"
STAND-ALONE THRILLER

"Shell Game" is a thriller that uses the economic environment created by the capital markets meltdown that began in 2007 as the backdrop for a timely, dramatic, and hair-raising tale. Badal weaves an intricate and realistic story about how a family and their business are put into jeopardy through heavy-handed, arbitrary rules set down by federal banking regulators, and by the actions of a sociopath in league with a corrupt bank regulator.

Although a work of fiction, "Shell Game," through its protagonist Edward Winter, provides an understandable explanation of one of the main reasons the U.S. economy languished for a decade.

"Shell Game" is a work of fiction that supports the old adage: You don't need to make this stuff up.

"Take a roller coaster ride through the maze of modern banking regulations with one of modern fiction's most terrifying sociopaths in the driver's seat. Along with its compelling, fast-paced story of a family's struggle against corruption, 'Shell Game' raises important questions about America's financial system based on well-researched facts."

—Anne Hillerman, *New York Times* Bestselling Author of "The Tale Teller"

https://amzn.to/2qBUdHT

ABOUT THE AUTHOR

Joseph Badal grew up in a family where storytelling had been passed down from generation to generation.

Prior to a long business career, including a 16-year stint as a senior executive and board member of a NYSE-listed company, Joe served for six years as a commissioned officer in the U.S. Army in critical, highly classified positions in the U.S. and overseas, including tours of duty in Greece and Vietnam, and earned numerous military decorations.

He holds undergraduate and graduate degrees in business and graduated from the Defense Language Institute, West Coast and from Stanford University Law School's Director College.

Joe is an Amazon #1 Best-Selling Author, with 16 published suspense novels, including six books in the *Danforth Saga* series, three books in *The Curtis Chronicles* series, three books in the *Lassiter/Martinez Case Files* series, and four stand-alones. He has been recognized as "One of The 50 Best Writers You Should Be Reading." His books have received two Tony Hillerman Awards for Best Fiction Book of the Year, been top prize winners on multiple occasions in the New Mexico/Arizona Book Awards competition, received gold medals from the Military Writers Society of America, the Eric Hoffer Award, and Finalist honors in the International Book Awards.

Joe has written short stories which were published in the "Uncommon Assassins," "Someone Wicked," and "Insidious Assassins" anthologies. He has also written dozens of articles that have been published in various business and trade journals and is a frequent speaker at business, civic, and writers' events.

To learn more, visit his website at www.JosephBadalBooks.com.